Set Up in SoHo

Also by Dee Davis

Set Up in SoHo

Dee Davis

 St. Martin's Griffin 🜂 New York

To Kim, Jennifer, and Hilary,

and to Kathleen, Dinah, and Julie—

sometimes it really does take a village.

SET UP IN SOHO. Copyright © 2009 by Dee Davis Oberwetter. All rights reserved. Printed in the United States of America. For information, address St. Martin's Press, 175 Fifth Avenue, New York, N.Y. 10010.

www.stmartins.com

Library of Congress Cataloging-in-Publication Data

Davis, Dee, 1959–
    Set up in SoHo / Dee Davis.—1st ed.
        p. cm.
    ISBN 978-0-312-36761-9
    1. Dating services—Fiction.   2. SoHo (New York, N.Y.)—Fiction.
3. Chick lit.   I. Title.
    PS3604.A9568S48 2009
    813'.6—dc22

                                                            2009017048

First Edition: November 2009

10 9 8 7 6 5 4 3 2 1

YOU ARE CORDIALLY INVITED TO ATTEND

THE OPENING OF

MANHATTAN MONTAGE

A SERIES OF PAINTINGS BY

STEPHEN HOBBS

8:00 P.M.

HOSTED BY ANNA AND GREGORY CARLSON

THE GALLERY

SOHO

CHAMPAGNE RECEPTION

BLACK TIE

REGRETS ONLY

Chapter 1

"Don't you think that dress is a little—revealing?" Althea Sevalas stared down the end of her nose at me, her withering glance serving as simultaneous judge, jury, and executioner. It was the quintessential mother's condemnation, except that Althea isn't my mother. She's my aunt.

"It's Alice and Olivia," I said, as if that explained everything. "From Bergdorf's."

"Well, I don't care where you got it, it's practically obscene." Althea sighed, sipping her martini. "You might as well take out a personal ad in a gentlemen's magazine. I can almost see your—"

"But you can't," I interrupted, flipping up the hem of the red silk bubble dress to reveal a pair of black boy shorts. "See, all covered."

"*Andrea,*" Althea protested.

I tried not to smile, but really, her look was priceless. "What? You thought I was pulling a Britney?" Okay, so I was probably overplaying my hand, but can you blame me? The dress was gorgeous. And short. But hey, it's the style. And I say if you've got it—well, you know the drill.

"I don't know, Andi," Vanessa Carlson laughed, emerging from the party's fray to join us, "flashing everyone might have livened things up a bit."

Vanessa and my aunt used to work together, but Vanessa—showing a great deal of wisdom, I might add—had decided to strike out on her own. The move created a bit of a rivalry, but then a little competition never hurt anyone.

"Poor Stephen probably wasn't expecting his first showing to be such a staid affair," Vanessa said, taking a glass of champagne from the silver tray of a passing waiter. "But then my mother doesn't know how to do anything without an excess of decorum."

Actually, Anna Carlson was the epitome of Upper East Side. Everything she did simply reeked of money and propriety. A combination I can do without, thank you very much. Although, considering my lineage, it's kind of hard to avoid. Anyway, despite her pre-Lagerfeld Chanel tendencies, she has a good heart—and a checkbook that guarantees that anything she attempts will be a fabulous success.

All of which boded well for Stephen's opening, even if the party was a bit dull. Most of Manhattan's elite had made their way to The Gallery in SoHo, and judging from the red dots decorating the paintings' placards, they were in a buying mood.

Stephen Hobbs is an abstract artist with a lot of talent and the sheer luck to have married into one of Manhattan's royal families. Not that it wasn't a love match. Cybil Baranski Hobbs is crazy for her husband. And despite Vanessa and Althea's sticking their noses into it (did I mention that they're matchmakers?), love prevailed and Cybil and Stephen are sublimely happy.

This was his first official showing. A social coming out, if you will.

"Well, I think the show is a rousing success," Althea said, echoing my conclusion if not the reasoning behind it. "Although Stephen looks a bit mystified by the whole thing."

"He's not used to all the attention," I said, grabbing a canapé from a passing tray. Shrimp in puff pastry. Pedestrian. But edible. It'd be better with a little cilantro and maybe a hint of cumin.

I probably should insert here that I'm a bona fide foodie, complete with a successful cable show called *What's Cooking in the City*. The concept is Martha Stewart meets *Entertainment Tonight*. Dishes from Manhattan's finest restaurants served up alongside gossip about who's eating where and with whom. Some of the biggest deals in Manhattan are struck over the perfect osso buco. And more than one tiramisu has been witness to illicit affairs of the heart. Inquiring minds and all that, but I digress. . . .

"I'll admit Stephen's a bit rough around the edges," Vanessa was saying. "But he's a good man. And he and Cybil belong together."

"Like you and Mark." Althea smiled. Mark Grayson was considered by some the catch of the century. And, quite understandably, he'd fallen for Vanessa. But she'd been a bit slow to read the memo and, as is often the case, things sort of got all mixed up. But in the end true love, as usual, had won the day, and they'd found their way together again.

Althea, naturally, was taking all the credit. She and Vanessa had made a bet about who could marry Mark off first—it had been Page Six fodder for months. But I suspect Mark would have managed without their interference. He was a "take no prisoners" kind of guy. Not the sort to give up, even with two meddling matchmakers standing in the way.

"So where's Dillon?" Vanessa asked.

"Here somewhere." I waved at the room with my champagne glass. My third. Staid parties call for serious libationary intervention.

"He's over there," Althea said, disapproval dripping from her voice like melting ice sculptures. "Flirting with Diana Merreck."

Dillon Alexander is my boyfriend (although saying it like that makes me sound all of sixteen). We've been semi–living together for a couple of years. I say "semi" because, although we invariably end up staying together at one of our apartments, despite pressure from Dillon I just haven't been able to commit to the idea of giving up my own personal space.

"He always flirts," I said with a shrug. "It doesn't mean anything." Truly, it didn't. Flirting was like breathing with Dillon. It was part of what I loved about him. Althea just liked the idea of getting in a dig. She can't stand Dillon. Thinks he isn't good enough for me. Which translates to "not of the right breeding." Dillon's California. His money's new, which in certain circles makes it completely suspect. And, according to Althea, he's got no ambition. Which is totally untrue. He's just got his own ideas about how to do things.

Which I find admirable.

Althea, not so much.

"It's not the first time I've seen him with her," she sniffed, taking a swig of her martini. Well, "swig" probably isn't the right word. Althea is nothing if not ladylike. Still, she can put away alcohol with the best of them, especially if it's served with olives. "And the truth is, I think you deserve better."

"Old song, same verse," I reminded her, wishing suddenly I hadn't felt so strongly about supporting Stephen. It's not like he needed me, and this was certainly not my idea of a good time.

"I just think you need to open your eyes and recognize the

truth. Dillon isn't the marrying kind." She scowled at me over the rim of her glass, arched eyebrows zooming up into her hairline.

"You don't know that. And besides, maybe I'm not the marrying type, either." We stood toe to toe, voices rising with each word. I knew better than to let her draw me into battle, but the champagne had loosened my tongue—and dulled my brain.

"Of course you want to get married, Andrea. You just have to find the right person. And Dillon simply isn't the right one."

"And I suppose you have someone in mind? Someone you'd like to fix me up with?" It was an old bone of contention. Althea was constantly trying to set me up with what she considered the perfect suitor.

Althea opened her mouth to respond, but Vanessa—God bless her—was faster. "Isn't that Bethany Parks over there? With Michael Stone," she inserted, neatly turning the conversation away from more dangerous ground. "I didn't know they were dating."

"This is the first," I said.

Bethany and I have been friends since our NYU days. We'd even roomed together for a while. Which is a huge undertaking, since she owns enough couture to open a Madison Avenue boutique. She needs one closet just for her shoes. Believe me when I say that Bethany lives by the adage "dress for success."

She's the kind of woman who takes the idea of Meals on Heels literally, delivering food to the apartment-bound elderly decked in her favorite Jimmy Choos. The idea of her tottering up five flights of stairs with a stack of Styrofoam containers would be laughable except for the humbling fact that she is also the kind of person who always puts others first.

Her date with Michael had come as a surprise, since she wasn't usually interested in trust-fund types. Not that there's anything wrong with Michael. He's just a bit stuffy for my taste. And, I'd thought, for Bethany's.

"Actually," Althea said, shooting me a triumphant glance, "I introduced them." So much for Vanessa's diversion.

"You set up my best friend?" I sputtered, trying to hang on to some semblance of composure. To say that I disapprove of Althea's meddling profession would be an understatement. Marriage—and love, for that matter—is not something that can be manipulated by facts and figures. It's a basic principle of science that like does not attract like. And making matches based on financial benefits and social commonalities is like throwing mud in the face of thousands of years of romantic tradition.

Not that I'm a romantic. Exactly. I just don't believe that people need intervention to find a relationship.

And I sure as hell didn't want Althea meddling in my friends' lives. Her manipulations had already cost me my mother. And I was still dealing with the fallout.

"I thought we had an agreement," I said, draining the last of my champagne.

"We had nothing of the sort. Besides, they're perfect for each other. And Bethany was just lamenting the fact that she wasn't meeting the right kinds of men."

"So you stepped in and made a match?" I swallowed, trying not to choke on my indignation.

"Not officially. I mean, Michael isn't a client. He's more of a friend. And I knew he was looking for the right someone, and Bethany's perfect. So I introduced them."

"It's still a setup. And when it goes south, I'll have to pick up the pieces."

"Who's to say it won't work out?" Vanessa asked. "I mean, Althea does know what she's doing. Michael's a good man."

"Spoken like a true matchmaker." I shrugged. "And I'm not saying Michael isn't good enough for Bethany. I don't even know him, really, except by reputation."

"Well, his background is impeccable," Althea assured me.

"That's just the point. Bethany's not going out with his background. She's going out with him. And wouldn't it have been better if they could have found each other on their own?" I sighed, realizing the futility of my words almost before I got them out. "Never mind. Stupid question, considering present company."

"Of course it's not stupid," Vanessa soothed. "It would be nice if the right people could find each other. But the truth is that it usually doesn't happen that way. And so we're here to help."

I sucked in a breath, and grabbed another glass of champagne. Vanessa was a good person, and I really wasn't trying to insult her. I just didn't believe in matchmaking. Particularly when it involved Althea and my friends.

"I just wish you'd keep your nose out of my life, Althea."

"But it isn't your life, Andrea. It's Bethany's."

"She's my friend. And you're my aunt. Which means her love life should have been off-limits."

"You're being ridiculous. Besides, it's not like I forced it on her," Althea said.

"She came to you?" I asked, surprised. Bethany knew my feelings about Althea's profession, and I'd thought she shared them.

"Not exactly," Althea said, not looking the slightest bit repentant. "I called her. But it didn't take much convincing."

"So you reached out to her, even though you knew how I felt?"

"Like I said, it wasn't about you."

"No. It never is, is it?" I sucked down more champagne and, with a tight smile, excused myself. I knew better than to get into it with Althea. There was no winning. I should never have engaged in the first place. But setting Bethany up crossed a line. An arbitrary one, to be sure. But still a boundary.

Not that Althea would recognize one of those if it hit her in the face.

Anyway, there you have it. My wonderful dysfunctional life.

But it is what it is. And except for Bethany's seeming defection, I wasn't going to let it get to me. I have my own life separate from Althea, and honestly our worlds only intersect at the odd social event. Okay, more than that, but the point is that I had broken free of all that Althea stands for years ago, and one little go-round was not going to set me back.

I stopped to exchange pleasantries with a couple of old friends, and to sign an autograph for a fan (which was somewhat surprising since the ladies who lunch hardly know where their ovens are, let alone how to tune in the Gourmet Channel). Still, the woman's gushing praise went a long way toward raising my spirits. And what that didn't accomplish, the rest of my champagne did.

I accepted a refill from a passing waiter and ignored the urge to confront Bethany with her betrayal. Best to let it wait until tomorrow. Besides, she really did look like she was having a fabulous time, and it's not as if I didn't want her to be happy. So instead, I went to congratulate the star of the evening, who was looking a bit dumbstruck by it all.

"It's a fabulous turnout," I said, waving at the glittering crowd. "And it looks like sales are brisk."

"I have no idea if they're buying because they actually like my work or if it's just fear of Anna Carlson," Stephen laughed. "But I'll take it either way. And the gallery has asked if I can extend the show."

"Well, I'd say that's an indication that the success is all yours. I mean, what's not to love?" And I meant it. Stephen's work speaks to me.

"I don't suppose you'd be willing to sell *Frenetic on Fifth?*" Cybil asked, turning from another conversation to join us. "I've had at least four offers for it."

"Not a chance. I love that painting."

Stephen had once offered me a painting and I'd chosen *Frenetic on Fifth*. And, because I think it's one of his best, I'd agreed to let him have it back for the show—strictly on loan. Which I suppose, in a weird kind of way, makes me an original patroness of the soon-to-be famous Stephen Hobbs. (Okay, maybe patroness is stretching it a bit too far. But I was definitely an early fan.)

"Never hurts to ask," Cybil continued. "I suspect you could get six figures."

"Well, kudos to Stephen. But no dice." I snagged another canapé. This one brioche topped with goat cheese and what appeared to be a bit of sun-dried tomato, although it better resembled damp cardboard. Fresh ingredients are the key to any good dish. And cutting corners is inexcusable. Especially when playing at this level.

"Don't say anything to Anna," Cybil said, eyeing the napkin where I'd discreetly folded the food. "She's used the same caterer for years, and Vanessa says she won't consider anyone else."

"I'd never say anything," I protested. "Besides, it's not bad. Just a bit pedestrian. And I'm overly critical anyway."

"You're an expert," Stephen said, loyally. "And actually, I agree."

"Me, too," Cybil laughed, "but we'll keep it on the QT."

"Hey, beautiful." Two arms encircled my waist as the words tickled my ears. "I'd wondered where you'd gotten to."

As more people stepped in to congratulate Stephen, I turned to smile up at Dillon. "Just mingling. How about you? Had enough of this party?"

"Hey, I'd had enough before I even got here."

"You should have been drinking champagne." I held up my half-empty glass as proof. "It has a way of making everything look rosy."

"Even Althea?" he queried. "I saw you talking with her and Vanessa."

"Couldn't be helped. She's hard to avoid. And besides, she wanted to gloat. Seems Bethany's gone over to the dark side."

"Dating Michael Stone, you mean? I always thought he was a bit too pompous for my taste."

"Well, you think anyone who lives above Fifty-first is pompous."

"True. But you agree with me."

"For the most part." I reached up to brush a wayward curl out of his eye. Dillon has the most glorious hair. The kind that God really should have given to a woman. But for some reason it never happens that way. Like eyelashes. Have you ever noticed that guys often have the most amazing eyelashes? It really isn't fair. "Anyway," I continued. "The relevant point here is that Althea set Bethany up."

"With Michael?" Dillon frowned. "I suppose it makes sense. But I thought your friends were off-limits."

"Apparently, the rules have changed. Only no one bothered to tell me."

"Well, there's no way it'll last."

"Exactly what I said. Anyway, what's done is done."

"Sounds like you're taking it all rather well."

"I wasn't. But as I said, I've had a few of these to dull my indignation." I shook my glass again for emphasis. "Besides, Bethany is a big girl. And if she wants Althea to set her up, I suppose it's not really any of my business. It certainly beats the hell out of Althea trying to set *me* up."

"I know she doesn't like me," Dillon said, still frowning. "But I really don't like her trolling for a replacement."

"She hasn't tried anything in ages. Although I'm sure she would if she could. You should have heard what she was saying about you."

"Anything I should be worrying about?" His expression was teasing, but there was something in his voice that gave me a moment's pause.

"Is there reason to worry?" I purposely kept my voice light, but my heart had stuttered to a stop.

"Of course not." He brushed a kiss across my forehead, but I wasn't convinced. "So what did the old battle-ax have to say?"

"Just that you were spending an unusual amount of time flirting with Diana Merreck." I laughed, but the resulting sound wasn't all that cheerful—I suppose, in part, because of all the people Dillon could have chosen to flirt with, Diana was the absolute worst. She stands for everything I hate about Manhattan society—a social predator who ranks her friends according to their breeding. She lives to judge others, and believe me, most are found wanting. To say she's a piece of work is an understatement, and the idea of Dillon spending time with her quite frankly made me sick to my stomach.

"I always flirt," Dillon said, finishing off his champagne. "You know that."

"That's what I told Althea, actually. But she implied she'd seen you together on more than one occasion." The last bit just sort of slipped out on its own, sounding much more accusatory than I'd intended.

"Really." There was definitely an underlying note in his voice. Not panic, exactly, but something very closely kin to it.

"Dillon, what is it?"

"Nothing," he said with what I considered a forced smile.

"Oh, come on," I said, stomach churning, "you don't even like champagne and you just drained your glass."

"There's nothing, I swear. You're just letting Althea get to you."

"No. I'm not." I shook my head, my heart threatening to leap right through my dress. "I know you too well. Something's up. So spill it."

"I don't think now is the right time. Why don't we head home and—," he started, but I was too wound up to let it go.

"Dillon. Whatever it is, just say it."

"I . . . ," he started, and then stopped. For a moment he just stared at his feet, then with a sigh he lifted his head, the look of regret on his face making my stomach do three-sixties. "Look, I didn't mean for you to find out this way."

"Find out what?" I snapped, working hard to keep my tone civil. It's just that I had the sudden impression that my carefully ordered life was about to spiral completely out of control.

His hands slid to my arms, palms massaging small circles as if somehow his touching me was going to make everything okay. And quite frankly, five minutes ago I'd have agreed with the idea. But that was then, and . . .

"I have been seeing Diana," he said finally.

I clenched my fists, nails digging into my palms as I struggled to comprehend the finality of those five little words. It couldn't be true. It just couldn't. This was Dillon we were talking about. *My Dillon.*

We might not have exchanged rings, but we were definitely committed. This was the man who knew me better than anyone.

My lover, my friend. The person I trusted most in all the world. I'd shared things with Dillon I'd never told anyone. Not even Bethany. We laughed at the same jokes, loved the same movies, shared a passion for Manhattan and for each other. Or at least that's what I'd believed until two minutes ago.

"It wasn't like I planned it, Andi," Dillon was saying, his words shredding what was left of my heart. "I mean, initially, I was just trying to help. She's throwing a party for a friend and she wants to have it at The Plumm. I have an in there, and so she asked if I could arrange things."

I sucked in a breath, fighting tears as I swallowed the retort forming in my head. I needed to take the high road. I needed to hang on to some semblance of normalcy.

"So anyway." He shifted uncomfortably, his hands dropping to his sides. "One thing led to another . . ."

"And you were having a private party for two?" Okay, so maybe I'm not so good at high roading. But it beat the alternative— completely and utterly falling apart.

"Yeah. But it's not like I was trying to hurt you." He actually sounded apologetic. As if in saying the last bit, he'd somehow make everything all right.

"Actually, I'm guessing I wasn't really on your mind at all in the moment." The first tears trickled down my cheeks, even as I struggled for composure. "So, was it just the once?" It was a stupid question, but you try being erudite when your boyfriend is telling you he's been schtooping someone you loathe.

"No." He shook his head. "But it's more than just sex. At least, I think it is."

Oh my God. Dillon hadn't just cheated on me. He'd gone and fallen for the woman. My gut clenched as I rejected the notion. This couldn't be happening. Not here. Not to me. I felt as if I'd blundered into some kind of alternate world. One where Bethany

needed a matchmaker and Dillon had the hots for Diana Merreck. And lest you think *I'm* being judgmental, you have to understand that Diana's all Hermès and pearls, while Dillon is
three-hundred-dollar vodka and partying until dawn. Like old
money and new money—they don't mix.

"So what?" I said, fighting to breathe normally, to keep some
semblance of calm. "You're dumping me for Diana Merreck?" My
heart had stopped beating altogether now. Although I suppose
that's impossible, since clearly I was still standing there listening
to Dillon destroy my life.

"No. I mean, yes. Oh, God, Andi, I don't know." Again with
the adorable confused look. Everything about him was so familiar. So much a part of me. And yet, it was as if I were listening to
a total stranger. Someone I barely knew.

"Well, you can't have it both ways." The words came out on a
strangled whisper, and I quickly downed the rest of my champagne in a vain attempt to find my balance.

"Why not?" he asked, his hair flopping onto his forehead
again. To my credit, I resisted the urge to yank it out of his head.
"You've always talked about our having a modern relationship."

"Yeah, but I didn't mean three-ways," I hissed through clenched
teeth, anger finally showing its wonderfully reinvigorating head.
"If you think you're going to have your cake and eat it, too, you're
out of your mind."

"I see," he said, looking defiant and apologetic all at the same
time.

"So that's it? Just like that it's over?" I half expected Ashton
Kutcher to jump out and tell me I'd been punk'd. Dillon wasn't
seeing Diana Merreck. It was all just a big joke. With me falling
for it lock, stock, and roasting pan.

"I don't want it to be. But I can't quit seeing her. I just can't."
So this wasn't a joke. Or some godawful dream. It was real.

Dillon was seeing someone else. He was seeing Diana Merreck. I'd trusted him with my heart and he'd made a complete and utter fool of me.

It was over. Just like that. Right here. Right now. In the middle of a fucking party in front of everyone we knew.

"Fine," I said, brushing angrily at my tears. I'd be damned if I'd let him be the one to cast the deathblow. "Then let's just end it now."

Without giving him a chance to respond, I turned and walked away with as much dignity as I could muster considering the circumstances and the fact that I was wearing four-inch heels. Okay, there was also the small matter of a little too much champagne. But hey, I was thankful for the insulation.

I swallowed my tears, smiled graciously at several well-wishers, ducked a conversation with a concerned-looking Vanessa, and even managed an air kiss for Kitty Wheeler. Which tells you right there how upset I was. Normally, I'd have avoided her like the plague. Besides being generally annoying, she's Diana Merreck's best friend.

Three minutes later and I was out on the sidewalk, hand extended for a cab. Except, of course, there wasn't one in sight. So I turned and started walking, reaction setting in, my body shaking as the tears began to fall in earnest. I still couldn't comprehend the enormity of what had happened. In less than two minutes my life had imploded, everything I'd believed to be true proving false.

Tears dripped off the end of my nose and I swiped at them, trying to keep my pain to myself. Fortunately, it wasn't that difficult a task. In Manhattan, no one really gives a damn. Which meant my breakdown was going pretty much unnoticed, except for a guy in a box on an abandoned stoop.

"Hey, lady," he called from his cardboard studio. "It can't be that bad."

I shook my head in answer, his words triggering the floodgates. Tears turned to sobs, and I closed my eyes, struggling for at least some semblance of composure. I could fall apart later. First, I had to get home.

I sucked in a breath, squared my shoulders, and moved forward, my foot landing on . . . nothing.

Nothing at all.

And, with an inverted jackknife worthy of an Olympian diver, I fell, butt first, into the abyss.

Chapter 2

Okay, not an abyss so much as a cellar.

I've lived my entire life in fear of falling through the hammered double doors that dot the sidewalks of Manhattan. When I was little I actually made quite a production of avoiding them. You know the drill—jumping over them. Running around them. Inching past the dubious ones, especially when the sidewalk was really crowded. But, as I got older, I realized that with a little prudence (and possibly a little less theatrics) I probably wasn't going to wind up squashed at the bottom of a dank old cellar.

Apparently, I was wrong.

The place was damp and smelled of mold. Thankfully, I'd landed on something squishy. Although on second thought, this was New York—home of Son of Sam, the Gottis, and eleven hundred episodes of *Law & Order*. My mind shifted into nefarious gear and I shuddered, trying to push to my feet.

But my legs were having none of that, and I immediately collapsed again, pain coursing through my leg and chest, something sticky dripping down my face. My left heel had broken off and my dress had a rip that made Althea's pronouncement of debauchery totally true. It was not only downright X-rated, it was impossible to repair. But, on the positive side, my shift in position had illuminated the source of my padded landing.

Cabbages—surrounded by crates of tomatoes, parsley, and what looked like turnips. I'd fallen into a vegetable market. Or, more likely, a bodega cellar.

So much for dead bodies.

"Are you all right down there?" A deep voice floated through the open doors above me. For a moment my mind played tricks on me, and my heart lurched, thinking that Dillon had come to find me. To rescue me (which was a ridiculous notion for any number of reasons, but I've always had a vivid imagination).

A dark head, clearly not Dillon's, appeared in the opening. "Should I call an ambulance?"

The idea of making a further spectacle was abhorrent. I shifted again, this time moving more slowly, anticipating the discomfort, and was satisfied that although the motion did make me a little nauseated, the pain wasn't completely unbearable. "No," I said, pulling together the tattered remnants of my dress. "I think I can make it home. I only live a couple of blocks away."

"Well, I'm coming down to make sure."

Just what I needed—a witness to my debacle.

"No, really," I called, "I can make it out. If you'll just give me a hand?" But before I could manage to move a muscle, he'd climbed down the steps (a much more sensible mode of entry) and was kneeling beside me.

"What hurts?"

"My head. A little. And my chest. Well, more my side, really."

He reached out gently to push my hair aside. "You've got a pretty nasty cut there."

"That explains the sticky stuff," I murmured. "I think I'd have preferred it be from a tomato or avocado or something."

He frowned, his fingers probing around the wound. "How hard did you hit your head?"

"It's a vegetable haven in here," I said, by way of explanation, waving weakly at a pile of potatoes in a corner. "And not that hard. At least I don't think so. Are you a doctor?"

"No." He smiled at that, and I was surprised at how much the gesture softened his face. "Just your average Good Samaritan."

I glanced up at the doorway, half expecting a crowd of faces. But the opening was empty.

"You said your chest hurts?" His hands moved down my shoulders, still palpating.

"I'm fine," I said, pulling away. "Really." Considering the situation, I was enjoying his ministrations entirely too much.

"Why don't you let me be the judge of that." He smiled again, and I nodded, grateful for the moment to let someone else be in charge. My head was starting to throb, and to be honest, I felt a bit woozy.

"So what happened?" he asked.

"I don't know. I was just walking and then boom, I landed here."

"Drinking?"

I searched his face for judgment, and seeing none answered honestly. "A little champagne." Okay—not so honestly. "But I needed it. I just broke up with my boyfriend."

"I see," he said, his words echoing Dillon's.

"No, it's not like that," I hastened to add, not sure exactly why I wanted to explain myself. "He'd just confessed to cheating on me. At a party. In front of half of the Upper East Side." Actually, I was making it sound worse. Go me.

"Well, that explains it all, then." His laugh was warm and

kind of gentle. It made me shiver. Or maybe it was the damp. Actually, it had to be the damp. The guy was a total stranger. I was just going into shock or something.

"Well, I don't think anything's broken," he pronounced, sitting back on his heels. "What do you say we get you out of here?"

I nodded as he slipped his arms underneath mine and lifted me upward. For a moment the world spun like crazy, then it cleared and I actually managed to stand on my own two feet. "Thanks," I said, clutching my dress. There wasn't much material in the first place, and thanks to some pretty provocative rippage it was not easy to stay covered.

"Here," he said, slipping out of his jacket. "Take my coat."

Well, blow me over with a feather. Chivalry is alive and well and living in a bodega cellar. Who knew?

"But I'll get blood all over it."

"So I'll get it cleaned." He shrugged. I slid in my arms as he held the jacket for me, grateful for the warmth. "How about I follow you up the steps?"

The "steps" were actually more of a ladder, and the idea of him following behind me (even though I was wearing his jacket) felt pornographic somehow. So I hesitated, standing on my one good heel, staring upward.

"It'll be fine," he soothed, as if talking to a child. "I won't follow that closely. I promise."

Embarrassment flooded my face and I looked again to see if he was laughing at me. But he wasn't. Just waiting patiently.

"Sorry. Guess I'm not thinking very clearly."

Holding a hand to my hemline, I managed to climb up and out, relieved to find that no one I knew was standing on the sidewalk. There were a few curious stares, but as I said, this was Manhattan, and frankly, my falling into a cellar didn't rank as

Gawker material. Although my minor celebrity might have elevated things a bit had the odd paparazzi happened by.

Fortunately, they had not.

My savior emerged into the light and I was surprised to see that his suit was, in fact, a tux. An expensive one at that.

"Oh my God," I said with a wash of guilt. "This is Armani."

"No worries. You clearly need it more than I do," he said, laughter coloring his voice as he took in my ragtag appearance. "Are you sure you don't want me to call for help?"

"No." I shook my head. "Honestly, I can make it from here. It's just a little way." In truth, I wasn't completely sure I could make it anywhere. But if I went to the hospital, they'd surely call Althea, and considering all that had happened, I simply wasn't up to a confrontation.

"How about I call someone?" he suggested, reading my mind.

I shook my head again, ignoring the pain. "I'd rather not make this any more public than necessary."

"But you're hurt. And you need someone to look after you."

"I've been looking after myself for a long time. Honestly. I can deal."

"Well, at least let me walk you," he said, offering his arm. Which I took gratefully. The world was starting to spin again.

"Thank you," I said, struggling to smile. "I really don't know what I'd have done without you."

"I suspect you'd have managed just fine."

I nodded my agreement, although it was an empty gesture, as I was having definite trouble just putting one foot in front of the other. We walked a couple of tentative steps, and then, without warning, I felt my knees turn to complete Jell-O.

His arms tightened around me as I opened my mouth to apologize, but my tongue clearly wasn't in the mood to cooperate.

Instead, my entire body sagged against him, my nose buried in the Egyptian cotton of his shirt as the world faded into a hazy shade of blue-black velvet.

The next thing I knew, I was lying in the ER listening to a screamer in the cubicle on the left and a woman behind the curtain on the right who clearly hadn't been happy about anything since sometime in 1966.

I had a vague memory of an ambulance and a rush of hospital personnel. Although, oddly, my clearest recollection was that my stranger had been there the whole time. Holding my hand, if my mind wasn't playing tricks on me. Of course, I probably hadn't given him much choice.

Anyway, apparently I was on my own now. Not even a doctor in sight. My purse had disappeared, along with my dress and his jacket. I gingerly felt along my hairline, my fingers encountering a gauze bandage just above my right eye.

"You had to have stitches." My aunt waltzed into the cubicle on a cloud of Opium, and I found myself wishing it were the real thing. "Seven along your hairline and five more under one rib. You're lucky you didn't break anything. But apparently you lost a lot of blood."

"That would explain the fainting."

"Yes, but not much else." Althea settled on the edge of the bed, her face lined with concern.

"How did you know I was here?" I asked.

"I got a phone call from a total stranger." She said it as if it were the most egregious of sins. "He had your cell phone, and apparently you have me on speed dial."

Stupid mistake.

"Sorry. Couldn't be helped. I was unconscious." I tried for an irritated frown, but only succeeded in a grimace of pain. "Is he still here?" There was no doubt in my mind who she was talking about. And just at the moment I really wanted to see him—to thank him, of course.

"No. He had to leave. Said to tell you not to worry about the jacket—whatever that means."

"Nothing, really. Did you get his name?" The answer suddenly seemed amazingly important, and I waited, holding my breath.

"Ivan or Aaron or something," Althea said. "I don't know. I wasn't concentrating on him. I was worried about you."

"Oh." Disappointment swelled, and I immediately felt guilty. It was the situation. Or some kind of reaction. What was it Patty Hearst had had? Stockholm syndrome? Well, I guess that's not the same thing, but you know what I mean. Clearly, it had to be some sort of illusion. I'd just lost Dillon. I couldn't possibly be interested in another man.

I shook my head, immediately regretted the motion, and then closed my eyes, waiting for the world to stop spinning.

"Are you all right?" Althea's worried gaze swam before my eyes. "The doctor said you might have a concussion."

"I feel a little woozy, that's all."

"So, want to tell me what happened?" she asked, taking my hand.

Of course I didn't, but Althea can be rather tenacious when it comes to extracting information.

I remember once when I was fifteen, Olivia Brookston and I snuck out to go to a club. We figured everything that was worth happening in Manhattan happened after our curfew. Armed with fake IDs, we managed to get in and were just high-fiving our success over Singapore slings (what can I say—I was a kid and umbrella drinks seemed really cool) when my aunt arrived and dragged us both home. I was grounded for a month, and to this day I still have no idea how she knew where we were.

The point being, Althea has a knack for knowing exactly

what it is you don't want her to figure out. Maybe that's how she manages to snare so many successful Manhattanites as clients. It wouldn't surprise me a bit. I mean, at the end of the day, knowledge is power.

Anyway, better to just come clean.

"I fell into a bodega cellar."

"I gathered that much. But your rescuer said something about your boyfriend?"

"Well, he didn't push me, if that's what you're thinking."

"Of course not." She shook her head, but I could tell that she wouldn't have put it past him. Which in some weird way was actually comforting. Even though it came from Althea. "But he did have something to do with it." She crossed her arms. Waiting.

I sighed. "Indirectly. You were right about Diana Merreck. He's been seeing her."

"Behind your back?"

"Is there any other way?" I asked, feeling miserable. As angry as I was at Dillon, I loved him. Or at least I had. No, I guessed I still did. Everything at the moment seemed a bit confusing. "Although after he came clean, he did suggest dating us both."

"And you told him to go to hell." Althea's tone made it a foregone conclusion. Which, thankfully, it was.

"Yes, but it wasn't as easy as you're making it sound. I've been with Dillon practically forever."

"Three years is not forever, Andrea," Althea said with a frown. "And besides, he was never right for you."

"Well, I thought he was." It was a stupid time to argue, considering that Dillon's recent admission had more than proved her right, but there was no way I was going to admit that. "And besides, maybe he'll get home tonight and regret the whole thing."

"And you'd take him back?"

"No. Well, I don't know. Maybe?" It wasn't the most definitive of answers, but the truth was I already missed him.

"Andrea, there's no way you'd take him back. Not after he cheated on you." She shook her head, and I could almost feel her disapproval. "Frankly, I'm surprised at Diana Merreck. I'd lay odds she hasn't mentioned the liaison to her mother."

"Can we talk about this later? Please? My head hurts." It did. Really. "I just want to go home and pretend none of this ever happened."

"Well, I hardly think that's going to be possible," a nurse said as she pushed through the cubicle curtains. "You've got a couple of bruised ribs, a gash on your belly, and a deep laceration on your head. All of which are going to be pretty hard to ignore."

Miss Congeniality reached for my wrist, checking my pulse, which had jumped alarmingly at her callous recitation of my injuries. "And to top it off," she continued, completely unaware of my discomfort, or quite possibly taking pleasure in it, "there's always the chance of concussion. So the doctor's ordered your discharge but only on the condition that you have someone who can watch over you for the next twelve hours or so."

"I can take care of myself," I said, moving to sit on the side of the gurney. The world tipped left and then right and I fought a wave of nausea. My aunt's perfectly manicured fingers closed on my arm, steadying me.

"I'm thinking maybe not," the nurse said with a snide smile of satisfaction. Definitely not a woman who'd chosen nursing because of her sense of compassion.

"It's not a problem," Althea assured her. "Andrea can stay with me."

I fought against another wave of nausea as the nurse handed me a little paper cup.

"For the pain," she said.

I swallowed the pills, wishing they'd magically transport me to a kingdom far, far away. But no such luck.

"Now, now, darling," Althea was saying as the nurse scribbled something else in my chart and then left the cubicle, "don't you worry. I'll take care of everything. I promise."

That's exactly what I was afraid of. Althea's promises tend to take on a life of their own.

"But I have to go home," I protested. "What about Bentley?"

"Bentley is a dog." A West Highland white terrier, to be exact.

"All the more reason why I need to go home," I insisted. The last thing I wanted was Althea's brand of "mothering." "He can't be left on his own."

"Fine," she said. "Then I'll call Dillon."

"No," I snapped. "He's my dog. Or at least he should be. I mean, possession is nine-tenths of the law. Right?" Technically, Bentley belonged to Dillon, but the truth was that he spent most of his time with me. Which had never presented a problem— until now. "Anyway, Bentley needs me." Or maybe I needed him. "So you can't give him to Dillon."

Althea considered the possibilities for a moment. She's not all that fond of dogs. But fortunately, she's less fond of Dillon.

"All right," she acquiesced, lifting a hand in surrender. "I'll have Wilson drive over and get him." Wilson Hartley is Althea's chauffeur. She has an entire staff, actually. Most of whom she inherited from my grandmother when Harriet decided to spend most of her time abroad. Anyway, I've known Wilson forever, which meant I could trust him with Bentley.

"Thank you." I sighed. It was a small victory. But I'd take the win.

"The important thing is that we take care of you."

The idea of Althea taking care of anyone was just this side of ludicrous. She wasn't exactly the "warm and fuzzy" type. That's why she has staff. But to be honest, at the moment, I didn't really relish being on my own. In one night, I'd been dumped, rescued, dumped again (if one considered my man of the hour's defection), and left alone with an aching body and a broken heart.

All of which made one overbearing aunt seem positively heavenly. Okay, maybe that's an exaggeration. But it did seem the lesser of two evils. I closed my eyes, shutting out the hospital, Althea, and the pain. I didn't need Dillon. Hell, I didn't need anyone.

And what's more—tomorrow was another day.

Which would have been comforting if Scarlett O'Hara hadn't been such a ninny.

Chapter 3

There's a moment when you first wake up, before your brain kicks fully into gear, when anything seems possible, and everything feels wonderful. The sun is shining, birds are singing. Okay, it's Manhattan, so think taxis honking. But the point is, life is fabulous.

For about two freakin' seconds—and then reality comes crashing in.

Some days it's worse than others (reality, I mean). And today totally topped the list. All I had to do was close my eyes and everything came back in full vegetated glory. Me, Dillonless, at the bottom of a very dark, dirty cellar. Can it get any more metaphoric?

Or awful?

I rolled over, burying my head under the pillow. Maybe if I stayed there long enough it would all go away.

"Andrea."

Then again, maybe not.

I braced myself and flipped over onto my back to face my aunt. "You're up early."

"It's not that early," she said with a shrug, pulling open the drapes. "Besides, I had an early meeting. And unfortunately, I've got another one in half an hour. I just came by to check on you."

"A matchmaker's work is never done," I said, grimacing as I sat up, every muscle in my body revolting with the movement. "Anyway, I'm perfectly fine."

"You don't look it." Althea sat on the edge of the bed, laying a hand across my forehead. "But you don't have a fever."

"I'm not sick," I protested, pulling back. "Just a bit banged up. I fell down the rabbit hole. Don't you remember?"

"Of course I do. I followed the doctor's orders to the letter, checked on you every two hours last night."

Which would explain the nightmares. "So how was your meeting?" I asked.

"Nothing important." She wrinkled her nose as she shook her head. "Potential client."

It never stopped. "Heard from Bethany?" Okay, so sue me, I was curious. And anyway, Althea required all her clients as well as their dates to check in afterward. Sort of a state of the union meeting, as it were. And I figured that even though Michael wasn't an "official" client, Althea would want to keep tabs.

"Not yet," Althea said, confirming my suspicions. "But Michael was really pleased."

"That makes it sound like he's just bought a new rug." I frowned, immediately regretting the movement since it stretched my stitches. Bentley emerged from the covers, poking a cold nose against my hand in a canine attempt at sympathy. But all it did was make me think of the carpet he'd ruined when he was a puppy.

It was African. From my mom. So it had meant a lot—to me, not Bentley. He'd relieved himself there not once but twice, and believe me, no amount of Resolve could . . . well, *resolve* the situation. So I'd consulted a Web site and, following instructions, I'd hand washed the rug the best I could and hung it out the window to air dry.

I had just been congratulating myself on a job well done when a gust of wind blew the rug off the sill and onto the top of a delivery van eight floors below. Apparently, the driver liked the new look, because he never even slowed down. Of course I ran down to the street, but by the time I got outside, the van was nowhere to be seen. I considered taking Bentley straight back to the breeder, but he'd looked so pathetically apologetic, I couldn't find it in me to take such drastic measures. Instead, we'd bonded over some Italian sausage and homemade linguine. And, except for the demise of a pair of old Manolos, we'd made it through the rest of his puppydom without incident.

But I still miss that rug.

"Michael enjoyed himself, Andrea," Althea was saying. "That's all I meant. I don't know why you have to be so prickly."

"Maybe because my life is a disaster?"

"Oh, please. Your life is fine. Or it will be after you've had some rest."

"I don't want to rest." I crossed my arms mutinously and Bentley let out a little yip of support. "I have to go to work. We're taping a segment today."

"Maybe you should postpone?"

"I can't. There's a strict schedule."

"But what about your face?" Althea asked, shaking her head like some kind of couture-clad schoolmarm. "There's quite a bit of bruising around the stitches."

I shifted so that I could better see myself in the mirror over the bureau. It wasn't a pretty picture, but with the right hair and makeup I figured no one would be the wiser.

"Even if they can camouflage the purple, what are you going to do about the pain?" Althea prompted, clearly following my internal train of thought.

"Vicodin." I picked up the bottle by the bedside table and gave it a shake.

"And your clothes?"

I was wearing the same scrubs the hospital had given me last night. Not exactly high fashion, but much better than my tattered alice + olivia. "Hello. I've got Wardrobe. It isn't exactly the big leagues, but there is a budget. Besides, we've already taped two segments of the show, so I've got to wear the same thing. And the outfit is at the studio."

"I suppose that's only sensible," Althea said, with a glance at said party dress. "Still, I don't like the idea of your trying to do anything so soon after your injury. The doctor said—"

"Twelve hours." I cut her off. "And it's been more than that."

"I should go with you," she sighed, "but as I said, I've got another appointment. Maybe I can reschedule."

"I don't need you to go with me," I protested. I'd been awake all of five minutes and already I was feeling smothered. "I can grab a taxi."

"Nonsense. But I do have a solution." She smiled as if she'd just achieved some kind of international accord. "If you insist on going, Wilson can drive you."

"But then who'll take you?" It wasn't infallible logic, but Althea did like traveling in style.

"I'll just call a service. Or take a cab." She nodded as if public transportation were an everyday occurrence. *Not.* "So we're agreed?"

"I suppose so." There was a compromise in there somewhere.

"Good, then it's settled. You'll do your taping and then Wilson will bring you home again. I should be back by then and we'll be able to make an informed decision as to whether you're ready to go back to your apartment."

We meaning *she*. Althea wasn't one for group decision making. Especially when it came to me. But just at the moment I really wasn't up to a fight.

"Oh," she said, "I almost forgot. Bernice made you breakfast." Bernice Hartley is Wilson's wife and the best cook in all the world. Really the absolute best. She makes the most fabulous blueberry muffins. I've been trying to figure out the recipe for years.

Althea waved her hand and, as if conjured, Bernie appeared in the doorway, breakfast tray in hand. In truth, I suspected she'd been listening at the door.

"So." Althea beamed as I sat back in bed and Bernie put the tray over my legs. "Everything is arranged. And I'll be back before you know it." She leaned down to give me an air kiss and then headed out the door.

"She certainly knows how to make an exit," I observed as Bernie sat on the edge of the bed next to me.

"She's really worried about you."

"I suppose. At least as much as Althea worries about anyone."

"Andi," Bernie chastised.

"I'm sorry. I guess I'm a bit out of sorts."

"Well, that's not surprising, considering all that you've been through. How are you feeling?"

"A little sore," I said, rotating my shoulder for emphasis, "but all things considered, it could have been worse."

"I meant about Dillon," she said. I should probably explain that Bernie has been listening to my problems since I was just a kid. She's been working for my grandmother since before I was born, and her kitchen's always been a place of refuge. Especially after my mother left. "I know you're hurting."

"Actually, I think I'm sort of numb," I said over a mouthful of blueberry muffin. "I had no idea he was seeing someone else."

"Well, maybe he's just sowing his oats, so to speak."

"He's sowing something all right." Diana-fucking-Merreck—if you'll excuse the pun.

"I don't blame you for being bitter, but men just have more doubts than women when it comes to commitment."

"Wilson didn't." Wilson had loved Bernie almost from the moment he saw her. It had been Bernie who'd taken a little time to come around. But in the end she'd fallen in love and the two of them had been together for over twenty years. No seed sowing in her hayloft.

"He was rather sure of himself, wasn't he?" She smiled fondly and then patted me on the leg. "Anyway, I'm sure Dillon will come to his senses and before you know it he'll be at the door, hat in hand." The idea of Dillon in a hat, let alone penitent, was laughable.

"So you really think he'll come back?" I'll admit, there was a certain amount of appeal to the idea, if only so that I'd have the opportunity to throw him to the curb.

"Yes, I do, actually. I've seen Diana Merreck, and she can't possibly hold a candle to you."

I smiled, feeling comforted in a familiar sort of way. "So," I said, changing the subject as I took another bite of muffin, "what about pepper? Could the missing ingredient be Madagascar pepper?"

"Guess the ingredients" was an old game. One we'd been playing for years. And I figured bringing it up now was as good a way as any to segue away from Dillon's philandering and the newly installed hope that maybe he'd just made a horrible mistake and, once realized, would come crawling home. Of course, there was also the fact that I really did want to figure out her muffin recipe, and I wasn't above using my current dejected state to advantage.

"It's not pepper," Bernie said with a sniff. "You're not really trying."

The truth is, Bernie is responsible for my love of cooking and I suppose de facto for my choice of career. As I said, I spent a lot of time in her kitchen. And like many unhappy kids, food had provided a nice distraction. (It's a wonder that I don't weigh three hundred pounds.)

Anyway, it became a game to try and guess the ingredients in one of Bernie's recipes. I started out with easy things like chocolate chip cookies or my favorite spaghetti sauce. And it seemed I had a knack for it. So once I'd mastered the basics, I'd moved on to more complicated challenges, like divining the secrets for making killer gnocchi or homemade tamales.

And from there I'd moved out of Bernie's kitchen, taking the whole thing to a higher level—copying the signature dishes of some of the finest chefs in the world.

I mean, this is Manhattan, a veritable bastion of culinary brilliance. What better place to taste a fabulous dish and try to identify all the different ingredients that make it so special? And it turned out I was good at it.

So good, in fact, that I managed to parlay it into a career—starting with a column in one of the dailies, followed by an early morning segment on one of the local shows. And that, along with a little divine inspiration from my friend Clinton Halderman, had led to my show on the Gourmet Channel.

Not bad for a little girl lost.

Anyway, without Bernie it never would have happened.

"I am trying," I said. "Pepper is a valid guess. There's a wonderful pound cake made with black pepper. And if someone didn't tell you it was there, you'd never know it. But the spice enhances the vanilla and in my opinion makes it one of the best cakes around."

"Yes, but it's not enhanced vanilla you're tasting, is it?"

I frowned, concentrating, and took another bite, savoring the flavor of the muffin. Blueberries, butter, eggs, cream, and coconut. The latter is what made Bernie's muffins truly unique and amazingly moist. But there was still something else. Some ingredient I'd never been able to put a finger on. I'd made batch after batch, but it was never quite right.

And Bernie wasn't telling.

"No, not vanilla. But I fell down a cellar so I'm not at my best." I sighed, resisting the urge to put hand to head.

"Nice try," she said. "But I'm still not telling. You'll figure it out. Eventually . . ."

I sighed again, just for good measure, and finished the muffin. "And if I don't?"

"Then maybe you're not as good as you think you are."

"Now that's a dagger to my heart." I feigned horror.

"Oh, please," she said, leaning over to plump my pillows. "I'm your biggest fan. Wilson even TiVo's the show, and you know he normally doesn't watch television unless there's sport involved. What I want to know is when they're going to move you to prime time?"

"You and me both." I shrugged. It was actually a bone of contention. My producer believed that we were ready. But the network wasn't as sure. "My numbers are good, so I figure when the time is right, it'll happen."

"Which reminds me. I heard an interesting tidbit the other day." Bernie was always in the know about what was new in the city. Her network of in-house domestics rivaled the CIA when it came to extracting juicy bits of information.

"So tell," I prompted with a little smile, enjoying Bernie's obvious excitement.

"Philip DuBois is here in New York." As news went, this really was big. Especially in the culinary world.

Philip DuBois was considered one of the most talented chefs in the world. Originally from France, he'd opened five-star restaurants in most of the world's hot spots, and a few not so hot, which interestingly enough had immediately put those cities on the map. In a world of celebrity chefs he was the certified king.

I'd been following his career for years, and Bernie knew how much I admired him.

"For a conference?" I asked. Manhattan's status as a culinary capital means the city's a draw for all kinds of events and seminars, and world-class chefs of DuBois' caliber are in high demand to headline such occasions.

"No," she said with a smile, clearly enjoying the moment. "He's opening a new restaurant."

"Where in the world did you hear that?"

"From Lois Miller—she had an interview for housekeeper. Apparently, he's bought an apartment and is hiring staff."

"That doesn't mean he's opening a restaurant," I said. "He's gone on record saying he'd never come back here."

Years ago DuBois had owned a restaurant called Bijou. It was a smashing success—a five-star affair—until he abdicated his role as chef to one of his staff. No one knows exactly what happened, but he left Manhattan and went back to France. And the rest is the stuff of legend. The man is an enigma. Which makes him all that much more fascinating.

"I guess he changed his mind." Bernie shrugged. "Lois was very definite on the matter. The place is going to be called

Chère, and it's supposed to open sometime this fall. DuBois is here to get it up and running."

"Did she say anything about cuisine?"

"French." Bernie nodded. "Something about going back to his roots, I think."

"Oh my God, this is huge. Any idea where the new restaurant is going to be?"

"No. Apparently, they're keeping that hush-hush. At least for now. But Lois is going back for a second interview. I suspect she'll know more after that." I'm telling you, never underestimate the domestics of Manhattan.

"Well, it's fabulous news," I said. "DuBois trained under major chefs like Michel Guérard and Roger Vergé. He's amazing. He'll be like the jewel in Manhattan's culinary crown. I can't wait."

"I'm just glad to see you smile." She glanced down at her watch. "Oh, heavens, look at the time. You're due downstairs in half an hour. So I'd best let you be getting on with it." With a last poke at the pillow, she smiled and left the room, leaving me alone—totally, completely alone.

Without Dillon.

Without anyone.

I patted Bentley, who was looking at me as if to say, *What am I, chopped liver?*, and felt a rush of self-pity. It really wasn't fair. But then, life wasn't about fair. And I wasn't a wallower. So with forced determination, I finished my breakfast, then headed for the bathroom, a shower, and some serious pharmacological help.

Less than an hour later, I was standing in Chelsea outside the doors to my studio wondering if maybe *three* Vicodin mightn't have been the better way to go.

Chapter 4

A hush fell over the normally bustling studio as I walked in, and I hesitated on the threshold, wondering how in the world news could travel so fast. But then, this was Manhattan. Clinton Halderman was the first to speak.

"You look like hell."

Clinton and I had met ages ago when he was opening his first restaurant in Manhattan. I was doing a feature on new chefs, and had scheduled an interview. Our conversation had lasted late into the night, and after several bottles of wine, a fabulous risotto, and the best crème brûlée I've ever eaten, I not only had a great article, I had a new friend and culinary adviser. So when I'd decided to try for my own show, it was only natural that I'd turned to Clinton for advice.

He'd seen the kernel of something interesting in my early morning segments, taken that tidbit, and fleshed it out. The result being *What's Cooking in the City*. Although billed as my creative consultant, he was actually the heart of the show, working on all aspects of production.

"Thanks for the charming endorsement," I said, wincing through a smile. "If it helps, it looks worse than it feels. You don't look surprised; how'd you find out?"

"You made the *Post*. 'Epicurean Socialite Tumbles into Black Hole of Despair.' Page Six. At least there weren't photos.".

"Oh, God," I sighed. "I didn't even think to look. What else did it say?"

"Basically, that Dillon's defection led to a champagne pity party that ended with a headfirst dive into a bodega cellar."

"There was no pity party," I insisted, shaking my head. "It was just an accident. I was upset."

"Justifiably," he sniffed. Clinton was loyal to a fault. "Anyway, it'll be old news by tomorrow. And I'm sure Margaret can do something to fix your face." Margaret was the show's makeup artist. "The prep work's already done. We've just been waiting for you."

"Where's Cassie?"

If Clinton was my right hand, Cassandra Harper was my left. An up-and-coming producer, Cassie was being groomed for the big time. Her love of food had landed her in my circle and, sharing common interests, we'd become friends. When Clinton had brought her the idea for the show, she'd instantly recognized its value, and, lucky for me, had the clout to make something happen. Three nail-biting meetings later she'd managed to convince the network that America wanted a little innuendo with their perfectly prepared bouillabaisse, and a month later, *What's Cooking in the City* had hit the airwaves.

"She's at a meeting upstairs. The big brass are in from Dallas."

A part of Texas-based Vision Quest, the Gourmet Channel was only five years old. Designed to compete in the burgeoning food-as-entertainment market, the network's chief competitors were the Food Network (also conveniently housed above Chelsea Market) and California-based Bravo, home to ratings-winning *Top Chef*.

The original idea for the Gourmet Channel sprang from Vision Quest's VP of artistic development, Tim Grubbin, who is also responsible for POW! (a ratings-busting superhero channel) and Two Hankies (romantic programming for women, taking on Lifetime, Oxygen, and WE). The baby of the group, Gourmet Channel was meant to feature high-end cuisine with a dash of glitterati thrown in for good measure.

"Did I know about this meeting?" I asked as I settled into the makeup chair, allowing Margaret to work her magic.

"No." Clinton sat in the chair next to mine. "Apparently, it was a last-minute thing. And judging from her face, not at all expected."

"That sounds worrisome." I frowned and Margaret tsked.

"No need to be concerned," Clinton assured. "Ratings for the show are up. And we've got solid national advertising support. I imagine it's just some sort of business thing. And frankly, that's why we've got Cassie."

"You're probably right. Besides, it's not like I don't have other things on my mind." I tilted my chin as Margaret gently rubbed foundation onto my skin to cover up my bruises.

"I really am sorry about Dillon," Clinton said.

"Me, too. But there's nothing I can do about it. So I'm just trying to soldier on."

"You sound like Althea. Soldiering is her kind of activity."

"I spent the morning with her. I guess it rubbed off. Anyway, it's useless to whine about something I can't change."

"That's a good attitude, but in my mind revenge is always the better avenue." His smile was a little wicked, and despite myself, I smiled, too.

"What have you got in mind?"

His grin broadened. "Well," he leaned in conspiratorially, lowering his voice, "it just so happens that Ms. Merreck owns a piece of Mardi Gras."

Once a month we do a segment reviewing the opening of a new restaurant in the city. Sometimes, if we like the restaurant, we have the chef on to cook one of his or her dishes. Other times, when we're not being so favorable, Clinton does the segment with me, and we cook an appropriate dish while discussing the restaurant's failures.

This month we were doing Mardi Gras. And the review wasn't good.

"How in the world did you stumble upon that little piece of information?"

He shrugged, opening his hands in the age-old sign for innocence. "Inquiring minds . . ."

"Oh, please, you were digging for dirt."

"And hit a payload." Clinton nodded, his expression smug.

"You're certain?"

"Absolutely. I had dinner last week with an old friend. He'd lost out on the sous chef position at Mardi Gras and was grousing about it. And in the course of the conversation he mentioned Diana. So this morning, I called around to verify. And it's absolutely positively true. Apparently, Diana has a small fortune invested. Which means that if it fails, she'll have eggs Benedict all over her plastically enhanced face."

"I have to admit the idea is appealing. But—"

"But what? You have her right where you want her—it's perfect."

I sighed, sorting through my cascading thoughts. I wasn't the vengeful type, but the restaurant honestly wasn't any good. So what harm could there be in twisting the knife a little? "I think you're giving me more power than I actually have."

"Maybe. But the truth is that people watch the show. And even more importantly, our reviews are often picked up by local print media. Which means that word will travel."

"And the restaurant really is awful. So it's not like we'd be lying."

"Absolutely not. But who can blame us if we pour it on a little thick. Boyfriend-stealing hussy." He wrinkled his nose with a disgusted shake of his head.

"I really do hate her." And Clinton was right, revenge would be sweet.

"So let's bring her restaurant down."

"All done," Margaret said, a smile lifting the side of her normally taciturn mouth. "And just for the record, if it were me, I'd go for it. Hell hath no fury and all that . . ."

Clinton waggled his eyebrows in agreement as I walked into the dressing room to change. A few moments later, suitably clad, I joined him on set.

Everything was ready to go, including three versions of the jambalaya we were cooking. With only thirty minutes to do the show, and only two segments of that dedicated to the dish of the day, there wasn't time to complete a dish on air. So, through the wonder of television, whatever I was cooking magically moved from one stage to the next in a matter of seconds thanks to the wonderful chefs in the network's prep kitchen.

Frank the cameraman signaled positions and, with a smile that was part Vicodin and part girl on fire, I opened the segment.

"Welcome back. Today we're celebrating the fiery tastes of Louisiana cooking. And in this segment we'll finish making our jambalaya and find out what our guest chef thinks of Manhattan's newest Creole restaurant, Mardi Gras. But first let's check our veggies. We've got chopped green pepper, onion, and celery sautéing in a little olive oil." I closed my hand on the handle of a saucier and gave the simmering vegetables a gentle toss.

"The Louisiana Trinity," I said to my invisible audience, "is the basis of all great Cajun and Creole cooking." I held up the pan and inhaled deeply. "Of course, nothing is perfect, and in my opinion, the Trinity is greatly improved with just a touch of garlic. But that could just be the Greek in me speaking. Still, it doesn't get much better than this." I held the pan out with a flourish and then placed it back on the burner.

"Next, we're going to take this base and turn it into a little piece of Cajun heaven. But before we go any further, I thought we'd bring in a little expert help. Join me in welcoming the owner and chef of Manhattan's award-winning Basil—my friend, Clinton Halderman."

The camera swiveled away from me as Clinton made his entrance, and I reached below the counter to retrieve a plate of already-chopped sausage. "Welcome, Clinton," I said, making room for him at the counter. "I was just telling these folks about the Louisiana Trinity."

"I have a good friend who swears nothing tastes right without it," he said, smiling at the camera. "In this part of the world we're not as wedded to it as they are down south, but I think we can all agree that aromatics, in whatever combination, are the basis of most great dishes."

"Jambalaya being one example," I said as the camera moved in for a closeup of the pan. "Now that our vegetables are nice and soft we're going to add some salt, pepper, and a little cayenne to raise the heat factor." I tipped the spices into the pan. "Once that's incorporated, we'll add about a pound of chopped andouille sausage."

"And while that's cooking," Clinton continued, producing a plate full of shrimp, "I'll get the shrimp ready for the pan."

I dropped the sausage into the saucier and stirred it as Clinton started to peel and devein the shrimp. "There actually aren't that many Cajun or Creole restaurants in the city," I said. "Which means the opening of a new one is something to celebrate."

"Except when it's not any good," Clinton added. "One thing I find outside the South is that the lines between Cajun and Creole start to blur."

"Creole," I said, picking up the train of thought, "is used to describe the cuisine of New Orleans. A more formal kind of cooking than rural Cajun fare, which refers to a specific type of cuisine brought to Louisiana by immigrating French Canadians back in the day."

"Unfortunately, Mardi Gras," Clinton said with a shake of his head, "the new eatery from chef Andre Lemont, is neither Cajun nor Creole, although it purports to be both."

"We recently had the opportunity to visit Mardi Gras," I explained to the camera as the monitor displayed an external photo of the restaurant, "and sample their menu."

"And sadly," Clinton continued, "it didn't live up to expectation."

"Frankly, I have to say I expected something better from Lemont," I added, my tone commiserating. "His Southern-themed Magnolia is elegant and always pleases. But his newest addition to the Manhattan restaurant scene was a dismal disappointment."

"When one eats Cajun one expects a little sizzle," Clinton said. "And that's definitely not what I got. My étouffée was cold and tasted more like bathwater than the spicy mix of crayfish and vegetables it's supposed to be." Clinton, who had made short work of the shrimp, set them aside as I added chopped tomatoes and some tomato sauce to the mixture cooking in the pan.

"It wasn't a very good start," I agreed, "and I didn't fare much better with my gumbo. The roux was overbrowned, the shrimp mushy, and the okra tasted like something left in the refrigerator too long." I sighed with an apologetic shrug for the camera, thinking about Diana and hoping Clinton was right and she'd sunk everything she owned into the restaurant. (Although it was a wishful thought, in actuality, since Diana's family had more money than they knew what to do with.) "I'm sorry if our review isn't making you long for Cajun cooking," I continued, pulling my thoughts back to the task at hand. "But I promise you *our* jambalaya won't disappoint."

I gave the ingredients in the pan a quick stir as the camera moved in closer. "After the sauce reaches a bubble you want to add your shrimp and cook just until it turns opaque."

"You can toss in a bay leaf at this stage if you like," Clinton added as I slid the shrimp into the pan. "But remember to remove it before serving."

The camera moved back out to encompass us both. "Anyway, back to our restaurant of the week," I said. "I was really hoping the main course would change my opinion. Unfortunately, that wasn't the case. My fish was overcooked and the sauce was uninteresting and overly bland." Maybe I was laying it on a little thick. But frankly, the idea of sticking it to Diana Merreck had taken on a life of its own.

"I had oyster pie," Clinton said, "and although it was better than my appetizer, it certainly wasn't anything out of the ordinary. Really, the only thing about the evening that wasn't mediocre was the fact that we were sitting at a table next to George Clooney."

"He had snapper. But he left most of it on his plate," I said, leaning toward the camera as if I were sharing a special secret.

"Not much of a recommendation, is it?" Clinton shook his head again.

In truth, Clooney had been two tables over and I couldn't actually see what he was eating. Although I did hear him order the snapper. So it was more or less the truth.

"When the shrimp has cooked through," I said, turning back to the jambalaya, "the only thing left is to add the rice and broth. Once that's done, just cover the whole thing and simmer for twenty minutes." I put the lid on the skillet and reached for another pan beneath the counter. "And now with a little help from the food fairies," I said, removing the lid with a flourish, "I present some of the best jambalaya this side of New Orleans."

"All it needs," Clinton said, "is some last-minute razzle-dazzle." He picked up a bottle of hot sauce and gave it a good shake into the pot.

I inhaled deeply with a sigh. "Simply fabulous."

"Unlike Mardi Gras," Clinton added. "To which I have to give a resounding thumbs-down." Again the monitor showed the exterior of the restaurant.

"Honestly, people—if you're craving Cajun, I'd give Mardi Gras a pass." I shrugged, then smiled for the camera. "Coming up . . . Clinton's going to help me make a fabulous eggnog bread pudding. An oh-so-sweet ending to our hot, spicy start. See you in a minute."

"And we're out . . . ," Frank said with a nod. "Good job."

"The jambalaya actually looks divine," Cassie said, walking onto the set. "But weren't you a little harsh on Mardi Gras?"

Clinton and I exchanged looks. "It really wasn't a good experience."

"Well, no matter," she said with a dismissive wave of her hand. "Controversy makes for good shows. Besides, I've got more important things to talk about."

"Your meeting?" I asked, my heart suddenly moving in double time.

"Yes, actually." She gestured us over toward a corner of the studio out of earshot of the various technicians still working on set. Then, with a frown, she studied my battered face. "God, Andi, you look awful."

"That seems to be the prevailing opinion. But believe me, it was a lot worse before Margaret got hold of me."

"I was sorry to hear about Dillon," she said. "But I'm sure you'll find someone new in no time at all."

"I don't want someone new," I said stubbornly, realizing that in fact I did not. What I wanted was Dillon. Or at least the Dillon I'd originally fallen in love with. The one who didn't cheat.

"Andi's going to be fine," Clinton said, matter-of-factly coming to my rescue, "and if memory serves, you had something important to tell us."

"Right. Yes. Of course." Cassie leaned in, lowering her voice. "I found out that Liddy McDermot is pregnant."

Liddy was the shining stone in the Gourmet Channel regalia. Her show, *Dining with Style*, was the network's centerpiece. Winning numerous awards its first year out, the show had raised the bar for similar programs. *Dining with Style* was a wonderful combination of simplicity, wit, and elegance. Of course, the fact that Liddy was a society maven didn't hurt matters at all. If Liddy said it was so—America listened.

"Other than maybe the political advantage of sending congratulations," Clinton frowned, "I'm not sure I see what the big deal is."

"That's because I haven't told you everything yet." Cassie crossed her arms, shooting him a narrow-eyed glare.

"So tell . . . ," I prompted, my moribund thinking morphing into something more positive.

"Liddy's leaving the show." She waited for her words to sink in, then continued. "Effective immediately. Her husband's never been too keen on the idea of her working, and apparently in light of her new condition he put his proverbial foot down."

"And since he pays the bills, Liddy had to listen." The idea appalled me on so many levels, there really weren't even words.

"To be honest, I think she's always thought of the show as a lark. Anyway, needless to say, the network is beside itself."

"Doesn't she have a contract?" Clinton asked.

"Of course. But she's also got the money to buy it out." Again she paused, then smiled. "Which means that the suits are scrambling to find a replacement."

"And they want me?" I squeaked, excitement making me sound like an overagitated Betty Boop as the full implication of Cassie's words sank in.

"Well," Cassie said, her tone cautionary, "they're considering you. Along with Ricardo Benavides and Missy Greenbaum."

"Ricardo's English is barely passable," I protested.

"But he's hot," Clinton said on a sigh.

"Point taken." I frowned. "I can accept that. But Missy? She's so . . . so . . . down home." Missy hailed from Georgia and her cooking reflected the fact. "The Gourmet Channel is about elegance. And what's more elegant than Manhattan dining?"

"Nothing," Clinton said, nodding his agreement.

"Your demographics do most closely match Liddy's," Cassie said, "but Clinton is right, Ricardo's a draw for completely physical reasons. And Missy's already in prime time."

"At seven thirty. In New York that's opposite *Wheel of Fortune*."

"Not in the heart of the country, and that's where most of the viewers come from. We skew eastern because people in the city like to hear about the dining scene. But the show hasn't been tested in prime time."

"But you said they're considering me."

"Yes. And to be honest, I think they're even leaning our way, but they want to be fair."

"Wonderful time for them to start that kind of thinking," Clinton said, sarcasm dimming his enthusiasm. "So what's the deal?"

"All three shows are being given the chance to come up with something worthy of prime time. No format changes or anything that dramatic. Just something kick-ass for a special show."

"I don't suppose they gave you any guidance?"

"Not in the meeting, no. But Bob Baker pulled me aside afterward. That's how I know they're leaning our way. He said all they were looking for was a ratings grabber. For our show he suggested finding a killer guest chef. Someone that Americans know about but haven't seen."

"Talk about impossible tasks," Clinton said as my stomach sank. "These days, thanks to all the cooking shows, most marketable chefs have already had their fifteen minutes of fame. Celebrity goes epicurean. How are we supposed to find someone who is part of the public consciousness and yet hasn't already been exploited?"

"I don't know. I'm just telling you what Bob told me. If we want to win we need to find the perfect guest. Someone who'll start a buzz from the moment we announce the show."

"So we're screwed." Clinton wasn't usually so much of a pessimist, but to be honest, he wasn't all that much off the mark.

"What do Missy and Ricardo have to do?"

"I've no idea," Cassie said with a shrug. "And frankly, that's not our problem. Finding a superchef is. Surely you all can think of someone. Between the two of you you know practically every chef in town."

"That's the problem," Clinton sighed. "The reason we know

them is because everyone does. At least the ones that are worth knowing about."

"Except Philip DuBois," I said, excitement cresting again. "He's coming back to New York. Opening a new restaurant. Bernie told me. If we can get him on the show, it'll be the coup of the year. It'll mean not only regular Gourmet Channel viewers, but most of society and all the epicurean world. The man is an enigma."

"Yes, but . . . ," Clinton started, only to have Cassie motion him quiet.

"I think you're on to something. The brass will love the idea. DuBois can cook with you and talk about his new endeavor. It'll be fabulous publicity for him and should skyrocket our ratings."

"But," Clinton insisted, still playing the role of killjoy, "he never gives interviews."

"It won't be an interview," Cassie gushed, still rolling on the momentum of the idea, her PR training kicking into high gear. "It'll be more like a master class. Andi cooking with a legend. This is inspired."

She was right. The whole idea was amazing—heady and seductive—me on prime time with Philip DuBois. This was it. My big break.

There was only one problem.

Clinton was right. DuBois never did interviews. Or anything else remotely connected with the media.

Which left only one alternative.

I'd simply have to change his mind.

Chapter 5

Saying I was going to convince Philip DuBois to come on my show and actually doing it were two completely separate things. And after the initial excitement of my pronouncement, I have to say I'd lost a little enthusiasm.

From my meeting with Cassie, I'd gone on to tape some teasers and do some prep work for the next show. Finally, finished, I'd fled the studio, hoping for a little R & R. Instead, I'd run into Bob Baker. He'd applauded my initiative and congratulated me on getting DuBois for the show.

Apparently, Cassie and her marketing mojo had taken my pie-in-the-sky idea and somehow morphed it into a confirmed reality, leaving Bob ebulliently counting the ratings and congratulating me on mission impossible.

Which meant, of course, that now nothing less than success would do.

To say I was panicked was a complete understatement. And so I'd retreated to the solace of Central Park. Well, actually, I'd gone to Althea's. She'd have just hunted me down if I hadn't. But I'd jumped at her suggestion of a walk in the park to clear my head, since the suggestion meant avoiding her constant hovering and endless questions. And truly, a leisurely stroll along tree-lined paths seemed just what the doctor ordered.

Of course, Manhattan is all about multitasking, so I'd brought Bentley along. Which meant, of course, that my stroll had turned into more of a brisk walk. The dog has never met a person, place, or thing he doesn't love, and I mean with his entire little canine heart. So far he'd stalked a pigeon, chased a squirrel, damn near climbed a tree, and peed on pretty much every tree and lamppost in this part of the park. To say that Bentley was enthusiastic would be a definite understatement.

Finally, though, his energy spent, we'd settled on a bench on the far side of Conservatory Water, content for the moment just to watch the world go by. It was a beautiful day, tulips poking their heads out of the ground and little radio-controlled sailboats gliding over the water, sails fluttering in the breeze.

A woman with a voice like a foghorn and an umbrella held in the air summoned a group of tourists to huddle around the statue of Alice at the north end of the pond. Thanks to a guy with a clarinet directly across from her under the shadow of an elm, she was having a little trouble being heard. It was sort of like dueling instruments. The guide would raise her voice, and the musician (and I use that word loosely) would increase the volume of his wail, the resulting cacophony scattering tourists and nontourists alike.

My dog lifted his head as the guide's voice reached chalk-on-blackboard levels, and clarinet guy, admitting defeat, gave me a grin and a shrug and headed off in the direction of the tunnel near Bethesda Fountain. The acoustics there are killer—better than Carnegie Hall, with a much less stringent dress code. Bentley gave a doggy sigh, and let his head drop back into my lap. The tour group lingered for a few more minutes and then the guide was off, umbrella bobbing through a sea of polyester and Nike-clad sixty-somethings as they made their way toward the Ramble.

I closed my eyes and let the sun-dappled warmth of the day envelop me, allowing, just for a moment, the idea that maybe everything would manage to turn out right. Diana Merreck's investment in Mardi Gras would go down the tubes, Dillon would come back to me, proverbial tail between his legs, and Philip DuBois would jump at the opportunity to be on my show. In short, life would be perfect again.

Of course, I should have known better. Just entertaining the notion of everything turning out all right was enough to wave a red flag at fate, tempting it to step in and show me who was boss.

With an excited bark, Bentley suddenly leapt off the bench, startling me into dropping the leash. And before I had the chance to correct the matter, he was free and running hell-bent for leather down the pathway after an equally wing-footed squirrel.

I screamed his name, gaining a leer from a fellow sitting two benches down, and a stern look of disapproval from a nanny with her sleeping charge. Ignoring them both, I called again, but the distance was increasing, and Bentley showed no interest whatsoever in slowing down. He didn't even pause to look behind him.

Sprinting—in flip-flops—I took off after him, alternating between cursing my dog and running through possible explanations I was going to have to create in order to break the news to Dillon that I had not only assumed ownership of his dog, but had managed to lose him as well. Completely oblivious to my turmoil, the canine in question disappeared around a bend without a backward glance, and for the first time I felt a tinge of panic. I couldn't stand it if anything happened to the little guy, at least not until I got hold of him and wrung his fuzzy little neck.

I took the corner, Jimmy Buffet lyrics ringing through my head. I'd never blown out a flip-flop but just at the moment it didn't seem that far outside the realm of possibility.

No sign of my wayward dog.

I tried to call for him again, but thanks to the unintended wind sprint was capable only of an asthmatic whisper. A second bend appeared and I rounded it, thinking I was screwed, but no, there was Bentley—joyfully accosting a jogger, tongue lolling, tail wagging. (The dog, not the jogger.)

I skidded to a stop. "I'm so sorry, he got away and . . . ," I stopped, my heart, which was already beating chaotically, moving into triple time as my brain registered exactly who it was that Bentley was accosting.

"I take it he belongs to you," my stranger said with a crooked smile.

"Yeah," I whispered, trying to make sense of this newest turn of events.

Okay, let's just stop right here and say that walking in the park to clear my head is one thing. I mean, it's just me and Bentley and a bunch of strangers. But running into the man who practically saved your life, wearing flip-flops, jeans, and a tatty T-shirt, is not the done thing. Especially when you add in the facts that I'd scrubbed off my makeup the minute we'd wrapped the show and that my hair, thanks to my recent wind sprint, probably resembled a Manhattan rat's nest.

I pushed said hair out of my face and strove for a calm I definitely didn't feel. "I'm afraid he got away from me." I looked down at Bentley, who was still eyeing my stranger with something akin to adoration. "He saw a squirrel and pulled free before I had a chance to react."

"Good thing I was here to head him off at the pass," my stranger said, still smiling, his dark eyes taking in my disheveled appearance.

"Yeah, I'm not exactly dressed for running." But he was. Sweats, T-shirt, hot, sweaty—did I mention hot? Why is it men look good covered in sweat? It isn't fair. Really. It's not. "Anyway, thanks for saving the day. Again."

"Not a problem," he laughed, shaking his head. "Just in the right place at the right time."

"Small world," I said with a wry grin.

"Well, it's a little island." He shrugged, reaching down to scoop Bentley up into his arms. My dog wiggled in doggy ecstasy as the man of the moment scratched him behind the ears.

"You left without saying good-bye." The words just came out of their own accord. But then my mouth had always had a mind of its own.

"I thought maybe under the circumstances you'd rather be alone. Besides, your aunt had arrived, so I left you in good hands."

"That's questionable, actually. But I understand. And I really do appreciate your help. You seem to be making a habit of riding to my rescue."

"Like I said, right place, right time," he said, walking over to drop down on a bench, my moonstruck dog still snuggling in his arms. I followed with a sigh. It wasn't like I had a choice. Really. He had my dog.

"So," I said, sitting awkwardly on the edge of the bench, still wishing an *Extreme Makeover* team would arrive with the precision of a NASCAR pit crew to comb, curl, clothe, and otherwise transform me into something a little more presentable, "I'm afraid you have me at a disadvantage."

He frowned for a minute and then smiled. "Ethan McCay. I

would have introduced myself last night, but you were kind of down for the count."

"Not my finest moment."

"So, who's this?" he asked, tactfully steering to a less awkward subject.

"Bentley." I smiled as said named dog stretched out on the bench between us, tail thumping like mad.

"As in the car?"

"Exactly," I said, nodding my approval. "My grandfather owned two of them. Classics from the fifties. And when I was little I loved riding around in them. So I guess it's a tribute to my grandfather. At least in part."

"Well, it's a great name for a dog."

"You really think so? Dillon never liked it."

"Dillon?"

"My ex," I said, wishing I'd kept my mouth shut. "The one I broke up with last night. Bentley is really his dog. Well, at least technically. But it turns out Dillon's not the nurturing type. At least when it comes to dogs. And since he spent more time at my apartment than his own, it just seemed simpler for Bentley to live with me. And now, under the circumstances, I figure—"

"Possession is nine-tenths of the law?" Ethan finished for me.

"Something like that. I really haven't had time to think it through. I just know that I'm not giving him up."

"Well, I don't blame you. And besides, I suspect Bentley's better off with you."

I waited for something more, but he went silent, and it stretched between us hovering somewhere between awkward and comfortable.

"I suppose we really should let you get back to your run," I said, more out of polite necessity than any real desire to see him go.

"It's all right," he assured me. "I was almost finished anyway. And it's nice to have company while I cool down."

"So you live around here?" I asked, trying to picture what his apartment would look like.

"Yeah, a couple blocks down from the Met." He nodded in the direction of Fifth Avenue. Or at least I assumed it was that direction. I'd sort of gotten turned around as I'd chased Bentley along the twisting paths.

"Wow. Nice address." Actually, I abhorred it. But now wasn't the time for a diatribe on Upper East Side living.

"I'm just staying there until I find a place of my own. I've only been back in the city a couple of weeks."

"Really?" I asked, immediately curious. "So where've you been?"

"Bouncing around. My family owns several companies and I've been traveling between them managing our legal affairs."

"You're an attorney." Upper East Side and a lawyer. Two for two—and I don't mean that in a good way. Still, he had saved my life . . . or very close to it.

"Yes. Corporate. But right now I'm just taking care of the family business. My dad had a heart attack, and I've been trying to help out."

Okay, very decidedly un–Upper East Side. "So you said 'back.' I take it that means you've lived here before?"

"Yeah, I grew up in the city, and most of my family is still here or at least somewhere nearby. How about you?"

"Pretty much the same. Except that I never left. I grew up near Carl Schurz Park. With my aunt and my grandmother. Then, after a stint at NYU, I moved to SoHo."

"That's right, you said last night that your apartment was in the neighborhood. So isn't Central Park a little bit far afield?"

"My aunt lives on Fifth. Nine twenty-seven. You know, the

one with the hawks? Anyway, I stayed with her last night. The doctor seemed to think I needed supervision."

"Probably a wise idea." He nodded, his fingers ruffling Bentley's fur. "You could have had a concussion. So how are you feeling?"

"Pretty good, considering. I've got bruises on my bruises, and a lot of stitches. But all in all, I'd say I'm on the mend. I even managed to tape my show this morning."

"Your show?" he prompted.

"Yeah. I have a television show. On the Gourmet Channel." I explained about *What's Cooking* and my unexpected shot at prime time, as well as my overenthusiastic gaffe and the mess it had landed me in. I'm not usually a "spill your guts to strangers" kind of girl, but I couldn't seem to help myself.

"So basically," he said, still scratching Bentley behind his ears, "you've backed yourself into a corner. You've got to produce Philip DuBois or one of your competitors gets the slot."

"That basically sums it up. Which means that, thanks to my big mouth, I'm screwed."

"Surely you're not giving up that easily."

"Well, no. I'm not. But if I'd had the chance to think about it—I mean, really think—I'd never have made the suggestion. I kind of have a tendency to talk first and think later."

"But it sounds like your producer kind of jumped the gun."

"Well, it's part of her charm. Or at least her success. Anyway, the point is I've got no one to blame but myself. So now I've just got to formulate a plan. Hence the walk in the park."

"It's definitely a good place for thinking."

"Except that I haven't come up with much. The man's truly publicity shy. Which means that it's almost impossible to gain access of any kind. Still, I figure where there's a will, there's a way."

"If I had to bet, I'd definitely put my money on you."

"From your mouth . . ."

"I'm usually right about these things."

"Positive thought." I smiled, suddenly feeling a little shy. "Anyway, none of it is going to do me any good if I can't figure out a way to reach him."

"Well, if it helps, I'm pretty sure DuBois' company uses Metro Media to handle his PR. That might be as good a place as any to start."

"There you go, coming to my rescue again." I'd meant the words sincerely but somehow they came out sounding flip.

"Hardly," he said, the silence between us growing awkward again.

"I'm sorry, that didn't come out right," I backpedaled, cursing my overactive mouth. "It's just that, considering the circumstances, it's sort of odd that you'd know DuBois. I mean, first you rescue me, and then my dog, and now my business."

"Well, I only told you who handles his PR. What you do with the information is up to you. And for the record, I don't know the man personally. My family's company has done business with his a couple of times. That's all. Are you always this cynical?"

"No. Actually, I'm usually quite the optimist. It's just been a tough twenty-four hours. But it would have been a lot rougher if it hadn't been for you. I didn't mean to sound rude."

"You're fine. As you said, you're not at your best. And frankly," he said, waving at his running attire, "neither am I. So what do you say we try this again? Over dinner. Tonight?"

"Oh. I, uh . . . I can't. Really. I'm afraid I've already got plans." I didn't. And I wasn't sure exactly why I was pretending I did. Except that, to be completely honest, Ethan McCay scared me. I mean, I was in love with Dillon, and breakup notwithstanding, I shouldn't be thinking about another man. It was too soon.

"Okay." He shrugged, obviously unaware of my internal struggle. "Then how about tomorrow?"

"No. I can't." The words came out much stronger than I had intended, and I immediately wished them back.

"I see," he said, his voice cooling by a couple of degrees.

"I'm sorry," I rushed to explain. "But I've only just split with Dillon and I'm just not ready for another relationship."

His mouth twitched at the corner. "I wasn't suggesting we get engaged. Just get to know each other a little better."

"Of course. I didn't mean to suggest otherwise. It's just that everything's turned upside down right now. And I don't need any more complications. Not that you're a problem. You're great. It's just that I'm a mess. I mean, even if it weren't for Dillon, there's still the matter of my head, you know, my stitches—the concussion." I was babbling. Even Bentley was looking at me as if I'd grown two heads. "I'm sorry, I know I'm not making any sense at all. I appreciate everything you've done for me. I mean, gosh, I should be asking you to dinner. To say thank you. After all, I ruined your jacket. And quite probably your evening. But at the moment, I just don't think I'm up to it." I'd gone from muddled to addled in under fifteen seconds.

"It's okay," he said, laying his hand over mine. "I understand. Truly."

I bit my bottom lip, feeling all of about sixteen. "I'm sorry."

"Look," he said, reaching into his pocket, "why don't we do this. I'll give you my number, and if you change your mind, you can call me." He produced a business card and handed it to me.

I nodded, shoving the card into my pocket, words finally having completely deserted me.

Ethan stood up and Bentley jumped to the ground, tail wagging, ready to follow his new friend wherever he might be going.

I envied him his complete and utter trust. "Clearly, my dog adores you."

"So that's got to be a vote in my favor. Right?"

"You don't need a vote of confidence. There's nothing wrong with you. I told you, it's me. I'm just not in a good place right now. But I really do appreciate the thought. More than you'll ever know."

He reached over to tuck a wayward strand of hair behind my ear, bending close in the process, his breath mingling with mine. "So, call me."

Our gazes met and held, and it occurred to me that I was probably going to look back on this moment with great regret. But before I could find the courage to say anything, he was off—which was probably for the best.

At least that's what I told myself.

But I didn't really believe it. And judging from the expression on Bentley's fuzzy little face, neither did he.

Chapter 6

Home sweet home is supposed to denote a safe haven. A place where one can escape from the evils of the world. But apparently that doesn't apply when one's home was recently inhabited by one's ex. Especially when his stuff is lying literally everywhere. I'd never really thought of Dillon as a slob before, but the evidence was overwhelming.

I live on the top floor of what was once a factory and then a warehouse. In the sixties the building was abandoned and then invaded by struggling artists who set up studios and created the bohemian culture SoHo is still known for today.

By the time I came on the scene, though, it was just an apartment building. Granted, one with really high ceilings and large rooms, but nothing particularly special. I had a huge living area, a third of which was dedicated to a state-of-the-art open kitchen, and a smaller adjoining room that served as my bedroom. But even though I adored my kitchen, that wasn't why I bought the apartment. The real pièce de résistance was located at the top of a spiral staircase. The small doorway at the top opened onto what, in Manhattan, was equivalent to the holy grail—a rooftop garden with amazing views. And, thanks to a rather sizable inheritance from my grandfather, it belonged completely and totally to me.

As a result, I was definitely cash poorer, but with skyrocketing property values, I was sitting on a real estate gold mine. Not that I had any intention of ever selling. That had been the primary reason Dillon and I hadn't officially moved in together. He owns an apartment downtown in one of those high-rise, high-dollar monstrosities that are slowly replacing buildings with character. His idea of heaven is a staff and an amenity-heavy building. Character be damned.

I wouldn't sell. And neither would he. Of course I'd believed that eventually he'd come around to my way of thinking. Which, considering the fact that half of his worldly possessions were strewn across my living room, hadn't been totally unjustified. I mean, he had, for all practical purposes, been living here with me.

Which would have been fine if he hadn't been spending the rest of his time with Diana.

So color me clueless. Isn't that always the way?

Anyway, to add injury to insult, he'd left me at least five voice mails. The first couple were pretty apologetic, I have to admit, but the latest ones were all about getting his stuff, including Bentley. *Fat chance.* It was tempting to just burn the lot (not the dog, of course), but I figured it would just be easier to pack everything up and ship it off to his apartment.

So after deleting the rest of my messages, most of them unheard, I grabbed a FreshDirect box I'd stored in the closet and started gathering up the paraphernalia that apparently had defined my relationship with Dillon.

I'd miss his DVD collection. We both had a fondness for Cary Grant movies. I slipped his copy of *Bringing Up Baby* back onto the shelf. Surely I deserved a little compensation. I was the wounded party, after all. Next up were his CDs. Nothing here that I couldn't replace. In fact, I'd never miss most of it. Particularly his predilection for the Talking Heads. With the box half full, I moved to the bedroom, emptying hangers and drawers. Considering the man had his own apartment, he'd kept a lot here.

Bentley watched as I moved on to the bathroom and a second box. Then finally, in a fit of adrenaline-spurred anger, I stripped photographs of Dillon from picture frames scattered around the apartment. I was on the verge of cutting him out of two of my favorite group shots when the house phone started to ring.

I checked the security camera and recognized Bethany and Clinton standing at the front door. With a sigh, I buzzed them in, not certain I was really up to company but definitely not up to trying to explain it over the ancient contraption that passed as our building's intercom. For aesthetic reasons they hadn't replaced the boxes when they'd added the new security system. Which meant I could see the person at the door, but any attempt at conversation was accompanied by enough static to drive a sane person around the bend.

The only thing older than the intercom was the elevator. So I unlocked the door and returned to the granite-topped kitchen island and my cutting spree.

"What's with the boxes?" Bethany asked when she and Clinton finally let themselves into the apartment. "It looks like someone's moving."

"Dillon." I nodded as I clipped through his face with a satisfied smile. "I considered a bonfire, but figured the building board wouldn't approve. Seemed simpler just to message his things."

"Sans photographs," Clinton observed as I cheerfully slit another picture.

"I just didn't want to look at him."

"Looks like fun," Bethany said. "Can I help?"

"All done, actually." I smiled. "So what brings you guys to SoHo?" Bethany lived on the West Side and Clinton had a fabulous loft in the East Village, neither of which is exactly in the neighborhood.

"Just wanted to see how you were doing," Bethany said.

"And I brought sustenance," Clinton said, holding up a bag of groceries. "Got everything here for your favorite mac and cheese."

"The one from Artisanal?" Artisanal is a restaurant at Park and East Thirty-second that's known for its cheeses, particularly fondue. But personally, I love their macaroni and cheese. I swear it's the best I've ever tasted. The key is using good Gruyère, and majorly buttered bread crumbs. It's not diet friendly but it really hits the spot when you need a little comfort food. "Just what the doctor ordered," I said, tossing the last of Dillon into the trash. "You're wonderful."

"I try," Clinton said with a smile, laying the groceries on the counter and beginning his prep. "Anyway, we figured you could use a little TLC."

I smiled, suddenly feeling absurdly happy. "So what else have you got?"

"Bordeaux," Bethany said, flourishing a couple of bottles of my favorite French Médoc. "And chocolate. Martine's." She pulled the signature pink box from a Bloomingdale's bag.

"Perfect."

Fifteen minutes later, mac and cheese bubbling in the oven,

we settled down on my sofa and chairs with glasses of wine and a plate of freshly made crostini. It pays to have a chef as a best friend. (Not that I can't manage a spread when called upon, mind you. It's just that sometimes it's nice to have someone else do the cooking.)

"You don't look as bad as I expected," Bethany said. "I mean, you can hardly see the stitches, and your bruises are already fading."

"Actually, they've gone Technicolor," I laughed, lifting my T-shirt to show off the yellow, green, and purple staining my rib cage.

"Does it hurt?" she asked, wrinkling her nose.

"Only when I breathe." I laughed again, taking a sip of wine. "Actually, it really doesn't hurt that much."

"So how many Vicodin are you taking?" Clinton asked, reaching for a crostini.

"I'm down to one at a time. But I admit I'm still taking them right on schedule. All in all, though, I was pretty lucky. It could have been a lot worse."

"So what about your rescuer?" Bethany asked. "Has he called or anything?"

"Well, as a matter of fact," I said, a blush staining my cheeks, "I ran into him in the park."

"Small world," Clinton observed.

"That's just what I said. The whole thing was all Bentley's doing, really." Bentley's ears perked up at the sound of his name and he gave up hovering for dropped crostini, jumping up beside me on the sofa instead. "He managed to get off leash. Chasing a squirrel. And anyway, one thing led to another and there he was—my stranger. He was jogging and intercepted Bentley at a bend in the path."

"So did you find out who he is?"

"Of course. His name is Ethan McCay."

"Never heard of him," Clinton said. "But then even I don't know everyone in the city. Bethany?"

"The last name is vaguely familiar but nothing concrete is coming to mind."

"Well, it wouldn't," I said. "He's only just moved back to the city. He's an attorney. Works for his family's business."

"Sounds interesting. What else did you guys talk about?"

"Nothing specific, really. We talked about my accident. And I told him about my show and the mess I landed myself in. Which reminds me. He mentioned Metro Media. Thinks maybe someone there is handling DeBois' PR."

"If that's true," Clinton said, "it might just give us the in we need."

"I thought the same thing. The trick, of course, being to find out who it is."

"I might be able to help there," Bethany said. "I sold a sweet little co-op on West Eighty-second to a woman who works for Metro Media. She's really chatty. Do you want me to see what I can find out?"

Bethany's a real estate broker. With Corcoran. She spends most of her time squiring people around town trying to find the perfect space for them to land. And considering average apartment prices have passed the million-dollar mark, it's a pretty lucrative way to make your living. Anyway, in this city, once you find a good broker you tend to hang on to them, which means that Bethany has a very eclectic and often quite connected list of clients.

"That would be wonderful," I said, Clinton nodding his agreement. "I take it Clinton filled you in on my morning's misadventure?"

"Yeah. And I think it's a fabulous idea."

"Except for the fact that it's probably impossible," I said.

"Well, if anyone can convince Philip DuBois to step into the limelight, it's you," Bethany said with a nod.

"I appreciate your confidence. But let's just take it one step at a time."

"Yes, but *prime time*," she said, her exuberance catching.

"I know. It would be amazing." I sighed.

"And well deserved," Clinton agreed. "But Andi's right. We shouldn't get ahead of ourselves. First step is to get a name. And then an appointment. From there we'll see what develops."

"Ever the practical one," Bethany said with a shrug. "Anyway, Andi, you haven't finished telling us about Ethan McCay."

"Yes," Clinton added, walking into the kitchen, "was he as charming in the daylight as he was in the dark of night?"

"The cellar, you mean?"

"You're taking all the fun out of it," Clinton said, opening the oven door to check on the mac and cheese. "I think it's incredibly romantic."

"You think Hallmark commercials are romantic."

"Well, they are. Besides, what's not to love? Damsel in distress rescued by dark stranger dressed in Armani."

"I was lucky he was there. But considering the fact that I was covered in blood and vegetable guts, which I managed to get all over him when I passed out, I kind of think the romantic bit is a stretch."

"I wish it had happened to me," Bethany said on a sigh. "So are you seeing him again?"

"He asked me to dinner."

"What did you say?" Clinton asked, dropping back onto the sofa.

"I said no. I just broke up with Dillon. It's too soon."

"Sometimes fate has other things in mind."

"Well, not for me." Although a part of me was still regretting my decision.

"I can't believe you turned him down. I mean, a date might be just the thing you need to get your mind off of Dillon."

"Or make me think about him even more. Just because he dumped me doesn't mean that I'm over him."

"Well, first off," Clinton said, "you broke up with him. As I recall, he wanted to keep seeing you."

"And Diana."

"True. But you still get credit for the breakup. And in my book that's extremely important."

"I suppose you're right. But it still doesn't mean I'm ready to start something new."

"It's just dinner," Bethany protested.

"You sound like Ethan." And just for a moment I could hear his voice in my ear. See the soft brown of his eyes. . . . I shook my head, banishing the image. Clinton and his romantic talk were clearly getting to me. Or maybe it was the combination of pain-killers and wine.

Either way, I'd made the right decision.

"He's a nice guy. But I'm not interested. The timing just isn't right."

"Okay, fine. I'll stop pushing," Clinton said.

"Right. Like that's possible. Sometimes I think you're as bad as Althea when it comes to matchmaking."

"Perish the thought," Clinton said, lifting his hands in protest.

"Speaking of Althea," I said, shooting a significant look in Bethany's direction, "before my night quite literally fell apart, I seem to remember something about you letting her set you up? Funny you didn't mention that when you told me you were going out with Michael Stone."

I sat back, watching her struggle to find words, delighted that I'd managed to turn the conversation away from me and my train wreck of a love life.

"I was going to tell you, but I figured you weren't going to be too pleased with the news."

"Well, I don't like the fact that my aunt went behind my back to set up my friend, but that doesn't mean I'm not happy about you and Michael. That is, if you're happy about it?"

"I'm ecstatic. I mean, I can't really believe it. We had the most marvelous time. Incredibly romantic. It was like we'd known each other forever. We stayed up half the night just talking. It was magical."

"Sounds like something straight out of the movies," Clinton said.

"I know." Bethany nodded, grinning like a loon. "And all because of Althea. I think maybe we've underestimated her abilities."

"No way." I shook my head so vehemently my stitches hurt. "It's just a fluke."

"Thanks a lot."

"I didn't mean you and Michael," I said, regretting my outburst. "I just meant that Althea got lucky. Besides, she told me it wasn't a real match. I mean, Michael isn't her client or anything."

"Well, that's true. But anyway, the point is that I had an amazing time."

"Why didn't you call me and tell me?" I asked. After all, I am her best friend.

"Under the circumstances, I didn't think you needed to hear about someone else's happiness."

"It wasn't someone else. It was you."

"Well, I'm telling you now."

"And, Althea's part aside, I'm happy for you," I said. "So when are you seeing him again?"

"Lunch tomorrow." Now that I was really looking, I realized Bethany was positively glowing. "And then we're going out this weekend."

"Well, I want to meet him," Clinton said.

"I know—I'll give a dinner party. It'll be great fun." I clapped my hands with excitement as the idea began to grow.

"That's really sweet of you. I'd love it. Of course, I need to run it by Michael first."

"Of course." I nodded, already planning the guest list. "We can do it whenever you like. Just let me know. It'll be the perfect opportunity for us to get to know him and for you to introduce him to your friends."

"And you can bring Ethan," Clinton said, his smile just this side of goading.

Fortunately, before I was forced to answer, my phone rang, the sounds of "Macarena" filling the apartment. (What can I say? I can't hear any other ring when I'm on the streets. It's a little embarrassing but I don't miss calls.)

I pulled the Razr out of its base and checked caller ID, all thoughts of dinner parties vanishing as my heart threatened to beat its way right out of my chest. "It's Dillon."

"What the hell is he doing calling you?" Clinton spat, anger sparking in his eyes.

"He wants his stuff back—including the dog."

The phone continued its merry jingle as we all three stared at it.

"Don't answer it," Bethany said.

"It's tempting," I whispered. "But I can't dodge him forever. And he needs to understand that Bentley isn't going anywhere." I flipped open the cell.

"Andi," Dillon's voice filled my ear, and I steeled myself. "You haven't been returning my calls. I was worried."

"I've been busy." My stomach had joined my heart, the two of them together making my head spin. I squared my shoulders, praying for a calm I most certainly did not feel. "What do you want?" I could barely recognize my voice as my own.

"I heard about the accident. Are you all right?"

"I'm fine. Honestly. No major damage." If I'd been Pinocchio my nose would have hit the breakfast bar.

"Good. Glad to hear you're okay," he said, sounding relieved. "I was also calling about my things." There was an awkward pause, and my chest tightened. Just the sound of his voice made me weak. Damn it to hell. "I, uh, thought maybe I'd come over to get them," he continued. "If you don't mind."

"There's no need." The new, icy version of me would have been quite impressive if it wasn't for the fact that my hand was shaking so hard I could barely hold the phone. "I've already boxed everything up."

"What do you mean?" He actually sounded perplexed. Sometimes Dillon could be incredibly obtuse.

"I mean that there's no need for you to come over here. I'll have everything messengered in the morning."

"Andi," he started, but I hung up.

The phone immediately started to ring again, and I dropped it as if it had suddenly become radioactive.

Bethany grabbed it, and barked angrily into the receiver. "She doesn't want to talk to you."

There was a moment of silence as Dillon replied, and Bethany's eyes narrowed. "Well, that's not likely to happen, is it? You're lucky she didn't burn the lot. As far as I can see, you don't have any rights at all here. Frankly, I think you're a son of a bitch and I hope you rot in hell." She clicked the phone shut and Clinton applauded.

It's nice to have friends.

"Thanks," I said, my voice now as shaky as my hands. "I don't think I could have talked to him again." I licked my lips, and drew in a breath. "So what did he say?" I know I shouldn't care, but old habits, right?

"You were right. He wants Bentley."

"Maybe I should give him up," I said, my fingers tangling in Bentley's silky fur. "I mean, technically, he does belong to Dillon."

"No fucking way." Bethany never curses. And she'd just done it twice. Which gives you some idea of how angry she was. "You've taken care of him since he was a puppy. Bentley belongs to you."

"You're right. I just had a moment of weakness. I may have lost my boyfriend. But I'm not giving up my dog. Dillon can take a flying leap."

"Which is pretty much what we told him," Clinton said. "So now you've just got to hold on to your guns. Or however it goes."

"I'm proud of you," Bethany said, lifting her glass in salute.

"This is just so damn hard."

"Which is exactly why you need a distraction," Clinton said, his eyes narrowing in a way I knew meant that he was about to suggest something I wasn't going to like. "I think you should go out with this McCay fellow."

"I told you, I'm not ready for that."

"Yes, well, you weren't ready for a television show, either, and look how that's turned out."

"Dating is a completely different thing," I argued. "And in case you've forgotten, my track record isn't all that great."

"And Ethan McCay isn't Dillon," Bethany said.

"You don't know that."

"Call him," Clinton said, holding out the phone.

"I can't just call him."

"You're right," Bethany said, and I shot her a grateful smile. "You need fortification first." She held out my wineglass. "Drink. Then call."

I shook my head, even as I dug Ethan's card out of my pocket. "I can't."

"Sure you can," Clinton cajoled. "Just press the little buttons. Technology is an amazing thing."

"That's not funny," I said with a glare.

"Maybe just a little bit?" He smiled.

"Honestly, this is a great idea," Bethany said. "If for no other reason than because this is a small town and once the word gets out that you're dating again, Dillon will know that you've moved on."

"But I don't want to go on a date. And I don't want to move on." Except that I did—at least a little.

"Yes, but what about revenge?" Clinton asked.

"I got that when we dissed Mardi Gras."

"That was Diana," Clinton said. "This is your chance to show Dillon that you honestly don't care."

I drained the contents of my glass as Bethany held out the phone.

"You really think I should do this?"

"Yes," they answered simultaneously.

And so, as the slow burn of the wine spread through my chest, I dialed.

The phone rang three times, and just as my thumb covered the button to disconnect, Ethan picked up.

"Hello."

I swallowed, the butterflies in my stomach doing a mambo. "I, um, this is Andi Sevalas. You know, from the cellar." Talk about stupid intros.

"Yes," he said, laughter lacing his tone. "I remember."

"I know. It's just that, well, I was thinking, and, if you haven't changed your mind . . . not that I'd blame you if you had, I mean, it would be perfectly understandable under the circumstances, but if you haven't . . ." Clinton was making motions for me to breathe and I tried to comply, but for the life of me I couldn't remember how.

"You'd like to go out to dinner with me after all," he thankfully finished for me.

"Yes," I answered breathlessly, feeling like an idiot. "I would."

"Great. How about Saturday?"

I nodded, then realized he couldn't hear me. "That's perfect. Where?"

"Nino's. The one on First? At eight?"

He had me at Nino's. One of my favorite Italian restaurants, it might not have the buzz of some of its more nouveau competition, but what it didn't have in gastronomical cutting edge it more than made up for in old-world ambience.

"That would be great. I'll meet you there."

"I think the way it's normally done, I'm supposed to pick you up." He still sounded amused, but for some reason the idea that he found me entertaining actually served to calm my jangling nerves.

"You've been away from the city too long," I said. "No one picks anyone up here. Besides, you're all the way uptown. I'll just meet you there."

There was a pause and then an audible laugh. "All right, have it your way. I'll see you at Nino's on Saturday."

"At eight," I repeated, to dead air. Ethan had already rung

off. Clearly he wasn't big on small talk. Which was just as well, considering I was apparently incapable of forming coherent sentences.

"I've got a date," I whispered as Bethany and Clinton exchanged high fives. "On Saturday. With my stranger."

Oh. My. God.

Chapter 7

The next three days passed in a whirl of activity. I shipped off Dillon's belongings (sans dog and a couple of DVDs). For the better part of valor, I continued to duck his calls, had my locks changed, and kept Bentley with me as much as possible. It was hard to think of everything ending this way. But what's the T. S. Eliot line? "Not with a bang but a whimper?" Maybe there's something to that.

Still, it wasn't easy. I'd honestly believed that Dillon and I were the real deal. Destined for a long life together. We'd met almost by accident, at a fundraiser my aunt had forced me to attend. It was beyond boring and I'd snuck out to a terrace for some fresh air. Dillon had had the same idea. He'd been leaning out over the balustrade drinking in the city.

There's nothing quite like Manhattan at night. Lights glittering like jewels accompanied by the myriad sounds that make up the city after sunset. And there's no better way to view it than from on high.

There hadn't been any small talk at all. Just an instant and intense connection that had made my stomach jittery and my heart skip beats. Newly arrived from La La Land, Dillon was still in the first throes of falling in love with the city. And I'd been delighted to show it to him. Along the way, we'd discovered that we had all kinds of things in common. His parents, jetsetters who loved to travel, had left him on his own a great deal as he grew up. That was something I could totally identify with.

But the commonalities didn't end with our lack of familial support or our love for the city. We both loved breakfast at all hours of the day. We hated the trappings of society, but not so much the amenities money could buy. We loved modern art, long walks in the Village, and little pubs and shops where people knew your name.

In short, we loved. Truly, madly, deeply. (A movie we both adored.)

And now, suddenly, without any warning, I was questioning all of it. I mean, not only had he fallen for someone else, he'd fallen for *Diana Merreck*. She was the epitome of everything he'd purported to despise. She was old money with attitude and no tolerance for anything beyond the ermine-lined comfort of her Upper East Side world.

It was as if I'd fallen down the rabbit hole, the world at the bottom turned inside out without so much as a by-your-leave.

And then, if all that wasn't enough, there was Ethan—and the D-A-T-E.

I'd spent almost as much time obsessing about it as I had Dillon's defection. And that, in and of itself, was enough for some major consternation. I mean, if I was really in love with Dillon, how could I possibly go out with another man? But if Dillon had left the building, why in the world should I stay at home wallowing in self-pity?

Ethan seemed on every level to be a great guy. Why shouldn't I share a meal with him?

And so it went. Back and forth. Great idea . . . bad idea . . . Andi's lost her mind. . . .

Of course, in the middle of all this introspection, I'd also managed to get my hair cut, my nails done, and my brows waxed. I hadn't had a date in almost three years, so I figured I needed all the cosmetic help I could get. (Clinton actually suggested Botox, but I declined, citing my recent hospitalization and stitches. A girl can only endure so much.)

Anyway, physically, I was pretty much as good as it gets. Emotionally, I was roller-coastering between depression, sheer terror, and that age-old adolescent shimmer of excitement. And intellectually, at least according to Bethany, who'd had to endure much of my overthinking, I was certifiable.

Fortunately, however, for both my sanity and my friends', I had a career to occupy at least some of my time. At midweek the Mardi Gras show aired, and wonder of wonders, the *Post* and the *Daily News* both picked up our review. Take that, Diana. Whoever said revenge was a dish best served cold missed the entire point of the act. Done without emotion it is meaningless. I mean, if it doesn't give you a thrill, then what's the point? And I have to admit that I took great joy in the fact that I'd dealt her, at the very least, a symbolic blow.

We'd also begun taping our next show, and, as always, getting into the kitchen provided great escape. There really is nothing like chopping onions, pounding veal, or just beating the hell out of a perfectly aromatic bread dough to ease one's tension. Besides, no one ever argues with a woman holding a seven-inch chef's knife.

That said, there was still the nagging problem of how I was going to manage to serve up Philip DuBois to the network execs.

Bethany, as promised, had contacted her client, and the woman had been only too happy to help.

Unfortunately, DuBois' publicist wasn't cut from the same cooperative cloth.

Monica Sinclair had represented DuBois for something like fifteen years. Which meant she was more than adept at keeping him out of the limelight. In fact, when Cassie had first contacted her about a meeting, she'd responded with a categorical no. But Cassie, being Cassie, had managed to cajole her way right into an interview, and so here we were at the corner of Sixth and West Forty-eighth on our way to Metro Media.

"You ready for this?" Cassie asked as she signed us in at the front desk of the Simon & Schuster building. Metro Media was the third-largest PR firm in the city, and they handled some of the biggest names in entertainment. Athletes, musicians, movie stars, even a couple of politicians. Celebrities from every occupation. Including chefs. Philip DuBois in particular.

"It's just Monica, right? DuBois won't be there," I said as we stepped into the elevator.

"No. I don't think she'll have even talked to him about it yet. This is strictly a chance for us to more fully explain what we have in mind. Then, assuming we can sell her, she'll take the offer to DuBois."

"And convince him to forget about his aversion for public displays and come on the show. Like that's going to happen. I should never have suggested getting DuBois."

"It's a fabulous idea," Cassie said, reaching over to squeeze my hand. "It's just going to take a little finessing. But we're good at that, right?"

"*You're* good at that," I conceded.

Cassie really was a rising star when it came to the world of television. She had an eye for nontraditional topics that could be made commercially viable. As well as my show, her company had produced specials for PBS, a mockumentary for HBO, a science fiction series for one of the major networks, and a hit reality show about circus performers.

She'd won numerous awards, including an Emmy, a Golden Globe, and a CLIO for some early commercial work. I was honored that she'd agreed to work with me. And, of course, grateful to have her as a friend. She was definitely the kind of person you wanted to have next to you when riding into battle.

As if on cue, said ride ceased, and the elevator doors opened.

"This is it," I said, my voice quavering.

"We're in this together," Cassie assured. "First up, DuBois' publicist. Once we get her on our side, she'll convince DuBois and the next thing you know, he'll be on the show. Just wait and see."

"Famous last words."

"We can do this." Cassie's tone was just this side of dictatorial. Which was exactly what I needed.

Squaring my shoulders and sucking in a deep breath, I nodded my agreement as we walked into Metro Media's eighth-floor offices.

The lobby had been decorated in that calculated minimalism that had been considered cutting-edge just a few years back. Black leather dominated the waiting area, wrought-iron torchieres reaching toward the ceiling like some sort of modern-day torture implements. In truth it was sort of Goth meets ergonomic gone Danish mod.

After we introduced ourselves, the receptionist paged Monica, and before I had time to flip through the latest issue of *People*, we were seated in her office.

In contrast to the lobby, Monica Sinclair's space felt light and airy. Soft beige walls were accented with mauve carpets and deep purple upholstery, the colors enhanced by simple birch furniture and the muted tones of two lovely oil paintings.

Like her office, Monica Sinclair epitomized understated class. Dressed entirely in gray, her dark black hair in an immaculate chignon, she looked surprisingly French, which, all things considered, probably made sense. DuBois had grown up in Provence and spent most of his working life in Paris. Subdued elegance would be something familiar. Inviting trust. And I could see that he would be drawn to a publicist who embodied these qualities.

"So as I understand it," Monica said, getting right down to business, "you need Philip to appear on your television show." I'd been right about France. Monica had just the barest hint of an accent. Carefully cultivated away, no doubt, it still gave her an air of exotic authority.

"We *want* Chef DuBois," Cassie corrected. "Would be honored to have him, in fact."

"Yes, well, my sources tell me that in order to move your show to prime time, you must produce Philip." She sat back, one eyebrow arching upward with controlled amusement. I suspected I'd quite like Monica Sinclair if my entire career didn't rest in her perfectly manicured hands.

"Your sources are correct," I said. "Or at least partially so. I do have a shot at moving to prime time. And that means coming up with an amazing show. But the idea to ask Chef DuBois was entirely mine. I've been a fan of his forever. Bijou is practically a legend and I go to his L.A. location every time I'm there. And last year, when my boyfriend and I went to Paris, we ate at La Mangeoire."

"Paris is a very romantic city," Monica said.

"It was a fabulous trip." And, I'd thought, one Dillon and I would repeat nostalgically as we grew old together. So much for

romance. "I still remember the striped bass in sun-dried tomatoes. And the profiteroles."

"They're everyone's favorite." Monica smiled at my enthusiasm and, banishing bad memories, I smiled back. Bonding over
food was not something new for me.

"Well, you can imagine my excitement when I heard that Mr.
DuBois was here in Manhattan to open a new restaurant. The
news is huge."

"Except that no one is supposed to know about it." Monica
frowned. "Who told you?"

"Someone with an inside track," I said, thinking of Bernie
and her friends. "But not anyone who'd wish Chef DuBois ill. My
friend found out inadvertently and only told me because she knew
how much I admired the chef's work, and how excited I'd be to
know that he was coming back to New York. Anyway, all of that
added together is why I want him on the show."

"To elevate *What's Cooking* to prime time," Monica repeated
pointedly.

"Of course." I nodded, facing her implications head on. "Who
wouldn't jump at that opportunity? Having Chef DuBois on the
show would certainly help advance my career. I'd be the first to
admit it. But quite honestly, for me this is much bigger than that.
It's a dream come true. The chance to cook with a master."

"And," Cassie inserted smoothly, "it's an opportunity for Chef
DuBois to publicize his new restaurant without the media frenzy
of a full-on interview. We're talking about a cooking show. And
a very positive slant both on DuBois and his return to the city."

"I saw this week's show." Monica steepled her fingers. "A restaurant named Mardi Gras, no? Not exactly a positive spin on
the restaurant."

I sighed. "Once a month we review new restaurants. In this

case the food simply wasn't up to par. And it's my duty to be honest with my viewers. I'm sure if you check our archives you'll find that there have been as many good reviews as bad ones. Mardi Gras just wasn't one of the winners, I'm afraid."

"The point is," Cassie was quick to insert, "that we won't be doing a review of Chef DuBois' restaurants. We won't be doing a review at all. With the exception of our monthly review show, Andi spends most of her time talking with area chefs about their dishes and their restaurants."

"As well as patrons and personal lives. I've seen the show on more than one occasion."

"I'm flattered," I said. "But if you've watched the show, then you know that it's all done with good intention. I love Manhattan and I love its restaurants. So it's a privilege for me to get to bring some of the greatest cooking in the city into the homes of my viewers."

"And that's what you intend for Philip?"

"Exactly." Cassie nodded. "We want to feature his cooking. And, at the same time, give our audience a chance to get to know the real man. It would be a special show dedicated to one of the world's foremost chefs."

"But the world already loves him," Monica said. "Or at least his cooking. So what does Philip gain by doing your show?"

"On an international level he is definitely considered one of the greats," I agreed. "But here in the city his reputation isn't quite as stellar." Cassie shook her head, but I ignored her. Unless I'd totally misread Monica Sinclair, she was the type of woman who responded best to honesty. "You know as well as I do that when he abandoned Bijou there were some hard feelings in both the financial and gastronomic communities. And both have very long memories, I'm afraid."

"And you think your show can help alleviate some of these 'hard feelings,' as you call them?"

"I think it's a chance to show people that the past is the past. And that Chef DuBois is coming back to the city to cook, not to stir up old stories. It's an opportunity to announce that he's bringing some of the phenomenal success he's had worldwide back to a place where he has roots. Bijou was actually his first real success, wasn't it? So there's history. And New Yorkers love history. If the story is spun properly, DuBois will be treated like the prodigal son."

"An interesting take, certainly," she said, her eyes narrowed in thought.

"Most importantly, it's a chance for him to do what he does best. Cook. And share his love for all things culinary with a like-minded audience. It's win/win for all of us."

Cassie nodded her agreement, all but shooting me a thumbs-up.

"He hasn't done anything like this in years," Monica said, cocking her head to one side as she considered the possibility. "But to be quite frank, you're right about his reputation. It's totally undeserved, of course. There were extenuating reasons for his leaving New York. Personal ones. But since he is an extremely private person, it's not something he's ever going to explain. Which means the topic would be strictly off-limits for your show."

"I can totally understand that." I nodded. "And I think we can make sure that you have that in writing. I have no interest in probing into the private areas of Chef DuBois' life. I simply want the opportunity to cook with him. And to share that with the people who watch *What's Cooking in the City*."

"Well, I have to admit, I'm drawn to the idea of presenting him in a fresh light."

"But we would, of course, want to talk about his professional history," Cassie said, her voice taking on a decidedly businesslike tone. "His background gastronomically speaking as well as the various restaurants in his culinary empire. It's part of the appeal of our show."

"I think that would be acceptable." Monica nodded. "As long as there are clear limits, and we've approved the topics beforehand."

"So we're actually going to do this?" I said, unable to contain my excitement.

"I think you could say that I'm cautiously optimistic about the idea. Of course, I still have to present it to Philip. And he's never very receptive when I'm talking about the press."

"But I'm not the press. Not at all. I'm just a lucky woman who gets to make her living meeting and cooking with some of the city's best chefs. It's pure joy. Believe me."

"I do, actually." She smiled. "That's one of the reasons I'm considering your request."

"Good," Cassie said, ever the professional. "Then we're agreed. I've prepared an information package with ratings and a demographic breakdown. I think you'll find that it skews nicely in the direction of Chef DuBois' intended customers." She laid a large packet on the desk. "In addition, there's a full proposal outlining our ideas for formatting the show should the chef decide to become involved in the project. There's also a DVD with several episodes of *What's Cooking in the City* similar in format to what we have in mind for Chef DuBois."

"Excellent," Monica said, rising to shake our hands. "I'll review this and present your ideas to Philip."

"I'm sure you'll understand that this is time specific," Cassie said. "We've only a short window to make this work."

"Absolutely. And quite honestly, Philip isn't the type to dither over making a decision. So hopefully, I can get back to you quickly."

I nodded, and sat back in my chair, content to let Cassie and

Monica hash out the nuts and bolts of our potential agreement while I enjoyed my small moment of success. Cassie had been right; with Monica on our side, the idea that I might actually share a saucier with *the* Philip DuBois, on national television no less, suddenly seemed entirely possible.

Prime time was within my grasp.

Chapter 8

Saturday night arrived way before I was ready and with enough rain to float an ark down Broadway. I sat at the window, trying to come up with a legitimate reason for canceling my date with Ethan. Don't get me wrong, part of me really wanted to go. But another, stronger part of me was just plain terrified.

Anyway, I'd picked up the phone about a hundred times, tried on pretty much every dress I owned. And basically come to the conclusion that I was a complete and total freak when it came to men. I couldn't hang on to the one I had and then, presented with the opportunity to get to know someone new, I panicked.

With a sigh, I picked the phone up yet again, and was just starting to dial when it rang, surprising me so much I dropped it into the sink. Thankfully, sans water. Grabbing it, I checked caller ID.

Not Dillon. Plus one.

Not Ethan. Minus two.

Althea.

Game over.

I sucked in a deep breath and answered. (I could have ignored it, but she'd have just kept trying.)

"Hello?"

"Darling," Althea gushed. "I didn't think you'd be home."

"It's Saturday night," I said, perversely, "where else would I be?"

"Well, you could have met someone wonderful."

"Yeah, right." I know. I know. I was lying. But the thing is, Althea has this tendency to take over. Especially if it involves my love life. And, as has already been pointed out, I'd practically already decided to cancel. So it wasn't really that far off the truth.

"Well," she sighed, "one can always hope."

There was nothing to say to that so I just left it to dead air.

"I really just called to check in. You're feeling better, I assume?" she asked, ignoring my silence.

"Much." I nodded, even though I was on the phone. "The bruises are fading and my stitches are starting to itch, which Bethany says is a good sign."

"How is Bethany?" she asked, her voice just a tad too innocent sounding.

"Like you don't know. Isn't she reporting in?"

"Well, yes, but she might not be telling me everything."

"They're supremely happy, Althea. You should be delighted. You've made a match."

"I do what I can," she said, and I imagined her hand-to-head shrug. "Anyway, I'm glad it worked out."

"So far, so good," I couldn't help adding.

"You sound like you don't want them to be happy," she scolded.

"I do. I swear I do. It's just that I don't like your meddling."

"Andrea, we've been down this road before." There was a moment's silence and then she said, "I saw your show. It was really good. The jambalaya looked delicious. I even asked Bernie to make some."

"It was her recipe in the first place," I admitted. "But I'm glad you watched."

"Thought you were a little hard on poor Mardi Gras. Was it really that awful?"

"It was, actually. But I'll admit I was spurred on a bit by the fact that Diana Merreck is part owner."

"Did you know that before . . ." She paused, searching for the right words. ". . . well, Dillon?"

"No, actually. Clinton figured it out after the fact."

"Go Clinton. I always liked that boy." Since said "boy" was pushing forty, her comment was particularly amusing. But from Althea it was a rare vote of confidence in one of my friends. "Hit them in their pocketbooks, that's what I always say."

"Well, it doesn't really even the score, but it did make me feel a lot better."

"I'm glad to see you're standing up for yourself. Women like Diana always think they've got the upper hand." Considering the two of them were cut from the same cloth, I was sort of surprised to hear Althea say it. "Anyway, you're worth two of her any day and Dillon's a fool not to see that."

It was tempting to tell her about Ethan. Really tempting. But if I told her, I'd be committed to going. And even buoyed by Althea's support, I still wasn't sure I was ready to go out with someone new.

As if in support of the thought, a thunderclap rattled the windows as it echoed down the street, a renewed hail of rain pummeling the glass.

"Well, darling, if you're really certain you're okay, I should ring off. I've got a charity dinner in an hour, and I'm not even dressed." A likely story. Althea's idea of dressing down was to change her jewelry. She still had her hair done once a week, and slept on satin pillows in a hairnet to keep her "do" fresh in the meantime. "You can come with me if you'd like."

I'd left myself wide open for that one. "Not worth getting out in this rain. I'll just cozy up with a bottle of wine and an afghan." And just like that my decision was made. I'd call Ethan and cancel.

I disconnected and walked over to the window, watching the city lights as they reflected in the wet pavement below. Hunched figures with umbrellas made their way through the pounding rain as lightning flickered in the distance and the thunder rolled.

Definitely not a night to be out and about.

I picked Ethan's card up off the table, hit the first three numbers, and then the buzzer went off. Apparently this was my night for company. I walked over to the security monitor and Clinton waved from down below. I punched the button to let him up, walked over to pour myself a glass of wine, and then opened the door to my very wet friend.

"What in the world brings you out on a night like this?" I asked, taking his dripping umbrella.

"The knowledge that you were most likely sitting here thinking of excuses for backing out on your date with Mr. Wonderful."

"I wasn't. I was talking to Althea."

"And you're holding Ethan's card because you couldn't remember how to spell his name?" He shot a pointed look at the card in my hand.

Busted.

"Okay, you got me. I *was* contemplating calling it off. The weather is awful. And the truth is I'm just not ready for this."

"Don't be silly. You know what they say—getting back on the horse is the best possible thing." He shed his raincoat and hung it on a hook.

"You make it sound dirty."

"Well, isn't that the whole point?" he asked with a wicked grin.

"You're incorrigible."

"I'm right. And I come bearing gifts." With a flourish he produced a garment bag I'd failed to notice with all the rain gear. "But first I need something to warm me up."

"I opened some wine," I said, tipping my head toward the bottle on the counter. "False courage."

"Wine would be great." He took the bag and laid it carefully on a chair, then took a seat on my sofa. "It's really nasty out there."

"My point exactly. Not a night to try and get a taxi."

"You're just making excuses," he said, accepting the glass of wine. "And I'm here to make sure you don't chicken out. Bethany would have come, too, but she had her own date to worry about."

"With Michael. I was just discussing them with Althea."

"So she really was on the phone."

"Yes. Digging to find out if I was up to anything this evening."

"And did you tell her about Mr. Wonderful?"

"No. I didn't. I mean, it didn't seem relevant if I'm going to cancel. And besides, you know how she is. If I tell her, she'll run a Dun and Bradstreet on him, check his heritage, and probably get the ladies at the Colony Club to vote him up or down."

"Well, I don't support this notion of canceling. But I can see why you didn't tell Althea."

"She was rather gushing about you, though."

"Really? I didn't think the old girl liked me."

"Well, she does. And she was really delighted that you helped me get one in on Diana."

"Will wonders never cease," he laughed, and sipped his wine. "I do think Althea did good by Bethany. She seems to be really smitten with Michael."

"You're the only person I know who uses words like 'smitten,'" I laughed. "Anyway, despite Althea's involvement, I'm delighted Bethany's happy. Did she tell you we finalized plans for the dinner party? You'll come, won't you?"

"If I don't have to bring anyone." Clinton had recently ended a relationship. It had been a long time in coming, and the breakup had been at Clinton's instigation. But that didn't mean there wasn't residual fallout. If I hadn't understood before, I certainly did now.

"I thought you were all for getting back on the horse," I reminded him. "You know, what's good for the goose . . ." I opened my hands in a shrug.

"I haven't met Mr. Wonderful," he responded. "*You* have."

"I wish you'd stop calling him that. And you don't know that he's wonderful, anyway. You haven't even met him."

"Well, if someone rescued me from the pits of despair, as it were, I'd damn sure give him a chance. Andi, this sort of thing doesn't happen every day and you're a fool if you don't take advantage of it."

"I know," I sighed. "I'm being a total idgit. But it's scary to think about starting something new."

"Of course it is," Clinton agreed. "But that's also why it's exciting."

"Well, I'm just not that brave."

"This, from the woman who conquered Metro Media and got us an interview with Philip DuBois."

"He hasn't agreed to be on the show yet. We've just got interest from his publicist."

"Well, Cassie said you were brilliant."

"I wasn't bad," I allowed. "But wasn't it you who said for us not to get ahead of ourselves? We just need to wait and see."

"Well, it sounds pretty positive to me. And I, for one, am excited at the prospect of meeting the man."

"Actually, I would have thought you'd have run into him somewhere or another. I mean you do move in the same circles, more or less."

"Thanks for the compliment." Clinton smiled. "But DuBois is in a category all unto himself. And he left New York long before I came on the scene."

"But he speaks, doesn't he? And teaches classes?"

"Not really that often. And usually only in Paris. I've always wanted to take courses there, but just never seemed to find the time."

"Me, too, actually. Someday. Right?"

"Yes. We'll make a point of it. But in the meantime, you're going to get a private lesson, as it were."

"Well, as I said, he hasn't agreed to anything. And we agreed not to talk about it until it happens. So how about I pour you some more wine?"

"How about we get you ready for your date instead?"

"I have nothing to wear," I said, threatening mutiny.

"Well, it just so happens I've got the solution to that. Aren't you going to ask me what I've brought you?" Clinton reached for the garment bag, holding it just out of my reach. "It's from Linda Dresner's."

Linda Dresner had a delicious boutique on Park Avenue. An institution, really, the shop catered to well-heeled clients interested in the latest European designs. She's cutting-edge and over-the-top expensive.

"What did you do?" I stuttered.

"Nothing that involved highway robbery. I promise. I merely called in a few favors. It's always easier to take a leap when you look drop-dead gorgeous. And I think you'll find that this little number will go a long way toward accomplishing just that . . ."

He pulled the zipper with a flourish and the garment bag fell to the floor.

The dress was gorgeous. Absolutely flawless, really. Silk georgette in black. It was softly draped in the front and back and cinched in at the waist with a wide silk belt. It put me in mind of Marilyn Monroe and subway grates.

"It's Hidalgo." Peter Hidalgo was the current "it" man in fashion. Newly split from his association with controversial designer Miguel Adrover, Hidalgo's new designs are known for their curve-hugging, hourglass perfection.

"I can't possibly wear that. It's too . . . too glamorous."

"Don't be silly. You'll look magnificent. I have an eye for these things, remember?"

"What about the bruises?"

"Well, the dress should cover the ones on your chest. And we already know how to deal with the ones on your head. Besides, it's not as if Mr. Wonderful hasn't seen you at your worst already."

"Well, I suppose there's truth in that," I said, laughing despite myself. The dress *was* fabulous.

"So go. Try it on. I'll pour us another glass of wine. Fortification and all that." He waved me off, and, with a sigh, I took the dress and the garment bag and headed into the bedroom, stopping in the doorway. The floor looked like a battlefield, rejected clothing covering every square inch of the floor. I'd tried everything I owned—even, in desperation, an old bridesmaid's dress. Needless to say, it hadn't passed muster.

Fortunately, Clinton had ridden to my rescue—again. Now if only the dress lived up to the promise, or more accurately, if only I lived up to the dress.

I kicked the bridesmaid's monstrosity out of the way, and slid out of my jeans and T-shirt. Then, with exaggerated care, I slipped the dress off its hanger. The soft silk felt like gossamer fairy wings or something equally ethereal. I slid it over my head and, holding my breath, turned to look in the mirror.

It was pure magic.

I might not be a society maven, but I'm not immune to the potency of feeling beautiful. Even my bruises seemed to fade under the graceful flow of the gown. As I smoothed the full skirt over my hips, I felt that time-immemorial rush of feminine power.

Clinton was a genius—or more realistically, I suppose, Peter Hidalgo was. Anyway, what's important was that I looked really good. I tightened the belt, and twirled in front of the mirror.

"How's it going in there?" Clinton called.

"I look like a princess or a goddess or something. It's amazing. Come on in and see for yourself." I twirled again, my heart fluttering along with the skirt hem.

"It's just a frame, Andi," Clinton said from the doorway. "The beauty's all yours."

"No more wine for you," I said, taking a sip from his glass. "You've gone poetic."

"I've only had a glass."

"Well, it's not me. It's the dress. It's absolutely fabulous. But which shoes?" I stared at the bottom of my closet and the tumble of shoes that covered the floor. "I'm afraid I don't own anything worthy of this dress."

"What's a beautiful dress without the right shoes?" He smiled, handing me the abandoned garment bag.

I'd been so excited about the dress, I'd totally missed the bulge in the bottom. I pulled out a box—Jimmy Choo. Bethany would be having an orgasm. And I'll admit my heart was beating a bit faster.

The shoes were almost as beautiful as the dress. Black patent sandals with gold-framed four-inch heels. I slipped them on and turned to face the mirror. The woman looking back had a cool elegance I'd never seen before.

Clinton came to stand behind me, twisting my normally unruly hair into a chic knot of curls. "Not bad at all, if I do say so myself." He fastened a sparkling clip to hold my hair in place and stepped back with a smile. "Now just a touch of powder on the bruises and you'll be good to go."

I twirled again, feeling ridiculously giddy. "Whoever said that clothes make the girl was on to something."

"Actually, the quote is 'Clothes make the man. Naked people have little or no influence on society.' Mark Twain."

"Well, he knew what he was talking about," I laughed, still twirling.

"On many levels," Clinton agreed.

Mark Twain and Cinderella's fairy godmother—who knew they had anything in common? But it turns out they were both right—it's all about the dress.

Chapter 9

Considering I've been dating for almost fifteen years now, you'd think I could handle almost anything. I mean, over the years, I've pretty much seen it all. Good dates, bad dates, half-remembered dates, completely unmentionable dates. You know the drill.

But somehow with Ethan McCay everything seemed different. Maybe it was the circumstances, or maybe it was the man, but I don't remember the last time I was this nervous about anything.

Thankfully, the rainstorm had played itself out. The taxi had dropped me on the corner of First and Seventy-second, but even though the restaurant was only a few yards away, I hadn't moved an inch. In fact, I was seriously considering retreat.

All I had to do was hold up a hand, hail a cab, and I was out of here. Of course, then I'd have to admit defeat. And I've never been one to do that easily. And besides, Clinton would never let me live it down.

Keeping that thought front and center, I stepped through the door into Nino's. There's something so wonderful about a restaurant that opens its arms to greet you. And in this case the greeting came from the man himself. Nino Selimaj. Nino's is the crown jewel in his restaurant kingdom, and I've got to say it's my personal favorite, although each has its own unique charm.

Positano, the midtown location, was more low-key, geared toward business lunches and corporate dinners. The West Side location, Nino's Tuscany, had that theater district vibe. You know, terminally happy patrons, live piano music—in general an atmosphere that appealed to the musical-bound masses. My Nino's, on the other hand, was totally Upper East Side—understated but elegant, catering to the fur-clad co-op crowd. It was the kind of place I sent out-of-towners who wanted a taste of old New York.

Nino kissed me on both cheeks and then asked after Althea (she regularly entertains clients here). I explained that I was meeting Ethan, and taking my elbow in that wonderfully continental way, he escorted me to a private table in a corner, where, with a smile and a bow, he left me to wait—alone.

Apparently, even with all my hesitation, I'd still managed to be early.

I sat down and made a play of looking at my menu. I know it's going to sound vain but I always feel like everyone is looking at me. There's just something so pathetic about sitting at a table all alone. Either you don't have anyone to eat with or you think you do, but they're not showing. It's horrible. So I've developed a routine. At first I pretend to have great interest in the menu, while surreptitiously checking my watch every few minutes. Then I go through the whole "sipping the water, eyeing the crowd as if they're here only for my amusement" routine. That usually works for about two or three minutes. And if that isn't enough time to produce my tardy dinner date, then I pull out my Razr.

Instant distraction. Honestly. A cell phone or PDA is the perfect solution for any awkward situation. You can check your messages, answer e-mail, catch up on the news, or even play a game. You're not required to actually talk with someone—that would mean admitting your stupid insecurities—but you do look busy. Which at least as far as the world is concerned moves the pity meter back down to a more palatable level.

Of course even that doesn't work forever. And eventually people at neighboring tables are back to wondering if maybe you're being stood up.

I hate it.

It's like I've become the floor show.

I glanced at my watch, toyed with my sparkling water, and debated the wisdom of ordering a glass of wine.

Really, I'm usually not so insecure. But it hadn't been the easiest of weeks. And I was on a date. My first in ages. Or I would be if said date bothered to show up. I lifted my head, and aimed a regal smile at the restaurant's other patrons. If nothing else I could pretend that I hadn't a care in the world.

And then, just as I was congratulating myself for my serene composure (and checking my watch for like the seventy thousandth time), the maître d' approached with Diana Merreck in tow. I kid you not.

Clearly I was under some kind of curse.

"Andi?" she said, smiling down at me as she lifted diamond-clad fingers to throat in feigned concern. "I told Dillon I thought it was you."

And then there he was, proof that life is indeed more horrifying than anything the subconscious could possibly dream up. I considered making a run for it, but I kind of doubted that Nino would appreciate my taking out diners and tables in the process.

And besides, I had my pride.

So instead of a fifty-yard dash, I straightened my new dress and pasted on a smile. "What a surprise running into the two of you here." When we were together, Dillon had always insisted Nino's was too stuffy.

"It's one of my favorites. So, are you here on your own?" Diana simpered, not waiting for me to answer. "We certainly can't have that."

Dillon, to his credit, looked like he'd rather have unanesthetized prostate surgery than share a table with the two of us, but even that couldn't cancel Diana's smug proprietorial smile.

"We'd love to have you join us." Right, and Jon Bon Jovi will be the next president.

"Actually, I'm meeting someone," I said, surprised to hear my voice sound so normal. Considering that I was having trouble drawing breath, it was a miracle, really. "But thanks for the offer."

I fisted one hand in my lap, digging my nails into my palm, trying to control the emotions surging through me—hatred being right up there at the top of the list.

"I saw your show this week," Diana said, her eyes narrowing to very unattractive slits, the tension between us tightening into something almost palpable. Dillon had actually retreated a step, making a great study of the top of his shoes.

"Really?" With sheer force of will, I maintained my smile, feeling like my face was going to crack into pieces with the effort. "I hope you enjoyed it."

"It wasn't what I'd hoped for," she said with a calculated shrug. "But I hardly think one bad review on one tiny little cable program is likely to have any real impact."

"You'd be surprised at how many people watch that tiny little program," I responded, trying to hold on to my rapidly escalating temper.

"I'm sorry I'm late." Ethan's voice came from somewhere over my left shoulder. Enter the cavalry. Perfect timing, as usual. He was definitely making a habit of riding to my rescue. Not that I was complaining.

"Ethan," I said, relief making me almost giddy. "I was wondering where you were."

"Sorry. My driver got stuck in traffic. Damn storm."

"This is Dillon Alexander," I said. "My ex?" Recognition dawned, and Ethan's jaw tightened. "And this is Diana Merreck," I continued, nodding in her direction. "Dillon's new girlfriend." The word rolled off my tongue with only the slightest bit of sarcasm, and I realized that with Ethan's arrival I'd actually started breathing again.

"Interesting," he said as Diana turned toward him, eyes widening in recognition. Her surprise was almost comical, except that it raised a number of rather disturbing questions.

Diana opened her mouth to say something (bitchy, no doubt) but Ethan cut her off. "It was nice of you both to keep Andi company, but now that I'm here . . ." His tone was just this side of dismissive, and from the pinched look on Diana's face, I guessed she'd gotten the point.

"Yes, well, we were planning on a romantic dinner for two anyway." Never let it be said that Diana Merreck wasn't capable of securing the last word.

Except that in saying nothing, somehow Ethan managed to trump her anyway.

They sidled away in a manner that I'm ashamed to admit I took great pleasure in. But then I've never claimed to be immune to the thrill of coming out on the winning side of an unpleasant situation, even when I had nothing at all to do with obtaining the victory.

"I hope you don't mind—," Ethan started, but I cut him off with a wave of my hand.

"I'm delighted. I can't think of anyone I'd less like to spend time with right now. You were great." And suddenly I was extremely happy that I hadn't chickened out.

"Well, normally," he said, "I wouldn't cut someone off so rudely, but I thought it was warranted, considering the circumstances."

"More than warranted. I'm not sure why, but Diana seems intent on rubbing my face in the fact that she has Dillon and I don't."

"She can be like that."

"So you do know her? I thought there was a moment between the two of you." I waited, biting the side of my lip, not sure I really wanted to hear about their connection.

"Yes. I know her. But we aren't exactly on the best of terms."

"Judging by her reaction, I thought maybe you were old lovers or something." I'd tried for light, but ended up sounding more accusatory. This dating stuff was hard. Especially when one threw one's ex and his new lover into the mix.

"Hardly," Ethan said, picking up his menu, signaling an end to my questioning.

"Sorry about the traffic," I said, taking the hint. His relationship with Diana Merreck really wasn't any of my business. "It took forever from downtown, too. I'd probably have been better off taking the subway, but there was no way I was going to try and negotiate all those stairs in these heels." I lifted a foot to prove the point.

"Well, we're here. And that's all that matters," he said with a smile. "And you look amazing, all things considered." I didn't know if he meant the rain or my run-in with Diana, but it was a lovely compliment either way.

"It's the dress," I said, feeling the warmth of a blush. "A friend gave it to me. For courage." The last bit came out entirely on its own.

"Dinner with me took courage?" he asked with a crooked grin.

"No. Yes. Well, it's been a while." I'd been reduced to babbling nonsense.

"If it helps, I think you're more than up to the task. With or without the dress." My blush deepened at the double entendre.

"Thanks, I think . . ."

"So," he said, thankfully changing the subject, "I take it you come here a lot? Nino was quite effusive when I told him I was meeting you."

"He's that way with everyone, actually. But it is one of my favorite restaurants. In fact, I was really pleased that you chose it. I've been coming since I was little."

"That's right. I remember you said you grew up near Carl Schurz."

I nodded and we sat in companionable silence as we read over the menu.

I already knew what I wanted—the homemade spinach and cheese ravioli in pesto is amazing—but I liked reading the menu anyway. There's just something comforting in seeing ingredients combined together in a way only a superior chef could accomplish. Quail stuffed with shredded duck served with polenta and black currant sauce, smoked salmon and asparagus in puff pastry. The only thing better than reading the daily offerings, in my opinion, was eating the food.

I closed my menu and the waiter moved in. "I'll start with the carpaccio and then have the ravioli, please." I smiled up at him.

"And I'll have the prosciutto salad, and then the Dover sole." Ethan looked across his menu at me. "Is white wine okay?"

I nodded, pleased to have been consulted.

"Great. Then we'll have a bottle of the Clos des Mouches," he told the waiter, handing him his menu.

I followed suit, not sure if I was more impressed with the wine (which was extraordinary) or the fact that he knew enough to order the sole. Only regulars were aware it was available, since it was never listed on the actual menu.

"I thought you said you'd been away from the city?" I asked, curious.

"I have been. Why?"

"Well, you knew to order the sole. That reeks of an insider."

Ethan laughed. "My father. He loves this place. And the sole is his favorite. I've had it a couple of times when I was here with him. But that was ages ago. I wasn't certain they'd still do it, but figured it was worth asking."

"You mentioned your father in the park. Something about a heart attack. Is he all right?"

"Yes. He's fine now," Ethan said as the waiter offered him a taste of the wine. "Although the doctors keep him on a pretty tight leash."

"I remember you said you'd been helping out. So where all did your travels take you?"

"I spent a year or so in the Far East. Malaysia. And then six months in Brussels."

"Sounds exotic."

"Only in the beginning. After a while all you really want is a good cheeseburger." He sipped the wine, then nodded his approval to the waiter, who poured two generous glasses.

"And fries. I can imagine. I remember the first time I was in Europe. I was about seventeen. My grandmother gave me the trip and took me to all the high spots. But my favorite memory is going to the Hard Rock Cafe in Berlin. American food. I was in heaven. Although I suppose I shouldn't admit that, considering my profession."

"I think there's room in any cuisine for a good burger." He

reached for his wineglass, leaning forward slightly, which gave me a perfect sight line to Diana and Dillon. Diana was laughing at something Dillon had said, his every gesture as familiar as breathing.

"You're staring," Ethan chided.

"I'm sorry," I said, shaking my head, focusing on the man in front of me. "I know I should just ignore them. But I'm afraid it's easier said than done."

"Would you like to go somewhere else?" The offer was so thoughtful I immediately felt guilty.

"No. We've already ordered. And I've got to face up to it sooner or later. It might as well be here—with you." I smiled, shifting slightly so that I could no longer see them.

"So did you have any luck with Metro Media?" he asked.

"Yes, actually, I did. We met with DuBois' publicist and things are looking hopeful. So thanks for the tip."

"My pleasure. I have to say, I'm a little surprised that you had such a positive meeting. DuBois being so media shy."

"Totally understandable. I was surprised as well, to be honest. But she said something about presenting him in a new light. Anyway, he still has to agree, so it's hardly a done deal. But progress is progress. And at least I've been temporarily saved from the fallout of me and my big mouth."

"Actually, I think it's one of your best features."

I ducked my head, feeling all of about sixteen. There was just something really unsettling about Ethan McCay. Fortunately, the waiter chose that moment to bring our appetizers.

When he'd finished delivering our plates, Ethan topped off our glasses and leaned back with a smile. "You've mentioned your aunt several times, and I know from the other night that she's your emergency contact. So what about your parents? Aren't they in the picture?"

An honest question. Sooner or later everyone asked. And for the most part people were usually compassionate, if a bit shocked. It simply wasn't the normal way of doing things in our set. Anyway, I always hate having to tell someone new. Especially someone like Ethan—whose opinion matters to me.

So I'd go with the *Reader's Digest* abridged version.

"They're still alive, if that's what you're asking. Only not in my life. My mother left home when I was just a kid. And my father . . . well, my mother is a bit of a flibbertigibbet. She has a penchant for the fast lane. The truth is, she never met a man she didn't like. And so it's not all that surprising that she managed to get herself pregnant without the benefit of marriage or even a clear memory of who it was exactly that contributed the winning sperm."

"So you don't know who your dad is?"

"No idea." I shook my head. "I'm afraid my mother was a poptart back in the day when the term still referred to a breakfast pastry."

"Must have been hard."

I searched his eyes for condemnation, but saw only compassion. "In some ways, yeah. But I think I came out okay."

"More than okay." He smiled. "So who raised you?"

"My grandfather when he was alive. And my grandmother. But I guess mainly it was Althea. Which is ironic when you consider she was the reason my mother ran off in the first place."

"What happened?"

"They had a fight. I was just a kid. But they were loud and it woke me up. I knew I shouldn't have been listening, but I couldn't help myself, so I hid behind the dining room door. Althea was telling my mother that she wasn't fit to take care of me. That I'd be better off without her."

"And your mom?"

"She was angry, too. Said that it was none of Althea's business. They kept at it for what seemed like forever. Althea goading, my mom defensive. Althea never approved of my mother's free spirit. And I couldn't stand to hear them fight so I went back to bed. Only I could still hear them yelling. Anyway, the next morning my worst fears were realized. My mom was gone. I haven't heard from her since."

"Not a word?"

"She sends gifts sometimes. And the occasional birthday card when she remembers. But that's it. Nothing else."

"And you blame Althea for her leaving."

"Yes, I guess I do. Meddling is her middle name. She even managed to turn it into a profession."

"A successful one, if the papers are to be believed."

"I suppose so, but to be honest, I find it a bit embarrassing. I mean, all that manipulating of people's lives and being front and center in the gossip columns. I could do without the notoriety."

"I can understand that. But it's all for a good cause. I mean, she does get people together who might not ordinarily find each other. Right?"

"You make it sound so romantic. With my aunt, believe me, it's far more calculating. She believes that people from the same background belong together. Especially when it comes to people with money."

"I think maybe you're selling her short, but then of course I don't really know her."

"I think you missed your calling," I said, shaking my head. "You should have been a shrink. I don't usually share my family secrets with strangers."

"But I'm not a stranger."

"Well, in point of fact, I only met you a few days ago."

"So we've covered a lot in a little time."

"All right," I laughed, lifting a hand in defense, "I'll agree that we're not strangers. But even so, I think I've shared enough about my family. At least for one night."

"Fair enough." He lifted his glass, touching the rim to mine.

We sat smiling at each other and I realized that I was actually happy. And all things considered, it was an emotion I hadn't felt in a while. Ethan was definitely intriguing, and, in all honesty, I was surprised at how easy it was to talk to him. To be with him.

Obviously, the wine had gone to my head.

When the waiter arrived with our food, I realized I'd hardly touched the carpaccio. Which says a lot right there, since it's really good at Nino's. Beef and bresaola served with arugula and shaved parmesan. Divine.

"So turnabout's fair play—why don't you tell me about your family?" I said. "I know your father runs the family business."

"Actually, my grandfather runs things. Everything belongs to him."

"So what exactly does 'the business' consist of?"

"Manufacturing, mainly. Other related industries. And then there are a series of investments. Mainly my grandfather's whims. He started in steel and expanded from there."

"Sounds impressive."

"Not really. It's just business."

"So your father is next in line?"

"No. Technically, he married into it all. I suppose my mother is the actual heir, although she has no interest in any of it. Anyway, none of it matters, since my grandfather's still going strong. Although I think in all honesty, Dad is ready to step down."

"Because of his heart attack."

"Exactly. Which is where I come in."

"The new heir apparent."

"Something like that."

"And your mother?"

"She just wants my father to be happy."

"Coming from my perspective, it sounds idyllic."

"I don't know." He shrugged, sipping his wine. "I always wished I had a more exciting family. Mine is about as predictable as they come. Stereotypical, even."

"You're certainly not stereotypical." The words came out before I had the chance to think about them. "I mean, you're definitely not what I expected." Great, I was just making it worse. "I'm sorry, that didn't come out right. What I meant was . . ."

"No worries. I'll take it as a compliment," he said, his smile amused.

"So there's nothing sordid in the midst of all that normalness? Nothing at all?"

"I have an ancestor who was a spy during the Revolutionary War. Does that count?"

"Only if he was working for the British." I raised my eyebrows, waiting.

But Ethan shook his head. "Nope. American to the core."

"So what else have you got? We're looking for something really torrid." I shook my head, laughing. "Like my grandmother. She snuck out of her prep-school dorm window to run away with my grandfather. Niko. He was a Greek immigrant decidedly not up to my great-grandparents' standards. So her parents disinherited her. Fortunately for me, she didn't care a whit, and my grandfather made a fortune importing Greek delicacies."

"You're Sevalas Food?"

"Well, my grandmother is. And I suppose, more or less, so am I."

"So you come by your love of food naturally."

"With the help of my grandmother's cook. I learned about olives and ouzo from my grandfather, but I learned most of what I know about food from Bernie."

"See? Fascinating. So what happened with your great-grand-father? Did he ever forgive your grandmother?"

"Are you kidding? Jackson Harold Winston never forgave anyone anything. The real question is whether my grandmother forgave him." I smiled, quite enjoying relaying this part of my history.

"Is she still living?" he asked.

"Absolutely. She still has her apartment on East End. But she's hardly ever there. Mainly she travels—seeing the world. Sowing her wild oats."

"Like your mother?"

"I think they have certain commonalities."

"And Althea is more like your grandfather."

"Actually, no. Althea is just Althea. My grandfather definitely wasn't immune to a good time."

"Well, I don't know how I'm supposed to follow up on that," he said with a mock frown. "My relatives just aren't that interesting. I think the last time anyone dared to buck authority in my family was in Scotland during the Jacobite Uprising."

"That sounds promising. Virile Highlander fighting for clan and rightful king."

"Actually, it was the lowlands. Although he did side with the Highlanders. Against the wishes of his father. But unfortunately it didn't end well. He wound up on the wrong end of a claymore. And that pretty much killed any further familial desire for rebellion. Although I suppose I've managed to buck the system a little. My father wanted me to go to Harvard. I picked Dartmouth. And no one wanted me to become an attorney."

"Well, there you have it," I said, trying to remember the last time I'd enjoyed a meal this much. "The blackest of black sheep. Your ancestors would be proud."

"Oh, yes, definitely walking the edge." He smiled and reached for the wine bottle, the movement clearing my view to Diana and Dillon's table. They were gone. And I hadn't even noticed.

The rest of the dinner passed almost too quickly, conversation ranging from the intricacies of making crème brûlée to the latest changes in international corporate tax law. In fact, we talked ourselves right out of the restaurant, into his town car, and down to SoHo.

The car pulled up to the curb outside my building and Ethan leaned forward to give the driver instructions before joining me on the sidewalk.

"You want me to walk you up?"

"No." I shook my head. "I'm fine. But thanks for tonight. It was cathartic."

"Not exactly the normal way of describing a first date."

"Well, considering the circumstances, it was hardly an ordinary date," I protested.

"Maybe not," he said with a devilish smile, "but it's been a hell of a start."

He bent down and brushed his lips against mine, the contact sexier than any full-blown kiss I'd ever received. I swear to God.

I watched as the car pulled away, heart pounding, all the while trying to remember the last time I'd felt this giddy.

Maybe never. And oddly enough—definitely not with Dillon.

Chapter 10

I'm not exactly sure what we all did before Starbucks. I mean, it's not like Manhattan didn't already have its fair share of coffee shops. But somehow it just wasn't the same. Not that I'm one of those "three nonfat lattes a day" people, mind you. In truth, I actually don't like coffee all that much. I prefer tea. Iced, mostly. But I've also developed quite the taste for one of Starbie's hot Tazo teas. I mean, really, who can resist walking to the counter and asking for a cup of "passion"? Especially if the barista is cute. (Honest to God, that's the name of the tea. It's made from, among other things, hibiscus flowers and poppies. Which in and of itself probably explains a lot.)

Anyway, the truth is no matter what you drink, there's just a vibe that makes Starbucks a fun place to hang. Then again, maybe that's the point—Starbucks as a destination. From a marketing standpoint I suspect that's as good as it gets. And, since Bethany has a penchant for caramel macchiatos, it had seemed the logical meeting place.

I hadn't seen her since my date with Ethan, and though we'd talked on the phone the next morning, she'd been a bit preoccupied with Michael. Not that I blamed her. There really was something exciting about the beginning of a relationship. Particularly when it looks as if it could lead to something lasting. (And just for the record, I'm still maintaining that the whole thing is in spite of Althea, not because of her. Score one for the exception to the rule.)

"Over here." Bethany waved from the milk bar as I pushed my way through the crowd. "Sorry to make this a rush job, but I've got an appointment in an hour. A couple from Texas. I don't know how in the world I'm going to find them something. I mean, they're used to four bedrooms in the suburbs with a laundry room and a pool. I'm showing them four *rooms* without a view and three tiny closets. I'm afraid it's all going to be a bit overwhelming."

"They'll be fine," I said, as we grabbed a table from a couple of tourists. "This is Manhattan, after all. People don't expect to find palaces."

"I don't know, everything is big in Texas."

"So they'll adjust." I shrugged with a smile. "Although honestly, I wouldn't want your job. Cranky people on limited budgets looking for the perfect apartment. I'm not sure the animal even exists."

"Well, you did pretty well for yourself."

"Pure luck."

"And a friend with an inside track." Did I mention Bethany found my apartment and showed it to me three days before it was actually listed?

"Yes, well, there is that. Anyway, all I'm saying is that even with the best agent, apartment hunting in Manhattan isn't exactly a euphoria-promoting event."

"Well, as clients go, I've certainly had worse. And I'm sure I'll find them something," she said, sliding into the chair across from me. "But we're not here to talk about the Jacksons." She waggled her eyebrows for effect. "Going out with Ethan clearly agrees with you. You're looking loads better."

"I'm definitely on the mend," I said, self-consciously tucking my hair behind my ear.

"You really were lucky. It could have been so much worse."

"Physically, yes. Although from a psychological point of view I think I might have hit it out of the proverbial ballpark."

"Well, at least the paparazzi weren't there. And there hasn't been anything more in the papers."

"Yes," I nodded, sipping my tea, "thankfully, they've moved on to a new celebutard."

"You're hardly in that category," she said with a shake of her head.

"No. I suppose not. But I definitely gave it my best shot with my fall from grace, as it were."

"Old news. I want to hear about your dinner. I can't believe you ran into Diana and Dillon."

"Actually, it was pretty unbelievable. I mean, we always joke about it being a small city, but what are the odds that we'd actually wind up in the same restaurant? Especially Nino's. Dillon hates it."

"Apparently, not as much as you thought."

"He's just kowtowing to Diana."

"So was it horribly uncomfortable?"

"Awful. At least until Ethan arrived. Although I think I managed to hold my own."

"And Dillon? How did he deal?"

"He looked pretty miserable, actually. At least until the two of them were alone." I closed my eyes, trying to banish the picture of him laughing and holding her hand. "But he did call to apologize."

"You actually talked to him?"

"No. I couldn't deal. But I listened to the message. And I've got to admit, it did make me feel a little better about the whole thing. Although I still can't understand what he sees in her."

"Nothing she doesn't want him to," Bethany said. "She's got him bewitched, but sooner or later he's going to wake up and realize just what he's done. Only you won't be there to pick up the pieces."

"I suppose not."

"You suppose not?" Bethany said, narrowing her eyes. "Come on. You *know* not. I mean, now you've got Ethan."

"I've only been on one date with him. And I shared practically forever with Dillon. It's not that easy to let go. Even knowing that I should. I think there'll always be a part of me that wants him back."

"I suppose that's understandable." She shrugged, taking a careful sip of her coffee. "Did Diana say anything about Mardi Gras?"

"Just that she saw the show. But if looks could kill . . ."

"Score one for you." Bethany smiled, then frowned again. "Which reminds me, I think I might have put my foot in it. Have you told Althea about Ethan?"

A shiver of dread traced its way down my spine. "Just the stuff from the night of my fall. Why?"

"Don't kill me." She scrunched her nose and I sighed.

"What did you tell her?"

"Just that you went out with him. She was talking about your weekend. And I just assumed you'd mentioned it. Anyway, I kept the details spare. I'm sorry. I shouldn't have said anything, I know. But I couldn't seem to help myself."

"Don't worry about it. Althea is good at extracting information. And besides, if you hadn't told her somebody else would have. So when did you talk to her?" Considering I hadn't heard a word, I suspected it had to have been recently. Althea wasn't one to hold on to news.

"This morning. I was checking in about Michael."

"I thought this wasn't supposed to be a 'real' match?"

"It isn't. But you know Althea, she likes to stay involved."

"That's an understatement. But I guess if you don't mind . . ." I shrugged, wondering why Bethany's alliance with Althea bothered me so much.

"I don't. Really. In fact, she's actually had some good advice. This whole thing has been moving really fast. And you know that my mom isn't the type to offer support." Bethany's mom wasn't the type to be a mother—period. It's one of the many things we had in common. "I just need the reality check. And Althea's been there. Besides, she really knows Michael."

"It's her job. And don't forget she's going to be predisposed toward making it work. She's competitive as hell, and even if this one's off the books, she'll still want to mark it off as a success. Which means keeping the two of you together."

"Which is exactly what I want."

"Good, then there's not a problem. But if that changes, remember that Althea's going to stick with Michael. It's just part of the game for her."

"You make it sound so cut-and-dried. It's a relationship, not a business merger."

"To Althea they're one and the same. So all I'm saying is take her advice with a grain of salt. Anyway, I'm just glad to see you so happy."

"You, too," Bethany said with a nod. "Every time I've mentioned Ethan's name you grin like an idiot. Have you heard from him since the date?"

"Just a quick call. But he sent flowers."

"Really? That's so wonderfully old-fashioned. I love it."

"It was sweet. But I'm trying not to build it up too much."

"You got flowers. When's the last time Dillon did that?"

"He sends them on Valentine's Day—usually." I shrugged. "Anyway, there's no point in comparing. Ethan isn't like anyone I've ever met."

"I knew it," Bethany said, flashing a triumphant smile. "You're falling for him. So when are you going out again?"

"I don't know. He said something about this weekend. But I've got your party."

"You haven't asked him? I just assumed you would."

"It's all so new. And this is supposed to be about you and Michael. Introducing him to your friends."

"Well, if Ethan is going to be a part of your life, then he should be there."

"Oh, come on. Aren't you jumping the gun a little?"

"Oh, please, it's not like you haven't leapt into relationships before. You and Dillon slept together after your first date. And as I remember it, he was practically moving in by date three or four."

"You're exaggerating. He never actually moved in at all. We just shared space now and then. And besides, look how that turned out. Maybe if I'd been more cautious I wouldn't have ended up getting dumped for Diana Merreck."

"I still can't believe it, really."

"That makes two of us. Anyway, the point is that considering all that's happened, I think the last thing I should be doing is jumping blindly into another relationship."

"Asking Ethan to my dinner party is not jumping into a relationship. It's just a date. And a safe one at that. You'll be surrounded by friends. Besides, he sent you flowers. That's got to count for something."

"I suppose." I ducked my head, remembering the crazy way I felt after he kissed me. "It's just that everything is so complicated. I haven't even had time to deal with the situation with Dillon. Surely I need some kind of mourning period."

"Life doesn't wait around for us to be ready, Andi. Sometimes you've just got to take advantage of what's offered when it comes. Even if the timing isn't perfect. Otherwise the opportunity will just pass you by. And you know as well as I do that there aren't that many chances when it comes to finding the right man in this town."

"Well, when you say it like that . . . but still, it could be a huge mistake. I mean, what do I know about him, really? He grew up in the city, but left to help run his family's business when his father had a heart attack. He's only just come back, and lives in a borrowed apartment on the Upper East Side. Come to think of it, I really don't know anything substantive about him."

"Except that he's got a chivalrous streak," Bethany said. "I mean, he's saved you what, like three times now?"

"That's hardly enough to recommend him. For all we know he could be a serial killer."

"Oh, please." Bethany lifted her hands in protest. "I hardly think that's likely."

"Ted Bundy was really charming."

"Yeah, right," she said with a snort. "Anyway, it's easy enough to fill in the details. Surely you've Googled him?"

"I hadn't even thought about it until now." I should stop here and say that I have a complete and utter aversion to computers. Don't know why exactly. They're just not my thing. Everybody I know has text messaging and MySpace pages. And I can barely turn my phone on, let alone figure out how to type on the tiny little keypad.

I know. I know. I'm living in the dark ages. But hey, at least it proves I'm adept at not giving in to societal pressures. Or something like that. Anyway, Googling might as well have been Swahili for all it meant to me.

"I'm convinced you were born in the wrong century," Bethany said. "I don't know how you manage. Really."

I opened my mouth to retort, but as if on call, said cell phone began to ring, the not-so-dulcet Latin tones eliciting a frown from the woman at the next table.

I shrugged and pulled it out of my purse, checking caller ID. "It's him," I mouthed, my stomach threatening to renege on the tea.

"So answer it, already," Bethany said, waving at the still-jangling phone.

"Hello?" I said, flipping it open, the sounds of "Macarena" thankfully going silent.

"Andi?" Ethan's deep voice sent familiar ripples of pleasure coursing through me. What can I say? I'm easy. "Am I interrupting anything?"

"No. I'm just sitting here having tea with Bethany."

"Good. I was afraid I'd interrupt a taping or something. Anyway, I've only got a minute. I'm in between meetings, but I wanted to check in." Checking in was good. Very very good.

"So did you accomplish great things?" I said, with complete lack of brilliance. What can I say, the man discombobulated me. "In your meetings, I mean."

"Pretty much what I set out to do. Although I'm afraid there were casualties."

"Sounds ominous," I said. "And very *Sopranos*."

"No dead bodies," he laughed. "But in order to maintain market share we had to take out a few competitors."

"As in they're now defunct?"

"For the most part."

"So you actually destroyed someone's company?" Put that way it sounded grim.

"More like took it over. It's just business. And for the record, if it hadn't been us, it would have been someone else. It's a tough world out there. Anyway, I didn't call to regale you with my business dealings. I just wanted to see if you were free for lunch tomorrow."

"Lunch?"

"You know, the meal in the middle?" Again I could hear a hint of laughter.

"Yes, I've heard of it."

"So are you free?"

"I can be. For you." Okay, at least I was starting to sound more like myself.

"Excellent. How about the Shake Shack? You can bring Bentley. I assume you're still trying to keep him out of Dillon's hands?"

"I am. Although he hasn't called since yesterday. And I had the locks changed. Still, it's sweet of you to remember."

"Well, Bentley and I are friends. Anyway, I've got to go, but I'll see you guys at two?"

"Sounds like a plan. Bentley will be delighted." I disconnected, a stupid smile plastered across my face. Apparently, my dog wasn't the only one excited at the prospect of sharing fries with Ethan McCay.

"So?" Bethany asked.

"We're having lunch tomorrow. At Shake Shack. With Bentley."

"Kind of an interesting chaperone."

"He was worried about Dillon trying to make off with him."

"How sweet."

"That's what I said. Anyway, sounded like he was having an awful day."

"So you said. Something about *The Sopranos?*"

"Apparently, he eliminated his competition. Some kind of leveraged takeover, I think."

"Doesn't sound like much fun. But then business rarely is. So are you excited?"

"I think so. It's all happening so fast. And I still don't really know anything about him."

"That's right. We were about to Google him." Bethany tapped his name into her BlackBerry and waited as the machine searched the World Wide Web. "Oh my God." She frowned down at the minuscule screen, her eyes widening as she read.

"That doesn't sound good," I said, leaning forward, suddenly very interested in modern technology and the knowledge it possessed. "What does it say?"

"That he works for Mathias Industries."

"Oh my God." I sounded like a bad echo. "You're kidding."

"Nope." She turned the BlackBerry so that I could see. "Walter Mathias is his grandfather. Says so right here." She tapped the screen for emphasis.

The Mathiases are old money with a capital "O." They even had an ancestor who signed the Declaration of Independence, although I've forgotten which one. Considered Manhattan royalty, the family were the bluest of bluebloods. A dynasty in the truest sense of the word.

Family members sit on all the relevant boards, and scoring a Mathias to headline a fundraiser is the social equivalent of knocking one out of Yankee Stadium. The family name appears on practically everything in the city. Parks, libraries, and museums, not to mention the myriad of profitable businesses all housed under the umbrella of Mathias Industries.

Walter Mathias, Ethan's grandfather, is an icon. The last of a generation of kingmakers, he buys and sells people and companies with a relish that is unequalled. He is the kind of man people speak about in hushed, almost reverent tones, partially in admiration, and partially in unadulterated fear.

And Ethan was his right-hand man.

The thought was staggering. It was akin to Cinderella realizing she was dancing with a prince—of Manhattan. If pricked, I suppose my blood would technically run as blue. But I have an equal measure of my grandfather's sturdy Greek ancestry. And to be perfectly honest, I take greater pride in the latter. As I've already said, I'm not one to stand on ceremony or breeding. And yet here I was, going out with the heir apparent to one of the largest privately held companies in the world.

"Oh my God" was an understatement.

"And he didn't say a thing?"

"Just that he was working for his family's company. I suppose if I'd been thinking I could have put it together. He mentioned working in Asia and Europe. And that his grandfather started in steel."

"I think you can safely say that for all practical purposes, he is steel." Even Bethany sounded bemused.

"What am I going to do?" I asked, still staring down at Ethan's picture smiling up at me.

"Nothing. I'll admit it's a bit of a mindblower. But it doesn't change anything. Not really."

"Are you crazy? It changes everything."

Okay, I know what you're thinking. That I'm the biggest kind of reverse snob. And maybe I am. But you've got to remember where I come from. My grandmother may not have cared about my great-grandfather's rejection. But my grandfather did. He hated the idea that money and breeding could interfere in something as basic as a father loving his daughter. And he was determined to raise his daughters differently.

Of course, that sort of thing rarely goes as planned. My mother, the flit, was totally indulged when a stronger hand might have led to a different life. And Althea . . . well, she definitely seemed to reject her father's beliefs in favor of my great-grandfather's notions—like attracting like and all that.

Anyway, what I'm trying to say is that Niko Sevalas wasn't a man to stand on ceremony. He believed the worth of a man wasn't in his breeding, but in his character. And that most of the people occupying the world of high society aren't gifted with the latter.

And I agree.

So, the real honest truth of the matter was that I'd been angry at Dillon for jumping ship for someone like Diana Merreck. And at Bethany for signing on with Althea and Michael Stone. But all the time, I was hobnobbing with the cream of the crop. A Mathias. And not just any Mathias, mind you. No. I was dating the heir to the throne.

Which made me, what? Potential princess of Manhattan?

My grandfather was probably rolling in his grave.

Chapter 11

May is always a dicey month in Manhattan. It's almost as if the weather can't quite make up its mind. One day it's balmy and springlike, then the next, the temperature has dipped back into frigid territory and raindrops are pounding down on fledgling plants and spring couture. In any case, it's best to dress in layers and carry an umbrella.

Fortunately for me, however, the day had turned out bright and beautiful—a hopeful harbinger of good things to come. And so at the appointed time, Bentley and I arrived, pressed and dressed (well, me more than Bentley), at the Shake Shack.

As the name implies, the outdoor venue features burgers, shakes, and the most divine soft-serve ice cream you've ever taken a spoon to. But, unlike its roadside inspiration, the Madison Square Park restaurant is equal parts homespun pleasure and epicurean delight. Americana served up with a Manhattan twist.

I scanned the long line winding its way through the park for signs of Ethan, but he was nowhere to be seen. My heart sank even as my brain reassured me that he was probably just running late. Fifteen minutes later, as I inched forward in line, checking my watch, I wasn't so certain.

So it was with great relief when Bentley started yapping, his tail thumping a mile a minute as he spotted Ethan making his way through the crowd. He lifted a hand in a casual wave, and my stomach started the now familiar mambo.

"Sorry I'm late," he said, bending down to give Bentley, who was practically climbing his legs in a bid for attention, a scratch behind the ears.

"Well, I'm glad you managed to get away. I was starting to think maybe you'd stood me up."

"Not a chance." He shook his head as we moved to the head of the line and placed our orders, Bentley still dancing around at his feet. "Just a rough morning. My meeting went long."

"I'm sorry. Anything serious?"

"Nothing I can't handle. Anyway, it's over now and I'm here with you." He smiled as he paid for our order, then carried the tray out into the park as we looked for somewhere to sit. The biggest problem with the Shake Shack is that it's practically impossible to snag a table. In fact, on nice days it can be so difficult, they've installed a Shack Cam. Seriously, you can check the Web site to ascertain how long the line is and decide if you're up for the wait.

Thankfully, though, we had Bentley on the job. Tail wagging and butt wiggling, he led us right to a recently vacated table.

"Nice trick," Ethan observed, as I slid into the chair across from him. "Can he get us a table at Pastis?"

"Wouldn't that be nice," I laughed. Although I sincerely doubted that Ethan McCay would have trouble securing a table at any restaurant in Manhattan, his familial ties providing a virtual key to the city as it were. "But I'm afraid most of the epicurean in spots aren't particularly keen on cold noses and fuzzy faces." As if to argue the point, Bentley jumped into my lap, his chin perched on the edge of the table.

"Pity," Ethan said with a smile. "I suspect Bentley would behave far better than some of the more celebrated clientele."

"It is her, Angie," an excited voice behind me interrupted. "I told you it was."

"Oh my God," her friend replied as the two of them moved up next to our table. Both women were in jeans, one sporting an I ♥ NEW YORK sweatshirt and the other a BeDazzled top with more glitter than a Chelsea sidewalk on a Saturday night.

"We love your show," the first woman said. "Watch it every week."

"Never miss it," her friend concurred. "You're our favorite."

They both nodded, and then the first woman held out a napkin and pen. "Could you sign this? To Liz and Angie?"

I nodded with a smile and signed the napkin.

"Pretty impressive," Ethan said, after they were out of earshot. "Does this happen a lot?"

"Not that often, really." I shook my head. "Once or twice a week maybe."

"I suppose it can be a real nuisance."

"Not at all," I said with a smile. "In fact, it's kind of a rush. I mean, it's nice to know people watch the show."

"With cultlike devotion, if Angie and Liz are any indication."

I laughed, and we sat for a moment in comfortable silence.

"So," Ethan said, finally, taking a bite from his burger, "how was your morning?"

"Uneventful, comparatively speaking. I went to the studio early to tape some promo spots and then spent the rest of the time testing recipes at home."

"That sounds interesting," he said. "Recipes you made up or someone else's?"

"A little bit of both, actually," I admitted. "I like to see if I can duplicate restaurant dishes. At the moment I'm trying to copy some agnolotti I had at Craft."

"I'd have thought pasta is pretty much all the same," he said, taking a bite from his hamburger. There were people who actually swore Shake Shack burgers were the best in the world. Which was entirely possible, I supposed, when one considered they were prepped across the park, at Eleven Madison Park, one of Manhattan's better upscale restaurants.

"It is. More or less. Although good homemade pasta is nothing at all like the stuff most of us are used to eating. But agnolotti is a kind of tubular ravioli—from the Piedmonte region of Italy. So, it's the filling and sauce that make it special. In this case, pureed sweet potatoes in a butter-pecan sauce."

"Sounds interesting," he said, his skepticism negating the words.

"Honestly, it's amazing. Deceptively light, and unbelievably good. Only so far I haven't managed to nail it. Something the chef added to the potatoes, I think. But I haven't figured out what. Anyway, you can't write it off until you've tried it."

"Well, once you get it mastered, maybe I will."

It was the perfect segue into asking him to the party, since I was planning to serve the agnolotti then. But I couldn't make myself do it. Partly because of my misgivings about his background, but mostly due to my complete and utter fear of rejection. Stupid, probably, but for better or worse I held my tongue.

"So you said you had a rough meeting," I said, surreptitiously breaking off the end of my hot dog for—well, my dog.

"I guess no more so than usual. Except that this one was a little more personal. One of our holdings received some bad press recently, and we're just trying to head things off at the pass."

"Defensive moves."

"Actually, this one is a little more on the offense. But you didn't come here to talk about my family's business," he said, pushing away his half-eaten burger in favor of the main event. Frozen custard—today's special being coffee-bean brownie. Even from across the table it looked fabulous.

"No," I shook my head, drawing a breath for fortification, "but I am curious to know why, when you were telling me about your family, you somehow managed to omit the fact your grandfather is Walter Mathias."

"It never really came up." He shrugged. "At least not specifically."

"But I told you all about my family," I said, giving Bentley more of my hot dog.

"And I told you about mine. I just didn't mention the surname. I find it has a way of shifting things. It shouldn't matter. But it always does. So how did you find out?"

"I Googled you."

"And I take it you have a problem with my heritage?"

"Not a problem per se. It's just that I've sort of made it a rule not to date 'connected' people."

"Now you're the one who's sounding like *The Sopranos*," he said with a laugh, placing the remainder of his hamburger on the ground. Bentley's ears went up, and then with a yip of pure delight he jumped off my lap, his attention firmly fixed on this latest bonanza.

"You're going to spoil him."

"Hey, you're the one who just fed him half a hot dog. Anyway, the point here is that I'm still the same guy I was before you looked me up on the Internet."

"True. And I'm here, so I'm obviously not entirely opposed to the idea of our seeing each other. It's just that I thought you should know how I feel."

"This coming from a woman whose ancestors founded Plymouth Colony. Not to mention the fact that your great-grandfather owned half of Massachusetts. Had they been in the same generation I expect Jackson Herold Winston would have given my grandfather a run for his money."

"It's hardly the same. My great-grandfather disinherited us, remember?"

"He disinherited your grandmother. But not Althea or your mother. And I assume, by succession—not you. And anyway, you're missing the point," he said as Bentley, the traitor, finished the hamburger and jumped up into Ethan's lap.

"Which is?"

"At the end of the day, we're not that different, you and me."

"Oh, come on," I said, reaching for a bite of his ice cream. "We're miles apart. My grandfather was an itinerant Greek immigrant."

"Who made a fortune with his import business. He may not have started out with the pedigree, but he certainly made a name for himself in Manhattan."

"It's still not the same," I protested.

"It's exactly the same. My great-great-grandfather started life as an Irish dock worker. He followed the same dream your grandfather did. Just a couple of generations earlier. Face it, your money is as aristocratic as mine."

"Put like that, I suppose it is," I admitted.

"But I'm not telling you anything you didn't already know. So why don't you tell me what's really behind this moratorium on Manhattan society types?"

"The same thing that's behind everything in my life," I said, wishing I'd never started the conversation. "My mother."

"I'm not sure I'm following."

"I told you my mother was a bit of a wild child. Suffice it to say her lifestyle wasn't exactly Miss Manners material. And in those pre–Paris Hilton days, following the rules mattered."

"And I take it society, as it were, wasn't kind?"

"Got it in one. They ridiculed her. Ostracized her. Basically made her life unbearable. So much so that she ran away."

"But you said she left because of a fight with Althea."

"She did. But that was just the straw that broke the camel's back. Don't you see? The fight with Althea just epitomizes the way society viewed my mother. They wanted her to change. To become something that she wasn't. And because of that, she was forced to leave."

"So why didn't she take you with her?" The question was abrupt and one I had never been able to find a complete answer for. So I did what I always did. I stood up for my mother—for what I needed to be the truth.

"She wanted to. At least, I think she did. But Althea wouldn't let her. She believed I'd be better off here in Manhattan."

"But you wanted to be with your mother."

"Of course," I said, trying to rein in my emotions. "Who wouldn't? Melina was amazing. Always laughing. You should have seen her. She lit up a room. Like sunshine or something. She made everything fun. I remember once she woke me in the middle of the night to see a meteor shower. We bundled up in blankets and went across the street to the park. We lay on the grass and watched the lights shooting over the river. It was magical. I'd have given anything to have gone with her. But Althea said I needed school and a disciplined routine."

"Not a bad notion, actually."

"I suppose not," I said, picking at my napkin, trying to find the right words. "But that doesn't change the fact that I lost my mother."

"You're carrying a really large chip on your shoulder," he said, pushing his ice cream away. "You know that, don't you?"

"Yes," I sighed. "I guess I do. Only it usually doesn't rear its ugly head in quite this vocal a way. It's just that when I found out who you were I felt like such a hypocrite. I've been so angry at Dillon for choosing Diana—the poster child for New York society women. And then at Bethany for her defection."

"I take it her new boyfriend is *connected*?" He asked, repeating my words, his lips quirking as he tried not to smile.

I nodded. "Michael Stone."

"He's a good man."

"That's what Bethany said. And I don't want to be judgmental. But Althea set them up. Which makes it so . . . so . . . elitist. And archaic. Like arranged marriages or something."

"But it's not like your aunt forced it on Bethany. I mean, her parents didn't give her an ultimatum, right?"

"No, of course not."

"Then it's not really the same thing. Althea just facilitated their meeting. Nothing more."

"You make it all sound so simple."

"Well, it is. You're angry with your aunt. Understandably so. But you've let that anger color your opinion of an entire population. Me included."

"But I explained . . ."

"Yes. You did," he said, cutting me off with a gentle smile. "And I'm more than aware of how judgmental certain people can be. But I don't think that's limited to one stratum of society. And besides, I think you've managed to miss one major point. Your grandfather married your grandmother."

"Yes, of course. He loved her."

"In spite of her background."

"Exactly." I nodded, not certain why he was making my point for me.

"So even though he distrusted the upper classes, and was disgusted by your great-grandfather's behavior, he still loved your grandmother enough to risk marrying her. Heritage and all."

"You're saying it's about the individual. And I agree with that. But that's simply not the prevalent attitude among the Upper East Side ladies who lunch."

"But you're not going out with them. You're going out with me. And so all that matters is what we think. And I, for one, am willing to overlook your somewhat anarchical point of view because, regardless of your opinion of our relatives, or maybe because of it, I find you fascinating."

"I . . . um . . . I . . . I don't quite know what to say," I stammered, for once at a total loss for words. No one had ever called me fascinating. Ever.

"Say that you'll go out with me again."

"I will." And I was surprised to find that I really meant it. Whatever else Ethan McCay was, he was intriguing as hell. "In fact, if you're up for it, you can come to a dinner party I'm having. That's why I'm working on the agnolotti. It's for Bethany and Michael. The party, not the pasta. So that he can meet her friends. Anyway, I'd love it if you'd come."

"When is it?"

"Oh, right," I said, shaking my head at my own ineptness. "This Saturday. Seven o'clock. My apartment."

"I'd be honored."

I released a breath I hadn't realized I'd been holding, surprised at just how very much I'd wanted him to say yes. "Good," I said, "that's settled then." I stared down at my hands for a moment.

And then at my dog, still nestled in Ethan's lap. "For what it's worth, I don't think you're anything at all like them."

"The ladies who lunch?" he said with an exaggerated shiver. "I certainly hope not. Look, I've had my share of run-ins with them. So I can't say that I don't understand at least a little of what you're saying. But as I said, I think to ostracize an entire social class for the sins of a very unenlightened few might be cutting off your nose, so to speak."

"At least when it comes to the two of us," I said.

"Just at the moment," he shrugged, with a crooked smile, "I think that's all that matters."

Chapter 12

I can't believe how stupid I was. You should have heard me carrying on like a crazy woman." I sighed, sorting through bunches of parsley until I found one that seemed really fresh.

The Union Square Greenmarket was one of the best places in the city to find produce, bread, cheeses, and even fish. The long-running farmers' market, a favorite of local chefs, was bustling even this early in the morning. I'd risen with the birds, so to speak, to score the freshest food for my party. And Clinton, not really a morning person, had thankfully agreed to come along.

"I can understand the reaction," he said as I sniffed tomatoes. "It's sort of a hot button with you. But it sounds to me like Ethan more or less took it in stride."

"Well, he agreed to come to the party. I suppose that's a good sign."

"I'd say so. And in some ways I think it's just as well that you got it all out. At least now he knows where you're coming from."

"But this can never work, Clinton. Can you imagine me getting serious about a Mathias?"

"Andi, you're not interested in 'a Mathias.' You're interested in Ethan."

"Yes, but if I got really serious about him, it would have to involve the whole family. I mean, ultimately, they could wind up being my in-laws. Can you imagine?"

"Don't hit me," he said, lifting his arms in mock defense, "but I can, actually."

"Clinton."

"Andi," he retorted with a shake of his head. "Aren't you getting a little ahead of yourself?"

"I suppose so. You know I always overanalyze everything."

"Well, stop it," he said. "For the moment why don't you just sit back and enjoy the ride?"

"Because I just went through a breakup and I don't want to set myself up for another."

"Again, you're borrowing problems you don't have."

"I know. And I don't mean to. Honestly, I don't. It's just that if I'd known who he was when I first met him, I'd never have agreed to go out with him."

"So maybe it's a good thing you didn't know. Sometimes fate steps in when you least expect it. Maybe Dillon met Diana just so you could find Ethan."

I paid for the parsley and tomatoes and we made our way between vendor stalls to my favorite baker. "Well, as lovely as that sounds, I hardly think Dillon was trying to do me a favor."

"I'm not saying that. I'm just saying that sometimes we're so caught up in the small dramas we miss the bigger picture."

"Focaccia, please," I said, pointing to a stack of loaves.

"I think the peasant loaf would be better," Clinton observed. "You're using it for bruschetta, no?"

"Yes. And I always use foccacia."

"Well, I think the density is better with the rustic round," he said as the vendor suppressed a smile.

"Fine," I said with a wave of my hand. "I'll take the peasant loaf." I'd learned long ago never to argue with Clinton when it came to food. He could be quite dogged in his opinions—and besides, he was usually right.

"Look," he said, continuing the conversation, "I totally understand your disdain for people who are quick to judge." Clinton was one of those people that sort of just sprang fully formed from the creative well of Manhattan. He never talked about where he'd come from, insisting instead that he had all the family he needed right here in Manhattan. Considering that I'd spent most of my childhood wishing that my relatives would be voted off the island, I could totally understand the sentiment. "But that doesn't mean that there aren't good people out there with sizable bank accounts and impressive social standing."

"That's what Ethan said, more or less."

"Smart man. Face it, the Mathiases might just be the exception to the rule."

"And how would you know that?"

"I've worked on several charity events with Ethan's grandmother. And I've done business with his father and grandfather over the years. Walter Mathias's company even invested in one of my early restaurants. So maybe you're the one being too quick to judge?"

"Well, it wouldn't be the first time, would it?" I laughed.

"So you'll give Ethan a chance?"

"Yes. I said I would. Besides, how can I not?" I smiled. "Bentley adores him."

"From the mouths of canines . . . or something . . . ," Clinton said as we stopped to buy some fresh mozzarella.

"I thought I'd find you here."

We turned to find Cassie, briefcase in tow, standing just beyond the cheese stand. I don't know that I've ever seen Cassie in anything but a business suit. Even on the weekends. She's just one of those people who is more at home at work. If that makes any sense.

"What are you doing here?" Clinton asked, clearly as surprised as I was. "You don't cook."

"I eat. And that's almost the same," she said with a shrug. "But actually, I came to find you two."

"How did you know we'd be here?"

"You're having a party tonight. And you weren't home. So it followed that you'd be here."

"I didn't realize I was so predictable," I protested, not liking the implication at all.

"You're not. Really," Cassie soothed. "It was just an educated guess."

"Not that we're not happy to see you," Clinton said, "but you could have called." He patted his cell phone in testament to the fact.

"Yes, but that would have spoiled the fun." Cassie's smile assumed Cheshire proportions. "So aren't you going to ask me why I'm here?"

"You suddenly had a yen to help with the party preparations?" Clinton teased.

"Right. And pigs are delivering the *Post*. No. I heard from Monica Sinclair."

"And . . . ," I prompted, my heart rate ratcheting up a notch or three.

"She's gotten us a meeting with DuBois. Says he's interested. Of course, it's not a done deal, but it's definitely a step forward."

"Oh my gosh, this is fabulous," I gushed, my heart still beating three to a bar.

"I knew it was going to work out," Clinton said, raising a triumphant fist. "Prime time, here we come."

"Not so fast," Cassie warned. "DuBois has granted us an audience, but we've still got to convince him to come on the show."

"Yes, but getting in to see him was half the battle," Clinton said. "I've got a good feeling about this."

"When's the meeting?" I asked.

"Next week. She's going to call with the exact time and place once she confirms everything with Philip. In the meantime, we've got to plan our attack. Figure out exactly the approach we want to take with DuBois."

"Not today," Clinton said. "Andi's got too much to do as it is."

I shot him a grateful smile. As I said, Cassie tends toward all business all the time.

"And besides, Andi seems to have nailed it the first go-round. I say our best bet is for her to deal with DuBois one on one."

"It's not a bad idea," Cassie agreed, "but there are still things we need to talk about. Anyway, I can't do it today, either. I've got a meeting with the network this afternoon."

"On Saturday?"

"Jameson Dinwiddy is in from Dallas and this was the only time he could meet." She shrugged. "Anyway, I want to be sure we've hammered out the specifics of what we'll be offering DuBois. As well as what's expected of him in return. That way I'll be able to guarantee network approval at our meeting, which means that if we can convince DuBois to sign on, it'll pretty much be a done deal."

"You're still coming to the party, right?" I asked. Cassie was notorious for last-minute cancellations. Blame it on her afore-mentioned workaholic tendencies.

"Absolutely, I wouldn't miss it. Don't worry, I'll be finished with the network in plenty of time."

"Good, we'll celebrate," Clinton said.

"Or at least drink to the possibility that we might just pull this off," Cassie corrected.

"Either way, it's all good." I smiled.

A few hours later, I'd finished my shopping and was heading upstairs to my apartment thinking that really my life had pretty much done a one-eighty since the night I'd fallen in the cellar. I'd managed to parlay a chance at prime time into a real opportunity, I'd met a really amazing guy, he was actually interested in me—despite my mouth—and I had a whole afternoon of cooking ahead of me. Totally my idea of paradise.

Things were definitely looking up.

I slipped my key into the door and, balancing my grocery bags, stepped inside.

"Andrea, where have you been?"

I dropped two of my bags, and almost had a heart attack. So much for things getting better. "Althea," I rasped, kneeling to pick up the fallen produce, as Bentley tried to beat me to the prize. "You scared the life out of me. How did you get in here? I've got new locks."

"Ah, but you hide your spare key in the same place as always," she said, lifting the pink and gold owl key ring for effect. "Not a good idea if you're trying to keep someone out."

No shit. Note to self: *move key*.

"So how long have you been here?" I asked, still juggling the groceries.

"Not long. Maybe half an hour."

I shot a surreptitious look around the apartment, relieved to see no signs of obvious pillaging. Althea has never been good at recognizing personal boundaries. Especially mine.

"I thought maybe something had happened to you," she said, with just a hint of condemnation. "I've been calling for days." I knew that, of course, but I wasn't about to admit that I'd been screening my calls.

"I've been really busy. With the show and the dinner party." I pointed at the bags, now safely sitting on the counter.

"Oh, that's right," she said, "for Bethany and Michael. What a lovely idea. Especially considering how much you despise the circumstances that brought them together."

"You mean you," I said, not willing to pull any punches.

She shrugged. "Although I can't understand why you'd begrudge Bethany her happiness just because it originated with a matchmaker."

"It's not just any matchmaker," I said, trying to maintain my calm. "It's you."

"Well, anyway," she said with an imperious wave of her hand. "I think it's lovely."

"Your meddling?"

"No." She shook her head. "Your party."

"Well, I'm glad you approve." Sarcasm was not so easy to control.

"And I'm glad you're okay. You are okay?"

"I'm fine. In fact, I just had really good news. It looks like I might score an interview with Philip DuBois. Which could mean a prime time slot for the show."

"That's fabulous—," she started, only to interrupt herself with a fit of coughing.

"Are you okay?" I asked, grabbing a glass and filling it with water. "Here, drink this." I gave her the glass and she took a sip, then another, fanning herself with one hand.

"Sorry," she said, putting the glass on the counter. "Something must have gone down the wrong way."

"You're sure you're all right?" I frowned.

"Perfectly fine." She nodded. "And I'm delighted to hear about your show. Prime time. Won't that be wonderful? Of course, it's still only cable." Talk about your mixed messages.

"Well, I'm really excited, although nothing's been finalized. But things are definitely looking good. So was there any other reason you came by? Besides checking on me?" It was a loaded question. But if I hadn't asked, we might have been sitting there all day. Better to just take the bull by the horns.

"Yes. Of course. I almost forgot. I wanted to tell you that your grandmother is coming into town." Not the topic I'd expected. Maybe I'd lucked out.

"I thought she was in Cabo San Lucas." My grandmother believes that life is meant to be lived out of a suitcase. Preferably at five-star establishments with people who unpack for you. It's something she and my mother have in common. That and a tendency to view life with a slightly altered state of mind. In my grandmother's case, with the help of martinis.

"She was," Althea confirmed. "But when she heard about your accident she insisted on coming home. To see you for herself."

"Didn't you tell her I was fine?"

"Of course. But you know she never listens to me." That was true enough.

"Well, she could have called."

"Yes, well, you haven't exactly been accessible by that route." I actually felt a little guilty. Maybe I'd been ducking calls more than I should. "Anyway, she wants to see for herself that you're fine. And I can't say that I blame her. I was terrified when I got the call from the hospital." Okay, the guilt was growing by the nanosecond. "So, in light of all that, I thought maybe I'd throw my own little party."

"I don't know," I said with a frown, "my schedule is crazy right now."

"Andrea." I hated it when she made my name a rebuke. "Surely you can find time for your grandmother." Put like that, though, I really couldn't say no.

"So what's the plan?" I asked, pasting on what I hoped was a breezy smile.

"Well, I'm thinking tomorrow. Brunch."

"Althea, I'm giving a party tonight. I'm not going to be up to brunch tomorrow." Even for my grandmother.

"It's not like you have to do anything except come," she said with infuriating logic.

"Of course," I said, the guilt peaking, "I'll be there."

"And you'll bring Ethan?" And just like that she dropped the bomb. I should have been better prepared, but she'd lulled me into believing I'd dodged the minuteman.

"I can't . . . I mean, I . . . It's just that . . . ," I stumbled through a few more ill-phrased words and then stopped—surely silence was better than me making a complete idiot of myself.

"It's just brunch."

"I've only started seeing him. I hardly think he's ready to be exposed to the entire family."

"Well, why in the world not? He's coming tonight, isn't he?" Bethany and her big mouth.

"Althea, I don't want to talk about this. My love life is my business."

"Love?" she queried, seizing on the word like a pit bull in a butcher shop. "So you're falling for him? I can certainly see why."

"I didn't say anything of the sort," I said, dropping down on a stool at the counter. "I've only been out with him twice. And I'm still getting over Dillon. So let's not jump to conclusions. Okay?"

"Fine. It's just that Bethany led me to believe—"

"Bethany should have kept her mouth shut. Now, can we just drop the subject?"

"I suppose so. But I still think you should bring him with you tomorrow. Your grandmother would love to see him."

"She knows him?" Something else Ethan had apparently forgotten to tell me.

"Actually, I have no idea if she's met the man, but she admires his grandfather. They've been friends for years." Apparently, I'd fallen into some kind of alternate universe, one where Althea was more plugged in to my relationships than I was.

"Well, I'm not bringing him."

"It's an open invitation." Althea had never been one to take no for an answer. "In case you change your mind."

"I won't."

"Honestly, Andrea," she said, picking up her Birkin bag, "I don't understand why you have to make everything so difficult. I'll expect you at eleven. With or without Ethan McCay."

I opened my mouth to argue, and then closed it again. Sometimes even I knew when to shut up. She gave me an air kiss and left the apartment, her perfume lingering like some kind of undercover operative.

"Honestly, Bentley," I said to my dog, in my best Althea impersonation, "I don't know why we bother." Bentley yawned, and I sighed. "Nothing I do is ever going to be good enough. It's just wasted effort."

And believe me, there have never been truer words spoken—except when it came to Ethan McCay. Now there was a man my aunt could thoroughly approve of.

Which of course was precisely the problem.

YOUR PRESENCE IS REQUESTED AT A
STARLIGHT DINNER HONORING

Bethany Parks

AND

Michael Stone

7:30 P.M.

HOSTED BY
ANDI SEVALAS

RESTON BUILDING, SOHO
REGRETS ONLY

Chapter 13

Dinner parties are a dying animal, I think. Especially in Manhattan. People just don't take the time anymore. Or have the space. And in a city full of fabulous restaurants, it's just easier to go out. But sometimes I think that we've lost something kind of crucial.

I remember, as a kid, helping Bernie polish the silver when my grandmother was throwing a party. The house would literally sparkle. Fresh flowers in every room. Heavenly smells coming from the kitchen. China and silver gleaming in the dining room. And just before the appointed time, my mother would come into my room, smelling of Chanel N° 5, her dress swishing as she walked. She always looked amazing.

Anyway, sometimes I was allowed to stay up and help serve the hors d'oeuvres. I took the job very seriously, offering Bernie's savory confections with a flourish. My mother would smile, my grandfather would wink, and Althea would tell me it was time for bed.

Killjoy.

Still, it was a magical time. But after my grandfather died and my mother ran away, we didn't have as many parties. It was almost as though my mother took the fun with her when she left. I think my grandmother just couldn't deal with her losses. And Althea had never been all that keen on entertaining. She'd always been the practical one in the family.

Anyway, from almost the moment I was old enough, I'd started having my own parties. For family and friends. Keeping alive the memories, I suppose. My grandmother had given me china and crystal and some of her silver. And I still delighted in getting everything ready. Making certain it was all just right.

And sometimes, when I was feeling particularly nostalgic, I'd even wear Chanel N° 5.

Today, though, I was concentrating on the present, and maybe even the future. Ethan was coming, and even though my common sense was issuing stern warnings, my heart wasn't having any of it. Instead, it just kept coaxing my brain into reliving his kiss. (Okay, kisses.) The one at Shake Shack had been even better than the one at my door. Deep, compelling, toe curling, and, well . . . *right*.

I smiled as I chopped tomatoes, and forced myself to focus on the task at hand. I had eleven people coming for dinner in less than half an hour. Best not to cut off my finger while lost in a pheromone-induced haze.

The agnolotti was finished. But there was still the sauce to prepare. The salad was washed, but not dressed, and the lamb, marinated and ready to skewer, was still waiting for its vegetable garnish. The custard tarts were finished, but still lacking their strawberry toppers. And although the peasant bread had been cut and toasted, I still had to assemble the topping for the bruschetta.

Okay, so there were still one or two things to do.

I'd gotten kind of sidetracked between Cassie's good news and

Althea's visit. Not to mention last-minute errands. And to be honest, I hadn't actually done a dinner party of this size on my own in a really long time. I'd always had someone helping me. Most recently, Dillon.

It's funny how you can fall into routines and not even realize you've done so. I'd almost forgotten the flowers altogether, only remembering them when I'd seen an empty vase I planned to use. Dillon had been in charge of flowers, and the bar, and numerous other details that I hadn't bothered to deal with in three years.

He might not have been much of a cook, but organizing was his middle name, and entertaining his forte. And even though I was well on my way to recovery, I still had a moment of regret. Of missing the little things that made up a long-term relationship. The normalcy, as it were.

I dumped the tomato in a bowl, pushing aside my maudlin thoughts. Tonight was about new beginnings. Bethany's and mine. And I wasn't going to let old memories get the better of me. Besides, I'd probably glamorized them, anyway. I mean, Dillon had been horrible at cleaning up. Prone to going to bed and leaving me with the lot. Or worse, insisting we both go to bed (okay, that part was usually quite pleasant), but then, the next morning, leaving me to face an apartment full of dirty dishes and abandoned party fare. Usually solo.

With a sigh I reached for the parsley, and had just started a rough chop when the buzzer sounded. Someone was early. Putting down the knife, I checked the security cam, smiling to see Bernie standing there holding a large sack.

I buzzed her in and unlocked the front door, then returned to my chopping, making short work of the parsley and moving on to chiffonade some basil.

"Look at you," Bernie said, stepping into the apartment, "the picture of domesticity."

"I prefer to think of myself as a gourmet celebrity. It's got a better ring. Don't you think?"

"If you're prone to putting on airs," Bernie snorted.

"So did Althea send you to spy?" I wouldn't put it past my aunt, but Bernie wasn't into subterfuge.

"She probably would have asked me if she'd thought of it," Bernie laughed, placing two Tupperware containers on the counter. "But she didn't. I just figured you could use a little help."

"And food?" I nodded at the containers.

"Just some crab puffs and cheese wafers." Bernie's crab puffs were lighter than air, and her cheese wafers legendary. "I figured they'd go with pretty much any menu."

"They're perfect," I said, mixing the herbs into the chopped tomatoes. "I was only planning on bruschetta as a starter. This will be much nicer."

"So I came to help. What can I do?"

I started to protest, then realized I'd only hurt her feelings, and besides, I really did need her. "There are onions and peppers in the fridge. They need to be chopped up for the shish kebabs."

I added olive oil to the tomato-herb mixture, and then transferred it to a crystal bowl set in the middle of a silver platter with the bread. One dish down. . . .

"So I hear you're coming to brunch tomorrow," Bernie said, skillfully alternating onions, peppers, and lamb as she threaded them onto skewers.

"Without Ethan, if that's what you're getting at. I'm not ready to subject him to the family."

"She means well, Andi," Bernie said.

"Althea?" I tried to keep the skepticism out of my voice, but failed miserably. "Hardly."

"You've just never understood her."

"Like you do?" I asked, walking over to the sink to wash the strawberries.

"I don't pretend to understand everything she does. But I do know that she does most of it for you."

"And I think you've been tippling the sherry."

Bernice smiled. "Well, maybe it's best that we agree to disagree on this subject."

"She's your employer, you have to take her side." The minute the words came out I felt awful about them. "I didn't mean that the way it sounded."

"I know you didn't," Bernie reassured. "And I also know that you know how much Althea loves you."

"I suppose in her own unique way." I shrugged as the buzzer went off. It seemed everyone was coming early. "But I'm still not bringing Ethan."

"Which is why I figured I ought to just come on over and see him for myself." Bernie grinned as she started to arrange the crab puffs on a baking sheet.

"Well, get ready," I said as I recognized Ethan in the security camera, my heartbeat ratcheting up to an uncomfortable rhythm, "because he's here." I shot her a look of sheer panic. "I'm a mess." I was wearing an old apron I'd liberated from Bernie's kitchen, and as usual it was spotted with bits of the dishes I'd been making. "And I haven't finished my makeup or hair."

"Well, buzz the man in," Bernie scolded. "Or he'll think you don't want him."

"But I don't," I said, trying to breathe normally. "At least not now."

"Go on, then. Get ready," Bernie said, wiping her hands on a tea towel. "I'll let him in."

"You're a godsend," I whispered, already heading for the bathroom and salvation in the form of Bobbi Brown. Ten minutes later, coiffed and lipsticked, I sucked in a deep breath and walked down the hall toward the living room, stopping just shy of the doorway so that I could watch for a moment, unobserved.

To my surprise, Ethan was standing beside Bernie, sleeves rolled up, chopping strawberries while she finished with the lamb. I'd worried that it might be awkward, but instead the two of them looked as if they'd spent many an evening chatting over a cutting board. I smiled, thinking how easily Ethan seemed to blend into my life.

"The two of you look like you've been working together for years," I said, stepping into view.

"Bernie's keeping me on track," Ethan said, and I smiled at his use of her nickname. As far as I knew, no one but Wilson and me called her Bernie. The fact that she'd shared it with him was only further proof of her approval.

"You're early," I said, feeling a little bit like the third wheel.

"I thought maybe I could help." Ethan smiled, nodding down at the growing pile of strawberries.

"Looks like you're doing a fine job," I said. "Bernie's always been good at commanding the troops."

"It's my business to know how to run a kitchen." Bernie shrugged with a smile.

"She was just telling me about your first attempt in the kitchen."

"Not the pancake story?" I rolled my eyes with an exaggerated grimace.

I'd been really little. Hardly big enough to hold a skillet. Let alone manage a recipe all on my own. But I'd been determined to make pancakes for my mother. And I'd seen Bernie do it a million times, so I'd gamely gathered milk and flour and eggs and made a batch of what would probably have been the worst pancakes ever. Except that in my zeal to perform like a pro, I'd decided to flip the pancakes the old-fashioned way.

Bernie had arrived in the kitchen just as I hefted the skillet with all the strength I could muster. The pancake had flown into the air with surprising gusto, sticking to the kitchen ceiling—along with three of its predecessors.

"I gather it wasn't much of a success," Ethan laughed.

"It was a disaster," I agreed, walking over to join them. "I think there are still pieces of pancake on the ceiling, and it's been repainted—twice."

"I tried scrubbing them off," Bernie said, "but they were like industrial-strength glue."

"My first cooking experience was hamburgers—in prep school. I tried to make them in my popcorn popper."

"I'm not sure I want to know how that worked," I said.

"Well, it was an old-fashioned popper. You know, the kind with the Teflon bottom. My roommate had done it. Or at least claimed that he had. Anyway, it seemed like it'd work. And actually, it went pretty well, until the grease caught fire."

"And you threw water on it," I said, already anticipating what was coming next.

"Exactly." Ethan grinned. "How did you know?"

"It's the single biggest reason for most kitchen fires—not to mention popcorn poppers," I said, trying to contain my laughter. "Don't tell me you burned down your dorm."

"No. It wasn't quite that bad. But the popper was toast, not to mention the carpet."

"Carpet?" Bernie choked on a laugh.

"I was cooking on the floor. Not very smart, I'll admit. But it was comfortable."

"And comfort beats logic every time." I nodded as if it made total sense. "I wish I could have seen it. How much trouble did you get in?"

"The headmaster called my father. Which was much worse than anything the school could have possibly doled out on their own. You see, my family has been attending Andover for generations. And my father was president of the school's board. Not surprisingly, he was fit to be tied. Threatened to send me off to military school, as I remember it."

"But you survived," Bernie said. "I mean, you graduated from Andover, if I remember right."

"And you know that because . . . ," I queried, surprised at her inside info.

"I looked him up on the Internet." If it weren't for the fact that I'd done the same, I'd have been angry with her. But the pot isn't allowed to call the kettle black.

"It seems to run in the family," Ethan said, shooting me a knowing look.

"I Googled him, too," I said with a shrug, pleased beyond words that he understood how I felt about Bernie.

"Well, inquiring minds and all that . . . ," Bernie laughed. And suddenly I felt everything was right with the world.

"So I've finished with the strawberries," Ethan said, pulling us back to the task at hand. "What else needs to be done?"

"I think we've done all the prep. I just need to put the final touches on the hors d'oeuvre trays. If you want you can put the cheese wafers on this tray." I reached behind me for a platter I had displayed above the sink.

"That's really nice. Italian?"

"Yes, from the Lake District," I said, pleased that he'd identified its origin. "It's one of my favorites. Mother sent it to me a few years back."

Bernie coughed, the sound a cover-up for her harrumph of

disapproval. She'd never really forgiven my mom for running out on me.

"You don't like the tray?" Ethan said to Bernie, his gaze only curious.

"There's nothing wrong with the thing." She shrugged. "I just don't think gifts make up for desertion."

I swallowed nervously, uncomfortable with the turn in conversation. "I think it's nice that she remembers."

Bernie just shrugged again, concentrating on skewering the lamb.

"I brought wine," Ethan said, the comment a welcome non sequitur. "I didn't know what you were serving so I brought red and white."

"Fabulous," I said, relieved at the change of subject. "Maybe we could have some now?"

"I think that's a wonderful idea," Bernie said, "you two have some wine, and I'll finish up here then head for home."

"Absolutely not," I protested. We might have different opinions about my mother and her gifts, but it didn't change how I felt about Bernie. "You have to stay for dinner. I know for a fact that Wilson's working tonight. So you can't use him as an excuse."

"I can't, Andi. I don't belong at your dinner. Besides, I'll make it an odd number."

"Actually, you'll be doing me a favor," I pleaded. "Clinton is coming on his own. So we're already an odd number. You'd make it a full party. And Clinton adores you."

"Bernie, you have to stay," Ethan confirmed. "We won't take no for an answer."

"Ethan's right." I shot him a grateful look, secretly delighted with his use of the word "we." "Please?"

"All right." Bernie held up her hands in defeat. "But give me something else to do. Your guests will be here momentarily."

I glanced at my watch. "Oh my gosh, I hadn't realized it had gotten so late. Bernie, can you check everything upstairs while I finish these trays?"

"Upstairs?" Ethan asked.

"The roof," Bernie said, pointing toward the spiral staircase. "Andi's got a veritable paradise up there. The best-kept secret in Manhattan."

"Sounds amazing."

"It is." I nodded, pulling the crab puffs out of the oven. "It's the main reason I bought the apartment. Why don't you go have a look. You can check the table for me while you're up there. And Bernie and I will finish up down here."

"Sounds like a plan." He sprinted up the stairs and disappeared from view.

"I like him," Bernie said, filling a doily-clad silver platter with cheese wafers. "More than Dillon."

"Not you, too? I thought you approved of Dillon." I set the finished tray of bruschetta on the coffee table, then gave the sofa pillows a final fluff.

"It's not like that. You know I'm going to support whomever you choose. All I'm saying is that I think Ethan is right for you in a way Dillon never was."

"Shush," I said, with what I hoped was a formidable frown, "he's just upstairs, he might hear you."

"He can't hear a thing." Bernie smiled as she moved to arrange the crab puffs. "And you know I'm right."

"Maybe," I conceded, although in truth I did think she was right, but the thought made me feel somehow disloyal to Dillon. Talk about ridiculous notions. "Anyway," I began, but was saved from further discussion by the buzzer.

"People are here." I pressed the button to let them in, then shot a final look around the room as Bernie placed the other trays on the table. The plan was to serve drinks and hors d'oeuvres down-stairs, moving outside for dinner.

There was a knock at the door and I threw it open to welcome my friends. Stephen and Cybil were the first to arrive, followed by Clinton.

"I hope you don't mind," Cybil said. "I left the door down-stairs propped open. Vanessa and Mark are just behind us. I saw them getting out of the taxi."

"No problem. I should have thought of that myself. We'll just need to be sure to close it after everyone's here."

"It smells delicious," Clinton said, already moving into the kitchen. Occupational hazard. "Is that Bernie's crab puffs I smell?"

"Just for you, Clinton." Bernie beamed as the two of them inspected my pasta sauce.

"You look great," Stephen said, holding both my shoulders so that he could inspect my face. "I was afraid it was much worse."

"Just some stitches, served up with a little humiliation."

"I couldn't believe it when I heard about Dillon and Diana. Of all people." Cybil pulled a face, shaking her head.

"It was a bit of a surprise, but I'm coping," I said with a smile, thinking of Ethan.

"Well, it's hard no matter how brave a face you put on it," Cybil said with a shiver of dismay. "I still remember how I felt when Stephen broke up with me."

Stephen and Cybil had had their ups and downs. Mainly be-cause Stephen had been uncomfortable with the huge gap in their economic and social backgrounds. But in the end love had prevailed.

"But things worked out," I said, smiling at Stephen, who typi-cally was looking uncomfortable with the entire conversation. Although to be totally honest, I wasn't feeling all that good about it myself, even though I knew that Cybil meant well.

"Well, it just shows that there's hope for you and Dillon," Cybil said.

"I certainly hope not," Ethan said, sliding his arm around me as he strode over to stand beside me. "It would kind of put a kink in my plans."

"Ethan," Cybil said, breaking into a wide but surprised smile. "I'd heard you were back in town. But I had no idea you knew Andi."

"He rescued me," I said, grateful for the warmth of his arm. "From the infamous cellar."

"You're Prince Charming?" Stephen said, quoting Page Six.

"I'm not sure about the moniker. Just right place, right time."

"Definitely for me," I said.

"For both of us," Ethan said, his arm tightening around me.

"Hi, everybody," Vanessa said as she and Mark seemed to blow into the room. Well, Vanessa more than Mark. He was her perfect foil. Cool and calm to her natural exuberance. "Sorry we're running late."

"Not at all," I said. "The guests of honor haven't even arrived yet."

"And we were just talking about Ethan and Andi." Cybil turned to her best friend with an accusatory tone as Mark and Ethan shook hands. "Did you know they were seeing each other?"

"Actually, Althea did happen to mention it," Vanessa said with an apologetic scrunch of her nose. "But I wasn't sure it was for public consumption."

"Well, we all know now," Cybil said. "And I think it's marvelous."

"Speaking of secrets," I gasped, my eyes falling to the ring on Vanessa's left hand. "Is that what I think it is?"

"Yes." Vanessa beamed, waggling her fingers, the large diamond flashing in the light. "We're engaged. Mark asked me last night."

"You knew about this?" I turned to face Cybil.

"Of course," she laughed. "But as Vanessa said, it wasn't my story to tell. Anyway, isn't it fabulous?"

"It's great," I responded, truly delighted for the two of them. "But shouldn't you be out having some sort of romantic tryst?"

"Actually, we covered that ground last night," Mark said, his eyes lighting with pleasure as he looked down at Vanessa. "And we couldn't think of anywhere we'd rather be than here with you."

"You're actually the first people beyond family to know." Vanessa's smile could have lit half of Manhattan.

"So you haven't told Althea?" I asked, thinking they must not have since my aunt hadn't mentioned the fact. But of course, the significance was huge. If Mark and Vanessa actually made it down the aisle (and that seemed fait accompli in light of their announcement), then Althea would win the bet.

And become completely insufferable.

"Not yet," Vanessa said. "We decided that we wanted to avoid the inevitable media circus for at least a day or so. And once Althea knows . . ."

"Everyone knows." I nodded, secretly pleased that for once I was actually in possession of vital information before Althea.

"Hey, what's all the hubbub?" Cassie asked as she came through the door. "I could hear you in the elevator."

"Vanessa and Mark are engaged," Cybil answered as Vanessa flashed her ring again.

"Wow. Nice rock." Leave it to Cassie to cut right to the chase.

"What happened to Stacy or Gracie or whatever her name is?" I asked Cassie, who had arrived suspiciously solo. Cassie has a habit of dating models and starlets. The relationships rarely lasted more than a couple of months. Which made it almost impossible to keep up with simple things like names.

"It's Macy, like the store." She sighed. "And she got a callback for a movie. In L.A. She left this afternoon. Just my luck. I actually was thinking I might keep this one around. Oh, well," she shrugged with a laugh, "it's not as if there aren't more fish in the sea."

"So who'd like a drink?" Ethan said, cutting smoothly into the conversation. "Seems to me like an engagement is cause for celebration. Andi, do you have champagne?"

"In the refrigerator." I nodded. "Left over from New Year's. The glasses are over the sink."

In short order Ethan was popping a cork, and I watched as he filled champagne flutes, everyone gathered around him laughing and talking. And suddenly I felt insanely happy. And not just because Vanessa and Mark were tying the knot. Although that was in and of itself wonderful news. No, what had me grinning like a loon was the fact that Ethan was acting for all the world as if he belonged here, in my apartment, hosting my party—with *me*.

"Andi," Ethan called from across the room, his eyes for me alone. "Are you coming?"

I nodded and, still smiling, went over to join my friends.

Chapter 14

The party was a smashing success. The food all turned out wonderfully, thanks in no small part to Bernie and Clinton. It was just so much easier with more hands in the kitchen. And Bethany and Michael had arrived to the popping of the champagne cork. Delighted with Vanessa's news, Bethany had been grateful, I think, for the shift of focus. It made it easier for Michael, who turned out to be a bit on the shy side.

Mark and Vanessa, not surprisingly, had made an early exit, followed by Cybil and Stephen and then Bernie, who had to forcibly be dissuaded from doing the dishes by Clinton and Ethan. The two of them had then volunteered for the task, much to my amusement and surprise, and Michael, not to be outdone, had gone downstairs to join them, although I suspected that had more to do with not being left alone with three women than any real desire to help with the washing up.

Anyway, left to ourselves, Bethany, Cassie, and I had moved from the table to deck chairs, the night surprisingly mild. Below us, Manhattan surged on, oblivious to the passing of time. Truly a city that never slept. But up here, it was peaceful. The quiet broken only by the occasional sounds from the traffic below.

"So tell me the truth," Bethany said, after shooting a quick look in the direction of the staircase. "What do you think of Michael?"

"He seems nice enough." Cassie shrugged. "A little quiet, maybe."

"He's certainly different from the men you usually date," I said.

"In a bad way?" Bethany frowned.

"No. Of course not," I backpedaled. "I was just agreeing with Cassie. He's quiet. And you've got to admit, most of the guys you've been with were a bit more outgoing." An understatement, actually. Bethany had always had a tendency toward men with big personalities. "Life of the party" types. And Michael was definitely cast from a different mold.

"I think maybe that's why I like him. Because he's different."

"You seem really happy," Cassie said. "In fact, both of you do. Almost makes relationships seem like something worthwhile."

"They are," Bethany said. "I mean, what's more important than finding the right person to spend the rest of your life with?"

"Having a good time." Cassie reached for the wine bottle to refill her glass. "Life is too short to waste precious time looking for something that I'm not even sure exists."

"But you said earlier that you were thinking of keeping Macy around. That sounds like a relationship to me."

"A momentary weakness." She shook her head. "I'll leave relationships to the two of you."

"Well, I'm hardly the poster child," I protested.

"So says the woman with a man downstairs doing her dishes. If that's not domesticity, I don't know what is."

"Ethan is wonderful. I'm the first to admit it. But that doesn't mean we're serious about each other. We've only just started going out."

"Michael and I haven't been going out that long and we're serious," Bethany said. "Or at least I think we are."

"You sound like you don't know." Cassie cocked her head to one side, waiting.

"I don't. He really is different. From other guys I've dated, I mean. And I mostly think that's good. But sometimes, well, sometimes I wonder if maybe sooner or later I'll wish he were more exciting—is that awful?"

"Of course not," I said, quick to reassure her. "I think it's natural to have doubts. Especially when a relationship is young. I mean, no matter how wonderful someone seems, there's always the fear that there's something else lurking underneath. Or that you're not seeing the real person. I mean, look at Dillon. If you'd asked me if I thought he'd ever cheat on me, I'd have been insulted, and absolutely positive he wouldn't. Especially with someone like Diana Merreck. They're like oil and water—you know?"

"But he did leave you for her," Cassie said, ever pragmatic.

"Exactly my point. I didn't know him at all. Even after three years. So how in the world are we supposed to make decisions about relationships after only a few dates?"

"Michael asked me to move in with him," Bethany said without preamble.

"You're kidding." Cassie's eyebrows rose in surprise. "Talk about jumping the gun."

"Well," she said, her tone defensive, "we've been spending practically all our time together."

"Did you say yes?" I asked, not certain which answer I wanted to hear. I mean, I wanted Bethany to be happy, but the idea of her spending the rest of her life with Michael just didn't feel right. Not that there was really anything wrong with him. He just seemed so—well, stuffy.

"No." She shook her head. "I mean, I haven't answered yet. I told him I needed some time to think. It's such a huge step. And well, there are so many things to consider."

"I may not be big on commitment. But I do believe in love," Cassie said. "And if you've found it, don't you think you'd know it?"

"I've always thought so," I said, "but then we're back to me and Dillon. So clearly I haven't a clue."

"What about you and Ethan?" Bethany nodded at the wine bottle, and Cassie passed it to her. "Do you feel that way about him?"

"I don't know," I said, shaking my head. "It's too soon. And we come from such different places."

"Or at least you'd like to think you do," Cassie said, the wine clearly having loosened her tongue.

"What's that supposed to mean?"

"Nothing. Really. It's just that you're always going on about uptown people as if you weren't one of them."

"But I'm not. At least not in spirit."

"Look, I'm not trying to attack your character. You know I adore you. It's just that people are who they are. And most of that is thanks to their backgrounds. For better or worse we're products of our upbringing."

"But we can change. You did."

Cassie came from a broken home in Jersey. Newark, to be exact. She'd bounced around foster homes and even lived on the streets for a bit. And then somehow she'd managed to turn it all around. Come out on top of the heap.

"Yes. But it's not despite my background. It's because of it. If I hadn't been through everything I did, I wouldn't have been able to find the drive that's carried me through the years and taken me to the top of my profession. Anyway, I'm getting sidetracked," she said, waving her wineglass. "We were talking about relationships. And what I'm trying to say is that people are attracted to whomever they're attracted to. And there are no other rules. It's just chemistry and, in my experience, there is absolutely no predicting it or denying it. So Bethany, either you want to move in with Michael, or you don't."

"It's not that simple," she said, folding her arms across her chest. "There are so many things to be considered."

"I'm with Bethany," I said, taking my turn at refilling my glass. Wine was great for lubricating conversation. "Trusting one's emotions is a surefire way to walk right into disaster. Especially if she's having doubts."

"Now you're sounding exactly like your aunt. Reasoned relationships based on weighed commonalities."

"That's not fair. You know I don't feel that way. It's just that I don't want to see Bethany make a mistake. Moving in with someone is a serious proposition."

"I agree," Bethany said. "That's why I asked for more time. But surprisingly, Michael comes down on the side of just knowing. Which means he sees my needing to think as rejection of some sort."

"You've been together for less than a month," I reminded her, not certain why I felt so strongly about caution. Probably just the fact that I'd been hurt so recently.

"I know," she said on a sigh. "I suppose that's the whole thing in a nutshell. Anyway, it's my decision. I just wanted to see what you guys thought."

"I think you should do whatever makes you feel happy," I said, reaching over to squeeze her hand. "And if that's choosing to move in with Michael, then I say go for it."

Cassie nodded her agreement. "You have to do what's right for you. That much I'm certain of. And for the record, you could do a lot worse than Michael Stone. He's worth a fortune."

"Well, it's definitely not about that," Bethany protested.

"Of course not," I soothed.

"But it never hurts," Cassie laughed. "And anyway, at least he asked you to move in. Macy just walked out the door without even looking back."

"You don't know that for sure," I said, shaking my head. "I mean, maybe she won't get the job. Or she will and she'll come back anyway. I mean, she'd be a fool to let you slip through her fingers."

"Thanks for that," Cassie said with a wry smile, "but if you'll excuse the pun, I made my bed. And now I've got to lie in it."

"God, relationships are a pain," Bethany said.

"I'll drink to that." Cassie raised her wine in salute, and we all clinked glasses.

"Still toasting Vanessa and Mark?" Ethan asked as we all flushed guiltily, and I prayed he hadn't overheard the conversation.

"Relationships in general," Bethany said.

"Or the lack thereof," Cassie added.

"I'll second that," Clinton said, as he and Michael emerged onto the rooftop, Bentley tucked under Clinton's arm. "I'm beginning to think my expiration date has come and gone."

"Don't be silly," I said, taking my squirming dog.

"Well, I suppose it was a bit of an overstatement." Clinton smiled. "Anyway, the kitchen's clean and I'm thinking it's time for me to head for home. Cassie, you want to share a cab?"

"Surely it's not time to go? There's still more wine." She picked up the empty bottle and frowned. "Well, there's some more over there." She waved toward the table, dropping the bottle in the process. Fortunately, Ethan snagged it before it shattered on the patio.

"Seems to me," Clinton said, "like maybe we've all had enough. Too much of a good thing and all that."

"Party pooper." She stuck out her tongue, but stood up, clearly accepting defeat. "It was a wonderful party."

"It was," Bethany said, standing as well. "But we probably should be going, too. It's really late." She linked hands with Michael, who looked almost comically befuddled by the gesture.

"It was great meeting everyone," Michael said. "And we'll talk next week about the project we discussed?" This last was addressed to Ethan.

"I'll look forward to it. I'll call and we'll set up a time for lunch." Birds of a feather . . . I quashed the thought before I could finish. Ashamed of myself. There was no comparison between Michael and Ethan, other than maybe their bank accounts.

I stood up, ready to head for the stairs, but Clinton insisted he could see everyone out, waggling his eyebrows suggestively behind Ethan's back. I shushed him and smiled as they all made their clanking way down the stairs. Laughter floating up through the open door.

"It was a nice party," Ethan said, picking up the wine bottle from the table. "Shall we finish the last of the wine?"

I nodded and sat back in the deck chair, Bentley curled up on my lap.

There is something wonderful about the end of a party. The hour or so after everyone leaves when you can sit back and really relax. Entertaining is fun, but it's also work. And tonight, there had been all kinds of potential minefields. My first party without Dillon. Meeting Michael. Sharing it all with Ethan. And even, by default, Althea. It was almost as if she'd been hovering there out of sight the entire evening, just waiting for me to screw up. Talk about bringing along specters from your past. Cassie would be having a field day.

Anyway, I'd survived it all. And Ethan was still here.

"So you're having a meeting with Michael?" I asked as Ethan handed me a glass of wine and settled into the deck chair next to mine.

"Yes," Ethan said. "His company is looking to diversify and we've got some investment opportunities that I thought he might be interested in. It might come to nothing, but I figure it's worth exploring."

"So you like him?"

"From what I know of him, yeah. And his background is impeccable."

"You sound like Cassie."

"I beg your pardon?"

"Nothing," I said, taking a sip of wine. "Just girl talk."

"You sounded like you were having fun up here. It's nice to have such good friends. Have you known them all a long time?"

"Bethany since college days. Stephen shortly after that. And I've known Vanessa in some capacity since I was a kid, and through her, Cybil."

"What about Cassie? I know she's your producer. But did you know her before that?"

"We moved in some of the same circles. But our business relationship has really cemented our friendship."

"She's certainly a character."

"And then some," I said, checking to make certain he wasn't being derisive, but his face only reflected curiosity. "But she's got a huge heart. And she's smarter than anyone I know. She's already made a huge success of her career, but I know she's going to achieve even more. I'm lucky to have her on my team."

"I can see that." He reached over to squeeze my hand. "But she's not the only one who's lucky. You're a good friend, too."

"You could tell that just from tonight?"

"I could tell that standing in the bottom of the cellar."

I ducked my head, concentrating on Bentley, embarrassed at his praise, but delighted nevertheless.

"So how about Clinton?" he asked. "How did you meet him?"

"At his restaurant," I said, walking over to look down at the traffic below, "over pasta."

"Now why doesn't that surprise me?" His laugh was warm and inviting. "The agnolotti was great, by the way. You were right about the sweet potato."

"I told you it was good," I said, turning to face him, leaning back against the wall. "And I finally got the right balance of garlic and pecans for the sauce."

"Has it ever occurred to you to just ask for the recipe? I mean, considering you're a television celebrity, I'd think most chefs in town would be glad to oblige."

"I'm not that much of a celebrity. And anyway, figuring out the recipe is half the game. I told you it started with Bernie. And I just never really let it go. I love trying to suss out what's what."

"And then we get to reap the benefits," he said, sipping his wine. "She's really great, you know. Bernie. And she was full of stories about you."

"Most of them probably things I'd just as soon not have had her share."

"Only a few," he laughed, coming to stand beside me.

"You'll have to introduce me to your family," I said. "Then they can return the favor."

"Perish the thought," he said with a faux shudder. "But seriously, I would like you to meet them. Particularly my grandfather. You'll like him, I think."

"If he's anything like you . . ." I broke off, embarrassed again, and Ethan reached over to take my hand, pulling me so close I could feel his breath on my cheeks.

"I've never met anyone like you before," he whispered. "You're so strong and yet so vulnerable." He shook his head, and I waited, letting myself get lost in his eyes.

And then he kissed me, and it was perfect. Amazingly, wonderfully, fabulously perfect. Like we fit together, his breathing became my breathing and, if you go in for all that romantic claptrap, I could have sworn our hearts were literally beating in tandem.

Honest to God.

Time passed and, well, you get the idea.

Finally, a bit breathlessly, we pulled apart.

"I should probably go," he said. "It's late."

"You don't have to," I said, not sure exactly what I wanted him to do, but quite certain that I didn't want him to leave. "I mean, you could stay, if you want to."

"You're sure?" he whispered.

"Positive." I nodded, my heart hammering as he leaned in to kiss me again.

Sometimes, it seems, in order to move forward, you have to jump off a cliff. But then nothing's ever gained without a little risk. Right?

Chapter 15

My first thought the next morning was that a bed is ever so much nicer with two warm bodies—or in our case, three, since Bentley had managed to leverage his furry little body between us sometime during the middle of the night.

My second thought was that the phone was ringing. And since it was on Ethan's side I was going to have to roll across him to retrieve it. How very morning-after awkward can you get? Not that I was having regrets, mind you—let's just say that I'm not usually a "three dates, hop in bed" kind of girl.

And my third thought was that, contrary to thought number one, the right side of the bed was actually empty.

Very bad sign.

"Hello," I said, picking up the phone, my heart sinking at the sound of the voice at the other end of the receiver.

"Good morning, darling," Althea crowed.

I grimaced, trying to listen and search for signs of Ethan at the same time. "What do you want?" I asked, cutting right to the chase.

"Is that any way to talk to your aunt?"

"I'm sorry, Althea," I said on a sigh. "But you woke me up." From a very nice dream about a very missing man. "And you know I'm never pleasant in the morning." Especially after what was apparently a one-night stand.

"True enough. I remember—"

"That I was a real problem child. I know. Same song, different verse," I said, frantically searching for a wallet, or keys, or pants, or something to verify that Ethan was still on the premises. "But I don't think you called just so that we could take a trip down memory lane."

"True enough," she sniffed. "I called to remind you that you're coming for brunch."

My heart sank. As if the morning hadn't started off badly enough. "Look, I had a really late night last night, and—"

"Your grandmother is so looking forward to seeing you."

"Harriet is probably already on martini number three—and it's only," I glanced over at the luminance dial of my clock radio, "eleven." So I'd managed to sleep in.

"Andrea, that was totally uncalled for." But totally true. Still, I loved my grandmother. And, martinis or no, she was my last real link to my mother.

"I'll be there in an hour or so. I promise." As soon as I sorted out what happened to my missing paramour.

"Good. We'll see you then."

I hung up the phone and sat up, accepting the sad truth that Ethan was gone.

I sighed and got out of bed, pulling on some sweats as I replayed the evening in my head. It had been a wonderful night. That much I was sure of. There'd been none of that first-time fumbling. Just the perfect coming together of his body and mine. Okay, I know—TMI. But I was trying to justify my apparently incongruous memories with the fact that the man in question was seriously MIA. And he just hadn't seemed like the "love 'em and run" type.

But then, considering my recent track record, maybe I wasn't the best judge of character.

The living room was equally devoid of the man or any sign of him.

I walked over to the breakfast bar and plugged in the teapot. A little caffeine would go a long way toward making everything make sense. And if not, it would at least jump-start my day. I was due at Althea's, after all.

I called for Bentley and was rewarded by a yap from the top of the stairs. In our enthusiasm to end the evening (or start it, depending on how you want to look at it) Ethan and I had apparently left the door to the roof open.

Good way to wind up in the police blotter in the *Post*.

I walked up the stairs, past my yappy dog, and was starting to close the door, when Bentley dashed past me out into the sunshine. Maybe he had the right idea. Nothing like a little blue sky to lighten a mood.

The rooftops of Manhattan are amazing things. Adorned with chimney stacks, water towers, faded copper cupolas, secret gardens, and the occasional helicopter, they're an unheralded architectural wonderland. When I was a little girl, I used to sit in my bedroom and gaze out my nineteenth-floor window at the myriad of terraces and gardens that stretched before me and try to imagine the people who lived there.

And now I was one of them.

It was a glorious day. The kind where there are no clouds. Just endless blue (well, as close as you can get in a city full of skyscrapers). At least SoHo provides more sky than most parts of the city. And believe me, sky is as much of a commodity in real estate here as closets and extra bathrooms.

I stood in the doorway, drinking in the morning, watching Bentley as he snuffled his way across the garden.

"Gorgeous day."

I spun around, clutching my chest, to glare at Ethan. "You scared the hell out of me."

"Sorry." He grinned. "I'm an early riser so I came up here to enjoy the morning."

Okay, so he hadn't jumped ship. But he *had* just scared ten years off my life.

"I thought you'd gone."

"Is that a good thing or a bad thing?" he asked.

"Bad," I replied, the word slipping out. "I thought maybe you'd left."

"You haven't got a very high opinion of me, have you?"

"More of myself, I think. Anyway, I was wrong."

He closed the distance between us, leaning in for a kiss. "Well, I'm sorry I scared you. But, believe me, after last night, you're not getting rid of me that easily."

I felt my face flame red, which was becoming the norm with Ethan in the vicinity.

"So who was on the phone?" he asked, stepping back, realizing perhaps that I needed the space in order to breathe.

"Althea," I said, my mouth on overdrive—again. "I'm supposed to go to brunch today. And I kind of overslept."

"Can't you just give them a rain check?" he asked, his eyes signaling that eating wasn't what he had in mind.

"There's nothing I'd love more," I said. "But my grandmother's here. She flew in just to make sure I'm all right. Dillon and the cellar and all. So I really have to go."

"I won't pretend that I'm not disappointed, but I do understand," he said with a shrug. "Want company?"

"Yes," I said, the idea of reinforcements momentarily overcoming my reticence to subject Ethan to my family. "I mean, no. I have to go. You definitely don't."

"It can't be that bad."

"I wouldn't bet on it." I sighed, immediately regretting dissing my family. "Look, maybe they aren't that awful. But they can be a bit overwhelming. And besides, Althea practically begged me to bring you, which means that if you come, she wins."

"And with the two of you everything is a competition," he said, the words a statement, not a question.

"Sort of. I don't know. It's complicated."

"Welcome to life," he said with a smile. And suddenly my fears disappeared. With Ethan at my side surely I could handle whatever Althea could dish out. Faulty logic, most likely, but standing there looking up at his crooked grin I wasn't exactly at my cranial best.

"Okay." I shrugged. "If you really want to come, I'd love for you to be there. I just want to be sure you understand what you'll be walking into."

"It'll be fine," he assured me. "Besides, I've met your aunt, remember?"

I felt a shiver of something I couldn't quite identify. But it wasn't good. "You know Althea. Why didn't you tell me?"

"You always jump to conclusions," he said, shaking his head. "I met her at the hospital, remember?"

"Right. Of course." I blew out a breath, embarrassed. "I'm sorry. Althea just has a way of getting to me. Even when there isn't a good reason."

"It'll be fine," he promised. "And if she gives you a hard time, she'll have to deal with me. How's that?"

"Comforting in a completely ridiculous kind of way." And just like that the bad feelings were gone, the day seeming full of possibility.

Two hours later, after a brief stop at Ethan's apartment, we were standing in the elevator up to Althea's apartment.

"My grandmother's name is Harriet. She's been on holiday in Cabo San Lucas. And there's a good possibility that she'll be tipsy. But in a good way. I hope. Anyway, there's no telling who else might be there. Althea's brunches sometimes take on a life of their own. Bernie will be there. And you might meet Wilson, Bernie's husband, although it's not likely. He doesn't usually work Sundays unless Althea has somewhere particular to go. He's the chauffeur. Did I mention that?"

"Andi," Ethan said, taking both of my hands, "deep breath. It's going to be fine."

I nodded, sucking in the suggested air. "You're right. I'm just nervous. I haven't brought someone to Althea's with me in a really long time."

"What about Dillon?"

I frowned, wishing I'd just kept my mouth shut. "He and Althea didn't really see eye to eye. So we kept contact to a bare minimum. And before that, well, there just weren't that many people I wanted to bring home."

"So I should either be really honored, or very worried."

"Both, probably."

The elevator doors slid open and we walked toward the apartment, Ethan's hand reassuringly on my elbow.

Althea opened the door before we even made it down the hallway. Thanks no doubt to her building's state-of-the-art security and a certain nosy doorman named Dan.

"Andrea, darling, you're here. And you've brought Ethan." She gave me a hug and surprisingly had one for Ethan, too. Which was weird, since my aunt wasn't exactly the demonstrative type. Especially with people she didn't know. But then, what the hell, nothing seemed to be playing out in a normal fashion these days. "Come in. Come in," she positively gushed. "Everyone else is already here."

The "everyone" turned out to be my grandmother, Althea, and Vanessa. Which was a good thing. Since this was likely to be a minefield of a meal, I was glad to only have Vanessa as an observer.

She was practically family, after all.

My grandmother, who had been sitting on the sofa, stood up as we walked into the room.

"Ethan McCay," she said, waving her omnipresent martini, "I'd have known you anywhere. You look just like Walter."

"So I've been told," Ethan said with a smile. "I understand you and my grandfather are old friends."

"I knew him when he was still wearing knee pants. Our fathers were friends." She sat back down on the sofa. "In fact, your grandfather took me to my first dance. Gave me a gardenia. It's still my favorite flower. After Niko died we sort of lost touch, but I've always carried a soft spot in my heart for Walter. And for your grandmother. I was sorry to hear she'd died."

"Thank you," Ethan said, perching on the arm of the chair I'd sat in. "We miss her. But she had a great life."

"That's all you can ask for," my grandmother agreed. "I've always subscribed to the theory that life is to be lived. Anything else is just a waste of time." She shot a significant look at Althea, who shrugged.

"We'll just have to agree to disagree, Mother."

"I'm sorry to have crashed the party," Vanessa said in an aside to me. "I just came by to share my news with Althea. I didn't want her to hear it from anywhere else."

"I'm glad you're here," I said. "The more the merrier. And you always seem to be able to manage Althea."

"I don't know, now that she's won the bet, I suspect she'll be insufferable. Not that I'm complaining. No matter what the papers say, I know I'm the real winner. I've got Mark."

"Can I get you something to drink?" Althea asked Ethan. "Vanessa and I are having mimosas. A little champagne to celebrate."

"Or if you prefer something with a little more bite," Harriet said, "there's a pitcher of martinis. Vodka. Can't abide gin."

"A mimosa's fine." Ethan smiled, standing up.

"Andrea," Althea prompted.

Straight vodka had its appeal. "I'll just have some champagne. But let me do it. I know where everything is."

"Lightweights," Harriet chided, brandishing her now empty glass. "But while you're up, I'll take a refill."

Althea's mouth tightened but she held her tongue. My grandmother's drinking was an ongoing battle between the two of them. Harriet usually holding sway. Since my grandfather's death, and my mother's defection, she preferred looking at life through a bit of a haze. And though at times it could be a bit trying, she never actually crossed the line from cheerful distraction to out-and-out drunk.

And in truth, she missed my grandfather more than she'd ever admit. Theirs had been a true love match. The kind that comes along only once in a blue moon—whatever the hell that actually means. And to make matters worse, she and my mother had always been very close. Cut from the same cloth, as it were. So my mother running away only exacerbated my grandmother's grief.

For a while, she'd sunk into a dark place, but then with typical aplomb she'd packed her Gucci bags and her Reed & Barton pitcher and never looked back. Anyway, all I'm saying is that I've always thought that a person has the right to choose their own escape. And for my grandmother, it's travel and martinis.

I mixed Ethan's mimosa, poured myself some champagne, and refilled Harriet's glass, adding a toothpick-skewered olive.

"Ethan," Bernie said, appearing in the doorway. "Nice to see you here. I didn't know you were coming."

"I didn't know I was, either." Ethan smiled.

"You know Bernie?" Althea said, her brows drawing together in confusion.

"Bernie had dinner with us last night," he explained. "She brought her famous crab puffs."

"I think I ate most of them myself," Vanessa said.

"Bernie was at your dinner party?"

"Yes." I nodded, enjoying Althea's flummoxed expression. "She was kind enough to fill in as Clinton's date."

"But . . ."

"It was a lovely party," Bernie said with a grin. "I was honored to be included."

"Times today are so much more open," Harriet said. "In my day, employees would never have been allowed at an employer's function."

"Well, Bernie's a lot more than just an employee," I protested.

"I think Harriet just meant that things have improved since her day," Ethan offered.

"Exactly." She beamed at him. "The world is more relaxed now. Less stuffy. Fewer rules. And I like it that way."

"The world is what it is," Bernie said with typical ambiguity, "but while we're standing here debating the intricacies of upstairs/downstairs relationships, the food I spent all morning cooking is going south. So might I suggest a change of locale?" Bernie's expression left no room for argument, and, drinks in hand, we moved quickly through the French doors that divided Althea's living room from her dining room.

Bernie had outdone herself. The buffet was lined with silver platters and tureens. Eggs Benedict and a cheese-and-egg casserole were accompanied by smoked applewood bacon, fresh croissants, and, of course, Bernie's amazing blueberry muffins.

"Mexican vanilla?" I asked as Bernie headed back to the kitchen.

"You know it's not," she said, disappearing through the swinging door.

"Vanilla?" Ethan asked.

"Andi's been playing 're-create the blueberry muffins' for the last ten years or so," Harriet said, taking two. "To no avail, I might add. It's like trying to crack a top government code. Only better, since you get to keep eating muffins."

"My money is on Andi." Vanessa smiled. "She's an expert, after all."

"At copying recipes," Althea snorted. "Not exactly a marketable skill."

"She's making a living, Althea," Harriet said, taking a seat at the head of the table. "A good one at that."

"Does Bernie always cook like this?" Ethan said, shifting the subject as he heaped food on his plate.

"Actually, she's cut back," Althea observed. "Now that it's only me. Which means that she loves it when I have people over. Sometimes I think I only have parties to please Bernie." Her soft smile was sentimental and completely un-Althea.

"So tell me about your bid for prime time," Harriet said, purposely giving Althea a chance to regroup. "Althea tells me that it's looking really good."

"I think so," I said, sitting down next to Vanessa. "Although I've still got to secure the interview with Philip DuBois."

"Did you say Philip DuBois?" Harriet asked.

"Yes, Mother," Althea cut her off. "He's a very famous chef."

"I know that, Althea. I'm not senile. I was just going to tell Andi—"

"She doesn't need your help," Althea said with a withering glance that was very much more in character than her earlier nostalgia. "She's got everything under control."

"Well, I appreciate the positive thoughts," I said, "but it's far from a slam dunk."

"Do you have a backup plan?" Vanessa asked.

"No." I shook my head. "I probably should. It's just that I've been channeling all my energy into the idea of getting DuBois to agree."

"Well, I think Vanessa's right," Ethan said. "You need to have an alternative ready. From what I hear, DuBois is a tough customer. And unfortunately, there's a very good chance that he'll turn you down."

"Thanks for the vote of confidence," I said, frowning across at him. It was surprising how quickly I'd come to count on his support.

"You know I didn't mean it that way." He shook his head. "I just think it's always good to have alternatives."

"Well said," Althea agreed. "But I'm sure Andrea will prevail. She has a way of taking the negative and turning it around into something wonderful." I was completely flabbergasted. Coming from Althea it was high praise. And somewhat inconceivable. There simply weren't words.

What a day this was turning out to be. Ethan hadn't gone screaming for the door. And now Althea was actually singing my praises.

Something was definitely off.

Maybe I was stuck in a dream. One where Althea was my

champion and things always fell my way. And any moment now I was going to wake up—alone and definitely deluded.

With a sense of both purpose and dread, I grabbed the skin on the inside of my arm and pinched. Hard.

Nothing happened.

Of course, if you believe in Murphy's Law then the cold truth is that when everything seems to be going right, something is most definitely going to go wrong.

Oh, bother.

Chapter 16

"That's a wrap," Frank said, closing out the shot as I lifted my signature glass of wine, signaling an end to this week's show.

After a weekend that can only be described as amazing, the last few days had been fairly uneventful. I'd managed to spend time with Ethan, of course, but between his business interests and mine, not as much as I'd have liked. After Althea's brunch, we'd spent the rest of the day together. In bed, if you want to know the truth of it. And it had been wonderful. But the advent of the work week had brought reality crashing in, which meant we'd only had time for a couple of quick lunches. Not exactly rose petals and satin sheets. Not that I'm complaining.

On the positive side, my bruises were almost gone, and the doctor had pronounced me healthy after removing my stitches. So at least now I could avoid the daily physical reminder of my fall from grace. If only the mind healed as quickly as the body.

And, so far at least, I'd managed to avoid Althea. Not for lack of trying on her part, mind you. She kept leaving messages. Most of them about Ethan. And how much they'd loved having him for brunch. She made it sound as if he'd been the main course. Although, considering her preoccupation with matchmaking, maybe the statement wasn't that far from the truth. Anyway, the point is I'd been able to avoid discussing any of it with her. It most definitely wasn't her business. Everything was so new with Ethan. The kind of thing I wanted to cherish. Not pick apart and analyze to death. I wouldn't be able to avoid her forever, but for the moment, let's just say I was still screening calls.

At least I hadn't had to duck Dillon. He'd actually stopped calling, which was a relief—sort of. I mean, if I was to be totally honest, there was some part of me that still wanted him to come crawling back. I know it's totally not healthy. But relationships seldom are. And so I was delighted and disappointed all at the same time, which probably meant I was overdue for a session with a therapist. But my family has a long-standing aversion to the profession. Quite possibly because we're all certifiable.

Anyway, even if he hadn't called, I couldn't avoid him altogether. Well-meaning "friends" made a point of letting me know that he and Diana had been seen out and about, hitting all the hot spots. The idea of Diana in those kinds of settings was almost laughable—except that she was tripping said light fantastic with Dillon. And no matter how much I was enjoying my burgeoning relationship with Ethan—Dillon's defection still hurt.

But at least his not calling meant that I could quit worrying about Bentley. Which was good news for us both. My constant attention was starting to wear on my normally affable dog. I mean, even a dog needs a little privacy now and then. And I was more than ready to drop the Fort Knox–style protection. Vigilance has its price. Mainly out-and-out exhaustion. It was nice to think that Bentley could go back to just being a dog. And that I could quit envisioning *Sopranos*-like wiseguys sneaking up my fire escape to snatch my pet.

And I suppose the most frustrating part of the week had been that we'd heard absolutely nothing from the DuBois camp. This despite Cassie calling—twice. I was trying to hang in. Tell myself that DuBois had agreed to see me. It was only a matter of finding the right time. But I'd be lying if I didn't admit I was starting to get a little worried. Then, to make things worse, the network bigwigs began making noises indicating that not getting DuBois might spell disaster for the show.

So in very short order, I'd found a new lover, lost an old one, ditched my aunt, saved my dog, and gone from having a great idea for a prime time segment to potentially killing my show.

But then what's life without a little adversity? Spices things up, right?

"Everything looked good," Clinton said as I walked off the set. "Another show in the can."

"Let's hope it's not the last one," I sighed, putting words to at least some of my fears.

"Still fretting over DuBois not calling?" he asked, not looking the slightest bit concerned at the thought.

"That combined with Cassie's news about the network brass," I said. "I never meant for us to lose the show."

"Stop talking like it's the end of the road. We're not going anywhere. The show's doing fine. The suits are just using the threat as a ploy to try and spur us into coming through and producing DuBois."

"Well, it's working. Except that we can't do a damn thing about getting DuBois. Hell, we can't even get him to return our phone calls."

"Calm down. Everything will turn out all right. You'll see."

"So what? You're channeling the Dalai Lama now?" Clinton

wasn't exactly known for his positive outlook. "Who fed you the happy pills?"

"Let's just say that you're not the only one with a new boyfriend."

"He's not my boyfriend," I protested automatically. Although even I had to admit the protestation was starting to wear a little thin.

"Honey," Clinton said with a wave of his hand, "he survived brunch with Althea and still came back for more. If that isn't the definition of commitment, I don't know what is."

"You've got a point." I smiled. "Anyway, for once this isn't about me. It's about you. And what I assume is the new man in your life . . . so spill."

"Well," he said, drawing it out to play up the moment, "I met him in a bar. I know, very cliché. But it was Vlada."

"Very chic. And you went on your own?" Clinton wasn't exactly a "cutting-edge scene" kind of guy. Dillon had always given him a hard time about his homebody tendencies.

"No. I'm not that brave. I went with a couple of friends. Rupert and Jason. You remember them. They worked for me a while back."

"Fun guys. I remember. Anyway, tell me more."

"Well, there was this amazing-looking man. And it turned out that Rupert knew him. So he introduced me. And voilà. Instant attraction." Clinton settled into the chair next to me as I started to rub Pond's on my face to remove my stage makeup. Believe me, the stuff is lethal to the complexion if you let it stay on too long.

"Maybe there's something in the water. First Bethany. Then me. And now you. Now all we need is to find someone for Cassie, and we'll have a trifecta."

"Actually, a trifecta means three, and we're four. So the analogy is a bit off, but I get your point," Clinton said, handing me a Kleenex.

"So do I know this guy?" I asked, wiping the cold cream off my face.

"I don't think so," Clinton said. "Paul Maroney?"

I shook my head.

"He's an investment banker. Worked on Wall Street for a number of years, then got sick of it all and opened his own on-line firm."

"Sounds promising." Like Cassie, Clinton tended toward artistic types. Blame it on our occupation. So it was nice to see him fall for someone less likely to jump ship at the slightest provocation.

"It is. At least I'm hoping so. We had a fabulous time. And then we went out again last night and it was even better. So you could say that I'm cautiously optimistic."

"It sounds wonderful. And you deserve someone fabulous."

"I know," he agreed with a grin. "But I don't want to jinx it. That's why I didn't say anything sooner."

"So are you going out with him again?"

"This weekend. We're going to see the play with Norbert Leo Butz."

"I heard it's good. And even if it's not, Norbert Leo Butz always is. I saw him in Twain's *Is He Dead?* It was hysterical."

"I know. I was with you. Remember?"

"Sorry. I'd forgotten," I admitted. Dillon was supposed to have gone, actually. A treat for my birthday. I adored Broadway. Dillon not so much. And so when the night had arrived, he pleaded a conflict, and Clinton had gracefully agreed to fill in. I guess I'd just pushed the whole thing out of my mind. For obvious reasons. "Anyway, sounds like a nice evening."

"That's what I thought. And of course we'll go somewhere for dinner afterward."

"Somewhere romantic," I agreed. "So when do I get to meet him?"

"I don't know. It's too soon, I think, for that sort of thing."

"So no dinner parties." I smiled.

"Definitely not," he said, holding up his hands to ward off the thought.

"Well, when the time is right. I do want to meet him. Party or no. And you've got to admit the one I threw for Bethany and Michael went rather well."

"Yes. Except that you were rather preoccupied."

"I don't know what you're talking about," I laughed. "I was the perfect hostess."

"Even if you did only have eyes for Ethan McCay."

"Guilty as charged," I acquiesced. "But seriously, I thought the party was a success. Didn't you?"

"Absolutely. And Bethany seemed pleased with it all."

"Except for her rooftop admission," I said with a frown. Bethany had shared the news of Michael's invitation with Clinton the morning after the party, so I wasn't breaking a confidence.

"Has she said anything else about it?" he asked.

"I haven't actually talked to her. I've left messages on her phone, but she hasn't been answering."

"Maybe she and Michael are shacked up in unmarried bliss."

"Oh, please, she'd have told us if she'd moved in." I sounded more positive than I actually was. Bethany had always confided in me, but with Michael it was different. Maybe it was Althea's involvement or maybe Bethany just honestly didn't know what she wanted to do. Either way, it was weird to feel like I was on the outside.

"You're right," Clinton agreed, without any of my self-doubt. "She would have. So that means she's still contemplating. Or something worse has happened."

"Like what?" I asked, wiping the last of the goop from my face.

"I don't know." Clinton shrugged. "I'm probably just making mountains out of molehills. I'm sure she's fine. If she wasn't we'd be the first to know. Right?"

"Of course." Still, I was worried now. And feeling guilty. I'd been so wrapped up in my own life, and in Ethan.

I played back the conversation from the rooftop. She'd sounded okay. Just unsure of what her decision should be. Clearly, she cared about Michael. Which meant that the decision was an important one. Hell, who was I kidding? It was *huge*. One I couldn't even conceive of—at least not with Dillon.

"What about Althea?" Clinton asked. "Did she mention them at brunch?"

"No. But that's not all that surprising. She was sort of fixated on Vanessa and her engagement."

"I'll bet. Althea triumphs again. She's probably sending out press releases as we speak."

"Well, it's not quite that bad," I laughed. "I mean, despite the bet, she is genuinely happy for Mark and Vanessa."

"As are we all. They're absolutely perfect together."

"I know. And to be honest, at first I thought Mark was a bit of a stuffed shirt."

"Which just goes to show you, you can't judge a book by its cover."

"You're talking about Michael again, aren't you?"

"I'm just saying . . ." He tilted his head and opened his palms, letting the sentence hang.

"I haven't been that bad. I was just upset about Althea and her meddling."

"Yes, but sometimes that works out for the best, doesn't it? Vanessa and Mark, case in point."

"We both know that Vanessa had as much to do with Mark falling in love with her as Althea did."

"Except that if it hadn't been for Althea, and a little shove from Vanessa's mother, I hardly think the two of them would have found their way back together after the debacle with Cybil and Stephen."

"So what do you want from me?" I asked. "A glowing endorsement of my aunt and her matchmaking? Not going to happen. I think the whole idea is archaic."

"Well, it is, in a way, I suppose. And, of course, I'm not asking you to accept something you're so fundamentally opposed to. It's just that I want you to tread carefully with Bethany. She puts a lot of stock in what you say."

"Oh, please." I frowned. "You're giving me too much power. And besides, I'm always careful about what I say."

Clinton responded with laughter, and I would have taken offense, except that it was Clinton, and in all honesty he was right.

"Look, when it comes to Michael and Bethany, I'll be the soul of discretion. I swear." I held up my fingers Girl Scout style.

"All right then." He nodded, satisfied. "Now that we've got everyone's love life sorted out, what do you say we go and find Cassie. I want to go over some of the ideas we have for next week's show."

We walked down the hall, Clinton still teasing me about my tendency to react without thinking, stopping in the doorway of Cassie's office as she looked up from a phone call, signaling us for silence.

"And you're sure about all of this?" she asked, the lines around her eyes indicating that she wasn't pleased with what the caller had to say. "I see. And there's nothing else to be done?" There was silence as the party on the other end answered. Cassie's frown deepened and she nodded. "I guess that's it then. Right.

Thanks for your help." She placed the receiver in the cradle and for a moment the only sound in the room was the ticking of her clock.

"That was Jeri Yost. Bethany's friend from Metro Media," she said finally, waving us into the chairs in front of her desk. "I called her after I talked to Monica Sinclair."

"You talked to Monica?" I asked, chewing the side of my lip, a nervous habit I'd carried over from adolescence.

"Yes," Cassie said, her tone brusque, another indication that she wasn't happy, "a few minutes ago."

"And I take it the news wasn't good?" I scrunched my nose up, a physical reaction to what I already knew I didn't want to hear.

"No," Cassie sighed, "it wasn't."

"DuBois isn't meeting with us," Clinton said, putting my worst fears into words.

Cassie shook her head. "Apparently, he changed his mind."

"But Monica said that he'd agreed to a meeting," I said, as if that made it irrevocable.

"Yes, but it was only a tentative agreement. And we already knew DuBois was gun-shy when it came to public outings."

"So it's over?" I asked, still trying to wrap my mind around the idea. "It can't be. Surely there's something we can do?"

"Not a thing. Monica was quite clear on the fact. There will be no meeting with DuBois. At least not for us."

"Did she say why he changed his mind?" Clinton asked.

"No. She gave no reason at all. In fact, the call was fairly brief. I got the idea that she just wanted to get it over with."

"Probably embarrassed to have led us on," Clinton groused.

"Well, anyway, that's why I called Jeri. I thought maybe she could get to the bottom of what really happened."

"And?" I prompted.

"At first she said she couldn't help. Not her account. You

know the drill. But after I emphasized how important this was to all of us and explained what was at stake, she said she'd do a little snooping."

"So she was reporting back just now."

"Exactly." Cassie nodded. "But you're not going to like what she found out."

"I don't see how it can get much worse," Clinton said. "I mean, with DuBois out that means our chances at prime time just sank to zero."

"Not to mention our credibility with the big brass."

"Don't worry about them," Cassie said. "I'll smooth things over. The show's ratings are solid. They're not going to drop us."

"But they're not likely to give us another shot at prime time, either."

"No. Not after this."

"So what happened?" I asked. "Why did DuBois change his mind?"

"According to Jeri, it was mandated," Cassie said, running a hand through her hair.

"By whom?" Clinton frowned.

"An investor. A major one, apparently."

"And someone DuBois listens to," Clinton said. "Did she know why they put the kibosh on the interview?"

"No. Apparently, it was all very hush-hush. Closed-door meeting. That kind of thing. But the long and short of it was that the investor made it clear that if DuBois didn't pull the plug on the interview, they'd pull the plug on DuBois."

"But that's blackmail," I protested.

"No," Cassie said on a sigh. "It's just business. And unfortunately, it didn't fall our way."

"So who was it that screwed us over?" I asked, fuming. "I want to know who the bastard is."

"No, actually, you don't," Cassie said, shaking her head.

"What the hell are you talking about?" I demanded, anger making my face hot. "Of course I want to know. And if possible make sure they pay for what they've done."

"Andi," Clinton reached over to cover his hand with mine, "nothing's ever accomplished in anger."

"The hell it isn't. Who is it, Cassie? I want to know now."

Cassie blew out a long breath. "God, I hate being the one to have to say this. But I don't see any way around it. If I don't tell you, someone else will."

"So just tell me," I said, my stomach twisting into a tight knot of dread.

"It was Ethan's company, Andi," Cassie said, her voice leaden. "Mathias Industries forced DuBois to turn us down."

Chapter 17

"Oh my God," I gasped, feeling as if someone had slammed me in the solar plexus. "It can't be true. There's got to be some kind of mistake. Are you certain?"

Cassie nodded, looking as miserable as I felt. "Jeri said she had proof."

"Look, Andi," Clinton said, taking my hand, "just because it's Ethan's family's company doesn't mean it's Ethan."

I jerked my hand away and walked over to the window, my mind reeling as my stomach roiled. "It's him. It has to be. He's taken over for his father as his grandfather's right-hand man. How could he not know?"

"But why would he want to hurt you?" Clinton shook his head, clearly as floored as I was.

"I think I can answer that," Cassie said. "Mathias Industries is also a major investor in Applause." Applause was a rival television network. Their niche, as it were, covered high-end entertainment. Theater, opera, dance . . . and high-end restaurants. "Based on what Jeri told me, it looks like when Ethan heard about Andi's plans, he realized what a gold mine the opportunity was."

"And decided to capitalize on it." Clinton nodded.

"So you're saying that he stole my idea."

"It makes sense," Clinton said. "He probably figured Andi wouldn't land the interview anyway. What with DuBois being so publicity shy. But then we managed to pull it off. Or at least get a very solid foot in the door."

"And so he had no choice but to kill it." I fought against my rioting emotions, trying to find sense where there probably was none.

"Unfortunately, I think it's the most likely scenario." Cassie sighed. "I'm sorry, Andi. But I have to call it like I see it."

"Of course you do," I said, as I struggled to breathe. The implications were unavoidable. Ethan had played me. Taken my trust and turned it to his advantage. "It's all just business. Right?" I could hear Ethan's words echoing in my head. "That's exactly what he said. I thought we were talking about some other business deal. But maybe it was his way of warning me. Of putting me on notice. He even suggested we ought to have a backup plan. At Althea's." I choked back tears. "God, I thought he was just being nice."

"Maybe he was," Cassie suggested, her tone indicating that she didn't believe a word of it.

"Yeah right. And Althea's going to give up matchmaking and join a knitting club," I said, anger thankfully overcoming my tears. "*Nice* would have meant being honest. Telling me that he was going to steal Philip DuBois and maneuver his company so that they came out the winner. Oh, but wait," I said, lifting a hand, "there isn't a way to turn something so devious into anything even remotely resembling civilized, is there? I mean, when would he have brought it up? When he was charming my friends? When he was sleeping in my bed?"

"Andi," Clinton began, only to have me motion him silent.

"No. This isn't business. This is personal. It's my show we're talking about. Our show. And he sabotaged it. For his own gain. There is nothing businesslike about that. And I'll be damned if I'm going to take it lying down." The irony of the last bit hurt more than I could ever begin to put words to.

"But there's nothing you can do," Cassie said, ever the voice of reason. "The damage is done. At least as far as we're concerned, DuBois is off the table."

"We could tell him what happened," Clinton said, his eyes narrowed as he considered the idea. "If nothing else, at least it would cast doubt on Mathias Industries."

"No." I shook my head, staring out the window. "DuBois is clearly already in their back pocket. He needs their money. And their clout. He's not going to change his mind."

"Andi's right on this one, I'm afraid," Cassie said. "There's nothing gained in going to DuBois. Besides, I doubt he'd talk to us anyway."

"So we're screwed," Clinton sighed.

"Probably," I said. "But that doesn't mean I can't give Ethan a piece of my mind." I turned from the window, fists clenched tight, my mind made up.

"Don't you think maybe you ought to calm down first?" Clinton asked.

"Not much chance of that."

"So, what?" Clinton frowned. "You're just going to hunt him down and let him have it?"

"Sounds pretty damn appealing."

"But it won't change anything," Cassie insisted.

"No," I said, already heading for the door, "but it'll make me feel better and that's got to count for something."

Thirty minutes later, wielding my anger like some kind of virtual Excalibur, I walked into Mathias Industries. The company headquartered in the Lipstick Building in Midtown, taking up three entire floors. Ethan's office was on the sixth. Clinton had wanted to come with me, insisted on it, actually, but I'd turned him down. This was something I had to handle on my own.

"You can go in now," the woman at the desk said, eyeing me warily. My insistence on seeing Ethan had bordered on aggressive, and I could tell she thought he was making a mistake letting me into his office.

And considering the circumstances, she was absolutely right.

"Andi," Ethan said, rising from behind the huge mahogany monstrosity that passed for his desk. "I wasn't expecting you."

"No," I laughed, the sound harsh and bitter. "I don't suppose that you were."

"Then . . ." He shook his head, having the actual audacity to look confused.

"I have a few things to say to you," I said, clamping down on my anger. I needed to stay clearheaded. Or at least keep from totally spiraling out of control. "And I figured now was as good a time as any. Sorry if I'm interrupting—*business*."

He frowned now, clearly recognizing that this wasn't a social visit. "I don't know what this is about, but—"

"It's about the fact that you screwed me over," I said, cutting him off with a wave of my hand. "That you fixed things so that DuBois would never do the interview."

"Andi . . ."

"Save the excuses. I know you did it. I've got proof. Mathias Industries is a major investor in Philip DuBois' new restaurant. Am I correct?"

"Yes. We are."

"And you own majority shares in Applause?"

"We do, but I—"

"And despite all the conversations we've had about my wanting to get DuBois for the show," I said, cutting him off, "you conveniently forgot to tell me about your own interests?"

"I just thought that considering your tendency to jump to conclusions, it might be better to wait to tell you about Mathias Industries' involvement with DuBois until you settled things regarding your show."

"You mean until you'd convinced him to turn me down."

"I didn't do that."

"Maybe not personally. But your company did, and you run the company. Which means you had to know about it. And you didn't even have the common courtesy to tell me about it. And please, don't tell me it's just business," I said, waving my hand again. "We've been sleeping together. Or was that just part of some bigger plan? Some *business* deal." I paused to suck in a breath, shaking my head when he tried to intervene.

"I didn't come over here to discuss this. Or to hear you make excuses. I just wanted to look you in the eye and tell you how despicable I think you are. You took my idea, and turned it to the benefit of Mathias Industries. You used me. And then when it looked like I might actually be going to pull it off—when DuBois agreed to meet with me—you torpedoed my chances by threatening to pull your support of DuBois. He really didn't have a choice, did he? God, what an absolute idiot I've been. I was right all along. We don't have anything in common."

And then, before he had the chance to rebut any of it, I stalked out of the office. In the elevator going down, I'll admit I had a momentary fantasy that he'd follow me. That he'd convince me that everything was going to be okay. That somehow the facts had lined up incorrectly. But when the elevator doors opened on the lobby, there was no one there.

Big surprise.

In the taxi on my way home, I called Cassie. But she wasn't answering. Probably trying to persuade the Gourmet execs to keep our show despite our inability to follow through on what turned out to be our very rash promises. I called Clinton next, but he wasn't answering, either. Maybe they both figured it was best to give me a little space. And in all honesty, they were probably right.

The adrenaline rush that had carried me over to Ethan's office and buoyed me while I gave him a piece of my mind had evaporated the minute I'd hit the elevators. And now all I was left with was the bitter aftertaste of my anger and disappointment.

I really had wanted to be wrong about Ethan. To believe that he was different. That he wasn't all about his heritage and his money and his privilege. But in the end, he'd been worse. Instead of showing his true colors, he'd managed to convince me that he was worth caring about—maybe even worth loving. And then when I'd trusted him enough to turn my back, he'd buried the knife.

And the worst thing of all was that I'd let him do it.

The taxi pulled to the curb outside my building, and after stuffing a twenty through the Plexiglas divider, I slid out onto the sidewalk, slamming the door behind me. It's funny how catastrophe can strike, everything in your life seemingly turned on end, and yet life goes on. Tourists still flocked down the street, craning their necks to see the carefully crafted ironwork or maybe trying to spot a star. The panhandler on the corner still sang his off-key songs, waving his cup, pleading for money. Businessmen in expensive suits, glued to their BlackBerrys, ignored both the tourists and the beggars, intent on making that next big deal or screwing some unsuspecting innocent.

Like me.

I went inside and headed for the stairs, too keyed up to wait for the elevator's ancient chassis to wheeze its way down from the upper floors. I reached the landing and pushed through the door to find the hallway already occupied. Bethany was sitting in front of my door eating from a pint of Ben & Jerry's. Chocolate Fudge Brownie. My favorite.

"The key wasn't behind the fire extinguisher," she said by way of explanation.

"Althea," I sighed. "She used it once too often. So I moved it." I pointed to the mirror across from the elevator. It served as the hallway's sole adornment and had seemed the perfect place for my key. "I attached it to the back with some tape."

"I should have thought of that." She smiled, pushing to her feet. "I brought ice cream. Although I'm afraid I've eaten most of it."

"How did you know?" I asked, opening the door just as a flying fur ball came barreling through, jumping at my feet with enough adoration to almost make a girl feel loved again. I bent to pick him up, my fingers ruffling his soft fur.

"Know what?" Bethany said, scrunching her nose as we walked inside and settled on the couch, Bentley happily ensconced between us.

"About Ethan. I just assumed, since you brought ice cream, that Clinton had called to fill you in."

"Actually, he did, but I didn't pick up," she said, looking honestly worried now. "Sounds like I should have. What's happened?"

"Fortification first," I said, reaching over for a bite of ice cream. Then with a sigh, I leaned back into the sofa, and filled her in on DuBois' defection and Ethan's duplicity.

"This calls for something stronger than ice cream," Bethany said, after I'd finished regaling her with my sordid tale. "Vodka tonic okay?" Without waiting for an answer, she walked over to the refrigerator and pulled out the tonic. "Are you sure about all this?" she asked as she poured generous portions of vodka into two glasses, followed by a splash of tonic.

"Yeah. Cassie says she has proof."

"I just can't believe it," Bethany said, handing me a drink. "Ethan seemed so nice at the party. In fact, I was a little jealous."

"For absolutely no good reason, it turns out." I sighed as a sip of vodka burned its way down my throat.

"What did he say when you confronted him?"

"I didn't give him much of a chance to talk. But he did admit the connection between his company and DuBois. And he didn't deny that getting DuBois for Applause would be a coup."

"So this whole thing was a ruse? He was using you the whole time?"

"No. That part still doesn't make sense. Maybe he thought he'd be able to have his cake and eat it, too. See me and steal DuBois. I mean, if it hadn't been for your friend on the inside at Metro Media, we might never have been able to suss out the real truth."

"Maybe he was going to tell you?" she suggested.

"After the fact? Big deal. I mean, did he think I'd just shrug it off and pull back the sheets?"

"I don't know." Bethany sighed, then took a long sip of her drink. "Men are pigs."

"Hey," I said, a new thought making its way into my over-loaded brain, "if you didn't know about Ethan, then there had to be some other reason for the ice cream." Since our college days we'd relied on Ben and Jerry—and each other—to get us through whatever calamity our lives managed to throw at us. Usually involving the aforementioned pigs. "What's up?"

"It's nothing," she sniffed. "I mean, in light of what happened to you, my problems sound pretty silly."

"Nonsense. Tell me what happened. Does this have something to do with Michael?"

She nodded. "He dumped me."

"But I thought he wanted you to move in?" I frowned, shaking my head.

"He did."

"And you told him you needed some time to think about it, right?"

"Yes. But what I didn't tell you was that he made a really grand gesture of the whole thing. He got Payard to make a chocolate box. And inside the box was a key to his apartment. He gave it to me when he came to pick me up for your party. As romantic gestures go it was lovely. But it also scared the hell out of me."

"That's totally understandable." I nodded to underscore my solidarity. "You'd only just started dating."

"I agree. But I could have handled it better. Anyway, we came to your party and I thought everything was okay. Until he took me home. I asked if he wanted to stay the night, and he said no, that he had things to do the next morning. And so I let him go. I thought that under the circumstances it might be a good idea."

"So what happened next?"

"He showed up at my apartment Sunday afternoon. And he'd had a few drinks."

"Never a good start."

"Exactly. Anyway, he basically just let me have it. Told me that if I wasn't ready to move in with him, then clearly I wasn't committed to the relationship and that he wasn't going to stick around to wait for me to kick him to the curb.

"I tried to tell him that he was wrong. That I'd been thinking about nothing but his request. But he didn't want to listen. Just said that he'd heard me describe him as boring. And that as much as he'd tried to get past the fact, he couldn't. He said that he'd thought I was different, but it turned out that I was like every other woman—only interested in guys I couldn't have. Guys with an edge. Not nice guys like him." She paused for a sip of courage. "You should have seen him, Andi. He was so angry. So self-righteous."

"Well, maybe you're better off without him. Maybe we're both better off."

"I'll drink to that," she said. We clinked glasses and drained the rest of the vodka. "But I don't feel better off."

"Neither do I," I said as I walked over to pour more drinks. "But I think maybe that's what men do. They sucker you in, pretending to be something they're not. And then—*wham*—when you least expect it, they revert to type."

"Assholes," she said, taking the glass I handed her. "And to think I thought he was different."

"Well, at least Althea won't have another notch on her belt," I said, feeling a little woozy from the alcohol.

"I guess there is that," Bethany agreed. "But I'd much rather that she'd won. I mean, I really did like him."

"Then maybe you should tell him you were wrong."

"But I wasn't. He shouldn't have jumped to conclusions. Or at least he should have given me a chance to explain my side of it. I don't respond well to ultimatums."

"It could have just been the alcohol talking," I said.

"No. That might have bolstered his courage, or made him be a little more harsh than he intended, but he still meant what he said. He couldn't handle the fact that I needed time."

"Well, I'm sorry," I said, reaching over to cover her hand with mine. "It just hasn't been a good month for finding Mr. Right. I'm actually two down, if you want to keep count."

"Dillon. I'd forgotten all about him."

"I wish I could. I mean, it's just too much to deal with, really. First my longtime boyfriend ditches me for the queen of Manhattan triviality. And then her counterpart wines and dines me right out of my chance for prime time."

"It's not fair," Bethany said, shaking her head. "They're all jerks."

"Now if only we can figure out how to live without them."

"More vodka," she laughed. Bentley barked as someone knocked on the door and I wondered what the hell had happened to the security in this building.

"Probably Clinton," I said as I pushed off the sofa to open the door.

"Good, he can join the wallowing."

"He can't, actually," I called over my shoulder. "He's met someone new."

"Well, at least one of us is having a success."

"I hope you brought libations," I said, throwing open the door. But it wasn't Clinton.

It was Ethan.

Shit.

Chapter 18

I, uh, think maybe I should be leaving," Bethany said, grabbing her purse as she made a beeline for the door, where I was still standing, staring at Ethan.

"No," I said with a visible shake of my head. "There's no need for that. *You* are welcome here."

"Actually, Bethany," Ethan said, his voice deceptively soft, "I think it might be best if you go. Andi and I have some things to talk about."

"I think we've said everything that needs to be said." My fingers itched to slam the door in his arrogant, aristocratic face, but my heart just wasn't buying into the idea, and besides, Bethany was in the way.

"*You* may have said what *you* wanted to, but I haven't had a chance for rebuttal." His eyes were like lasers pinning me to the spot. And too late I remembered that the man was an attorney. A rather good one, if present circumstances were any indication. "And if I remember first-year law," he continued, "our entire system of government is based on the right of the accused to face his accuser."

Okay, so I wasn't a poster child for innocent until proven guilty. But I still had the facts on my side.

"I'll call you tomorrow," Bethany said, inching toward the door looking decidedly uncomfortable.

"You don't have to go," I insisted stubbornly, shooting a narrow-eyed look at Ethan. If he thought he could intimidate me, he had another think coming.

"Yeah, actually, I do." She nodded. "You guys need to sort this out and I don't think I've got anything to add to the equation."

"We could use a referee," I suggested, tentatively.

"Andi—," Ethan warned.

"Fine," I sighed, accepting the inevitable, as Bethany scrambled out the door. "Thanks for the ice cream."

"Hang in there," she mouthed behind Ethan's back. And then, in a more audible tone, "I'll call you later."

I nodded, and stepped back to let Ethan into the apartment. Bentley, who apparently hadn't gotten the memo about the whole disastrous affair, threw himself at Ethan in unabandoned delight.

"Bentley," I called, leaning down to pick up my traitorous dog.

"This isn't a war, Andi," Ethan said, still using his overly calm tone.

"No. It isn't." I sighed, straightening to face him. "So what is it you came to say?"

"Can we at least sit down?" he asked.

"I'm sorry," I said, "duplicity tends to make me forget my manners." I hadn't meant to sound so snippy, but backstabbing boyfriends have a way of bringing out the worst in me. And lately, I seemed to have hit the mother lode.

I walked over to the sofa, still holding Bentley, and took a seat, waiting.

"There was no duplicity," Ethan ground out. "You've taken what appear to be the facts and assumed the worst."

"Can you blame me?"

"For connecting the dots, no. For not giving me the benefit of the doubt, I guess I expected more from you in that regard."

"You didn't deny any of it when I was in your office," I said, crossing my arms, trying to channel Jack McCoy.

"You didn't give me a chance." He walked over to the bar and poured a few fingers of bourbon. Okay, I'll admit I've got no idea what "fingers" of bourbon even are. But it sounds better than saying he sloshed some whiskey in a glass. And since the buzz from my vodka tonic had evaporated the minute I'd opened the door, I held up my glass, silently requesting another.

When he'd settled on the sofa, I took a long drink and then dove in. "So are you going to deny that Mathias Industries persuaded DuBois to cancel his meeting with me?"

"No. It's just that—"

"But if you're not denying it," I cut him off, frustration cresting, "then I'm not sure why we're having this conversation."

"For absolutely no reason at all if you keep interrupting."

My fingers tightened around my glass as I resisted the urge to throw it across the room. The impulse wasn't at all ladylike, and quite frankly, it was my good crystal. Instead, I sat back, and with what I hoped was a supremely regal air, waved for him to proceed.

"I didn't have anything to do with DuBois refusing to do the interview. Until you came barreling into the office, I didn't even know it had happened."

"I find that hard to believe. You told me yourself you'd stepped into your father's shoes. And Google clearly identifies him as the working head of Mathias Industries. And I've got proof—well, Cassie actually has it—but the point is that I know that Mathias Industries is responsible for DuBois' change of heart."

"I'm not denying that."

"But you just said . . ."

"I said that *I* wasn't responsible—"

"Ignorance is no excuse."

"I'm not pleading ignorance, Andi. I'm telling you that no one in my employ contacted Mathias."

"Then who . . ."

"It's complicated."

"Isn't it always," I said, still fondling my glass.

"Look, Andi," he said, looking altogether too serious, "there's something I should have told you the minute it came up. But you have to understand I didn't expect there to be any ramifications from the omission."

"There are always ramifications. It's a law or something. Anyway, why don't you just tell me," I prompted. Surely it couldn't get any worse than it already was.

"You remember at Nino's—when you ran into Diana and Dillon."

"Yeah. How could I not?" I shrugged. "Humiliation is always memorable. Although I'm not sure I see what that has to do with any of this."

"I know, but just bear with me," he said on a sigh. "Do you remember asking me about Diana? You thought that the two of us might have been involved."

I nodded. The idea had made me sick then, and despite the circumstances, or maybe because of them, the feeling was only stronger now. "Are you telling me that you *were* involved with her?"

"No." He lifted a hand in denial. "At least not the way you mean. Diana is my cousin, Andi. Her mother is my mother's sister."

"Holy shit." My stomach threatened revolt.

"Exactly." He nodded, reaching out to comfort me, but I waved him off with my hands. "Now you understand why I didn't want to tell you."

"Aside from the fact that it's something else you lied about, I still don't see what this has to do with Philip and the interview."

"Diana was the one who talked to Philip." And just like that it all made sense.

"She wanted to get back at me for dissing her restaurant," I said, surprised to find that my voice actually sounded normal.

"It would seem so. Although I suspect that was only part of it. I gather there's no love lost between the two of you."

"She stole my boyfriend, I hardly think that's grounds for best friends forever," I said, ignoring the flicker of hurt that flashed in his eyes. "Although to be honest, I've never really liked her. She's the perfect example of everything I hate about Manhattan society."

"Yet another reason why I was loath to admit that she was my cousin."

"But I still don't see how any of this happened without your approval."

"Diana didn't ask for approval. In fact, she didn't tell anyone what she was doing. She just called DuBois and told him in no uncertain terms that if he didn't turn you down, Mathias Industries would find somewhere else to invest their money."

"And he just bought into it? What is it about men and Diana?" The last was purely rhetorical, but Ethan answered anyway.

"Sometimes men just see what they want to see. Anyway, Philip listened to her because he believed she was acting on my grandfather's authority. My grandfather let her handle the original talks about our investing in DuBois' restaurants. So as far as DuBois knew, Diana was still speaking for the company."

"And you had no idea that she was doing any of this." I walked over to the counter to refill my drink. I had a feeling I was going to need all the fortification I could get. Me and my overactive mouth.

"None at all." He shook his head. "Except for the few words we exchanged at Nino's, our paths haven't crossed since I got back."

"But didn't she realize that eventually someone was bound to figure out what she'd done?" I asked, bringing the bourbon over to refill his glass.

"I think she thought that by the time we figured out what had happened, she'd have convinced my grandfather that getting DuBois on Applause was the right course of action."

"So does Diana actually work for Mathias?" Quite honestly, the image didn't fit. She wasn't exactly the nine-to-five type.

"Not officially. But I think she's always believed that when the time came for my father to step down, she'd be the one Grandfather tapped to take his place. I'd never shown any interest, so she figured it was a done deal."

"You never wanted any of it?"

"Not really. I mean, I love my family. And I'm proud of all that my grandfather's achieved. But I never really saw myself stepping into his shoes."

"But then your father got sick."

"My grandfather needed someone with experience. Someone who could hit the ground running."

"You." I tried to imagine how I'd feel if Althea suddenly needed me to run her business. It was a staggering thought—and fortunately one that would never become a reality. Althea was healthy as a horse, and frankly, I'm the last person she'd ever call on. The realization was more disquieting than it should have been. "So I imagine Diana was pretty pissed."

"I'm sure she wasn't happy about it. Although she never said anything to me."

"Did your grandfather lead her to believe that she was going to take over?"

"He says no. But he's always kept his own counsel, so I can't say for sure. The relevant point here is that I think Diana believed that if she could produce DuBois along with the idea of an exclusive interview on Applause, then my grandfather would see just how indispensable she really was."

"And if in so doing she happened to screw up my life, that would just be icing on the cake." I nodded, most of the pieces falling neatly into place, but there was still a big one missing. I took a sip of vodka and took the plunge. "What I don't understand is how exactly Diana found out about my interest in Philip. I mean, I might be a small-time celebrity, but my movements are hardly front-page news."

"That part was totally my fault." He sighed, leaning back. "I told my mother. I was just telling her about you. And your show is part of the package. Anyway, apparently she shared the conversation with my aunt."

"And your aunt told Diana," I said, finishing the thought.

"Actually, she was there. My mother just didn't realize that she was delivering you into the hands of your enemy."

"So let's see if I've got this straight," I said, my mind spinning. "You told your mother about the girl you were dating. She shared the information with her sister. And out of all that Diana winds up with a nugget that looks to set her up as a winner with your grandfather and ruin my life as an extra bonus."

"That's pretty much it in a nutshell." He shrugged.

"So how did you figure it all out?" I asked, my heart doing somersaults over the fact that Ethan hadn't intentionally torpedoed my life. My brain countering with the fact that if he'd just been honest with me about Diana everything would have played out differently.

"I can be pretty dogged when I put my mind to something," he said. "And I wanted to be able to prove to you that I hadn't betrayed your trust."

"After the things I said to you, I'm surprised it mattered all that much."

"You know it matters," he said, his words sending a shiver running down my spine. "Anyway, if I'd told you Diana was my cousin when the opportunity first arose, maybe none of this would have happened."

"You should have told me. But considering the situation with Diana and the way I flew off the handle this afternoon, I can understand why you didn't."

"That's not an excuse. The truth is that I was protecting my own interests. But you have to know I never meant for any of this to happen."

"If I hadn't engaged her in the first place, it probably wouldn't have. I shouldn't have made Mardi Gras the target of my anger. So part of the blame is mine. I know better than to try and exact revenge. It always backfires. Except, apparently, for Diana."

"I wouldn't say that," Ethan said with the shadow of a smile. "She threw around the company's name without any kind of authorization. And she threatened the business relationship Mathias has with DuBois. My grandfather is not about to let that go unpunished."

"So maybe what goes around does come around."

"Maybe. Although to be honest, I don't know that I care all that much about what happens to Diana. I'm more concerned about where you and I go from here."

Now there was the million-dollar question.

"I said some awful things."

"With provocation," he acknowledged.

"Yes. But you're right, I should have given you the benefit of the doubt. At least long enough to let you try and explain things."

"If you had, I'm not sure that it would have gone any differently. I didn't even know about Diana at that point. So all I could have done is work to convince you that I wasn't the one who'd talked to DuBois."

"It shouldn't have been so easy. To mess things up between us, I mean."

"Well, in the end, it wasn't, was it? I mean, we're both still here."

"I suppose so." The glimmer of hope blossomed into full flame. "So we're going to be okay?"

I nodded, certain that that was what I wanted, but not completely sure it was possible. "I won't stand for you lying to me again."

"But I didn't really lie," Ethan said. "It was only an omission."

"That's just semantics and you know it," I said, shaking my head. "If this is going to work, I need you to promise me—no more lies. By omission or anything else."

He paused, and I held my breath, heart hammering.

"Ethan, is there something else I should know?"

He waited a beat and then shook his head. "Nothing of consequence. Honestly."

I wasn't sure it was exactly the answer I'd been looking for, but there was no questioning his sincerity, and it wasn't as if I was without blame. At least a little.

And the truth of the matter was that I didn't want to lose him.

"So what do we do now?" I asked, turning my glass with nervous fingers.

"We move forward," he said. "A little wiser and hopefully still together. Although I understand if you want to part ways. Getting involved with me has proved to be a bit more than you bargained for."

"I think that's an understatement," I said with a wan smile.

"Well, no matter what you decide to do, I want you to know that everything is going to be all right. With regard to DuBois, I mean. I called him as soon as I found out what had happened, and explained the situation. He's not an easy man to convince, but I got him to agree to meet with us. Or just with you, if that's what you prefer. And my grandfather's going to talk with him as well. To assure him that I am, in fact, acting on behalf of the company."

"So I still have a shot?" I tried but couldn't contain the excitement in my voice. "For the show?"

"You do." He nodded. "Of course, you have to convince DuBois that cooking with you on air is the right move for him. But I have faith that you can pull it off."

I was humbled to think that he'd done this for me. After everything I'd said. And not even knowing if I was willing to give our relationship a second chance. "You didn't have to do this."

"But I did," he said, reaching over to cover my hands with his. "And I think you know why."

I nodded, words suddenly not enough to convey what I was feeling.

He leaned forward and our lips met. A covenant, if you will.

There was no way to erase what had happened, but maybe out of all the bad, something good was still possible. I wasn't certain of the fact. But I knew that I wanted to find out.

Hope springing eternal and all that.

Chapter 19

If we weren't willing to forgive them for their foibles there wouldn't be such a thing as a successful relationship. All men lie about one thing or the other," Harriet said as she perused her menu. "It's just a matter of degree."

"If you weren't absolutely right," Clinton laughed, "I'd probably be insulted."

"Well, present company is excepted, of course," my grandmother said, taking a sip of martini.

The three of us were having lunch at one of my favorite restaurants in the city—davidburke & donatella. Three parts circus, one part turn-of-the-century townhouse, the restaurant is a sublime combination of old-world elegance and eye-catching whimsy. Honestly, the decor really is almost as wonderful as the food. Particular favorites of mine are the lithographs of Tony Meeuwissen's deck of transformation cards that adorn the walls and menus, and a bouquet of life-size glass balloons that would make a Murano glassmaker proud.

"So you think that I did the right thing giving Ethan another chance?" I asked.

"Definitely." Harriet nodded. "I mean, he's rich, he's handsome, and he's clearly besotted. What's not to forgive?"

"Diana Merreck," Clinton said, rolling his eyes.

"He can't help who his relatives are," my grandmother said. "No one can."

"Guess I can't argue with that." I sighed, thinking of Althea. "But I still can't help but feel like the other shoe is waiting to drop."

"Well, here's hoping it's not a stiletto." Clinton shrugged with a wry grin.

"Very funny," I said. "But this isn't a laughing matter. I mean, I'm not exactly noted for making great decisions when it comes to men. And even though I know that Ethan isn't Dillon, I can't help but worry that I'm moving too fast."

"Have I missed a marriage proposal here?" Clinton queried.

"No. Of course not."

"Then I don't think there's a problem. Just take things day by day and see where they lead. It's called dating," Clinton said with a laugh.

"Sound advice." Harriet nodded. "Life is too short not to take a leap of faith."

Since I'd had that very thought myself, I could hardly argue. Still, I couldn't help but worry. "Bethany took your so-called leap of faith and look what happened to her."

"She panicked," Clinton said.

"What do you mean *she* panicked?" I frowned. "It's Michael who overreacted."

"Their reactions were both a little over the top, if you ask me," he said.

"When I met Niko," Harriet smiled, taking a sip of her martini, "I didn't think twice about running away with him. I just did it."

"No hesitation at all?" Clinton asked.

"Absolutely not," she said with a shake of her head.

"And you never had regrets?" I asked, fairly certain I already knew the answer. Like my mother, my grandmother was a free spirit—a woman who followed her heart, not the dictates of society.

"Of course there were regrets," she said, much to my surprise. "I loved my father very much. And there were times when I missed my family more than I can say. But that doesn't mean I made the wrong choice. I loved Niko so much that I was willing to give up everything for him. But even when you know what you have to do, that doesn't mean there isn't a cost. One simply has to be willing to pay it."

I'd never heard my grandmother sound so—well, pragmatic. And I wasn't all that sure that it suited her. Or maybe it's just not how I wanted her to be. I guess in my mind I'd always thought that she'd gone with my grandfather without a backward glance. The idea that she hadn't was a foreign concept.

But then maybe, as usual, I was putting too fine a point on things. I do have a tendency to overanalyze a bit. Anyway . . .

"I never know what to order here," my grandmother was saying. "I mean, what in the world is sea-soaked chicken? A last holdout from the *Titanic?*"

"No," Clinton laughed, "that'd just be really old chicken. Besides, it's not sea-soaked, it's sea*water*-soaked."

"Same difference. Who wants to eat a drowned chicken?"

"Harriet," I said with a smile, "it just means it was soaked in brine. That's what makes it so juicy."

"Well, then why don't they just say that?" She frowned, closing her menu. "I don't understand menus these days. They're so full of alliteration and fancy descriptions no one has any idea what it is they're actually eating. Everything is either crusted with something—which sounds hideous in and of itself—or topped with ingredients I've never heard of and usually can't pronounce, and then to top it off, everything is piled together so that you can't distinguish one thing from another anyway."

"It's called vertical cuisine," I said. "Food as architecture. In its heyday it was a completely new way to look at food. Giving chefs 'air rights,' if you will."

"Well, I prefer my sides on the side, thank you very much," Harriet sniffed.

"In a divided plate no doubt," I laughed as I handed the waiter my menu. "I'll start with the bisque and then the black bass." The fish came with fennel-cauliflower "risotto" and an artichoke and picholine olive–preserved lemon relish. It did sound exotic. But for me that only enhanced the experience. Seeing how the chef combined different elements to create the perfect meal was half the fun. And in this case, chef Eric Hara was a master at the game.

"I'll have the chicken," Harriet said with a beatific smile. "And another martini. What better accompaniment for overly hydrated chicken than an overly hydrated me?"

"I don't think vodka counts as hydration, Harriet," Clinton said after giving the waiter his order and handing over his menu. "So, are you planning to stay in New York for a while?"

"I don't think so," she said with a shake of her head. "I only came back to make sure Andi was okay."

But Andi wasn't okay. My whole life seemed to be teetering on the brink. Not that I was going to admit the fact. Still, it might be nice if she'd noticed.

"The truth is," Harriet continued, blissfully unaware of my

insecurities, "ever since losing Niko, I just don't feel comfortable in the city. Too many memories. There's just nothing here for me anymore."

"What about me?" The words just sort of spilled out on a wave of resentment.

"Oh, darling," she said, sounding exactly like Althea, "you know what I mean. Between your grandfather's death and your mother leaving I just need a little space. It has nothing at all to do with you. I came home the minute I thought you needed me."

"I know." I sighed. "I didn't mean to imply that you didn't care. But it would be nice to have you around for a while."

She reached over and patted my hand, signaling the waiter at the same time. "I believe I asked for another drink? Really," she said, before turning her attention back to me, "service just isn't what it used to be. Anyway, sweetie, you know I love you. But I'm expected in Paris by the end of the week. Count Barogie is having a huge party. Everyone will be there. I've even heard there's a chance that your mother will show."

And there you had it. The chance to see my mother outweighed anything I could possibly throw at her. Just for a moment I wondered if Althea felt the same sense of rejection, prodigal daughter taking first chair to the one who'd stayed at home.

Weird feelings. I shook my head, dismissing them. The last thing I wanted to do was empathize with Althea.

"You know she probably won't show," I said, referring to my mother.

"Does she do this often?" Clinton said, clearly intrigued by our dirty laundry.

"Melina tends to stay pretty much off the radar where I'm concerned," Harriet said, her tone dejected. "I've never really understood why. I wasn't the one who asked her to leave. Although

push come to shove I probably would have sided with Althea."
This was definitely a day for surprises. Harriet never sided with
Althea about anything. At least not until now.

"What do you mean?" I asked.

"Nothing, really," she said with a shrug. "It's all water under the
bridge. Melina's chosen her life, just as I chose mine."

"So you never actually get together?" Clinton asked with a
frown.

"Oh, once or twice a year our paths usually cross," Harriet admitted. "But never for very long. Melina isn't any better at staying
put than I am."

"At least you've seen her," I said, unable to keep the wistful
tone out of my voice. "I never hear from her at all."

"She sends cards," my grandmother said. "And gifts."

"When she remembers, but it's not the same." Actually, I
cherished everything she'd ever given me. And I kept the cards
in a box under my bed. It was a childish thing to do. Ridiculous,
really, when you considered that she never actually wrote anything except "love, Mother." The truth was that I was clinging to
a bunch of sappy sentiments written by some Hallmark staffer I
didn't even know.

"But at least it proves she's thinking of you," Harriet said. "She
just isn't the demonstrative sort."

"She used to be," I sighed. "I remember her here in New York.
Before Althea drove her away. She was a good mother."

"Memory is subjective, Andi. We all have a way of seeing
what we want to see," she said, leaning back as the waiter brought
her new martini. "Anyway, enough talk of Melina."

"My fault," Clinton said with an apologetic frown. "I brought
it up. I'm afraid I was just curious."

"Understandably." Harriet smiled. "Our family is a trifle unusual."

"Believe me," Clinton laughed, "yours has nothing at all on mine. And I can totally understand the need to get away."

I could, too, actually. Except that in this instance we were talking about getting away from me. And that really wasn't a particularly palatable thought.

"It was never about you, Andi," my grandmother said, reading my mind. "You have to know that."

"I suppose I do. But I'm still the one who got caught in the fallout. Anyway, you're right, it's all old news. Surely we can find something better to talk about."

"So catch me up on the latest developments with the show," Harriet said, her warm smile directed to me. And suddenly I felt better. My family might be weird, but in their own unique way they did love me. "I take it everything is on again with Philip DuBois?"

"Seems to be," I said. "Cassie is finalizing the details as we speak. Although I confess I don't think I'll breathe easily until we're standing in front of the man."

"He does appear to have a tendency to change his mind," my grandmother agreed.

"Or have it changed for him," Clinton said with a frown.

"You're talking about Diana again."

"Unfortunately," I sighed, "she seems to be the focal point of my life of late."

"Not a pretty picture." Clinton shuddered. "But at least for the moment she seems to have been vanquished back to whatever slime pit she crawled out of."

"With Dillon."

"If he's going to be that stupid," my grandmother said, "then I say he deserves what he gets."

I laughed, feeling a lot better. "We did manage to dodge her bullet, didn't we?"

"You bet your ass we did." Clinton raised his hand and we high-fived.

"Here's to the sweet smell of success," Harriet said, lifting her martini. We toasted, then leaned back as the server set our appetizers on the table.

My lobster bisque looked amazing. Steaming hot with a positively divine aroma. Angled jauntily across the bowl was a thin oblong crisp of lobster roll. It was almost too perfect to eat, as artistically appealing as it was appetizing. (I told you d&d was a fabulous restaurant.)

Polite silence descended. You know, like on an elevator full of strangers, everyone concentrating on the little numbers overhead as if they were crucial to their very existence. Only in this case it was lobster bisque, crab cakes, and sashimi.

Anyway, after everyone had had a chance to sample their food, Harriet brought the conversation back to the topic at hand. "So will you and Clinton both be at the meeting?"

"No." Clinton shook his head. "Just Andi and Cassie. And Ethan."

"I'm not sure I understand why Ethan needs to be there." My grandmother leaned back in her chair.

"You and me both," Clinton said, over a forkful of crab cake.

"I thought you were pro-Ethan," I protested. "Weren't you just telling me that I made the right decision when I forgave him?"

"Actually, I think it was a mutual forgiving," Clinton said with a suggestive waggle of his eyebrows. "You kind of jumped to some pretty harsh conclusions."

"With your help," I said, frowning at him with mock severity.

"True enough." He shrugged. "But the facts did seem to support the assumption."

"You know what they say about assuming," Harriet said.

"Yeah, I do," I laughed. "And it's absolutely, positively true. Believe me."

"Well, it seems to me that it all came out right in the end. But you've managed to get completely off point. What I want to know is what Ethan McCay has to do with DuBois and your show?"

"Well, for starters, he's the reason we got the meeting with DuBois rescheduled."

"Actually, it was Mathias Industries that opened that particular door," Clinton said.

"Yes, well, for all practical purposes they're one and the same. And even if that weren't the case, DuBois asked Ethan to come. An independent opinion, I guess."

"Hardly independent." Harriet shook her head. "Ethan's in this up to his neck. It was his cousin that caused the problems in the first place."

"Which is why I'm not completely comfortable with him being there," Clinton said on a sigh. "But there's nothing much I can do about it, so we'll just have to hope that it's all for the best."

"Maybe you should think about approaching someone else to be on the show," Harriet said. "Someone less mercurial. Even if Chef DuBois agrees to come on *What's Cooking*, who's to say he won't change his mind ten minutes later?"

"I've had the same thought," Clinton nodded, "but DuBois is as big as they come when one is considering celebrity chefs. And when you add in his aversion to public appearances, it makes him irresistible. A real ratings bonanza."

"And we're going to get him to agree. I know we are." If only I felt as confident as I sounded.

"If positive thoughts could move mountains . . ." Harriet smiled as Clinton's iPhone signaled an incoming text.

"Excuse me," he said, pulling the phone from his pocket to read the message.

"You young people and your multitasking," Harriet said. "I'd never be able to keep up."

"Actually, I'm right there with you." I smiled. "One task at a time. But I think, given the desire, it's probably pretty easy to get the hang of it."

"Well, I'm not sure I'd ever be able to master it. But thankfully, I don't have to. Anyway, in regard to DuBois I didn't mean to be a naysayer. I just wondered if there were other options. In light of everything that's happened, I just don't see how you can trust anything he tells you."

"If we can get him to agree to the appearance," Clinton said, still scrolling through the text message, "the network lawyers can make sure he hasn't got any room for wriggling out of the agreement."

"So all that's left is for me to convince him to do the show."

"Tomorrow," Clinton said, shoving the phone back in his pocket. "That was Cassie. Everything has been finalized. You're meeting at his offices."

"Just DuBois?" I asked, my stomach knotting in anticipation.

"No. Monica will be there, too. And, of course, Ethan."

"Right. Just the five of us. Maybe you should come."

"You don't need me," Clinton said, patting my hand. "You'll do fine. You always rise to the occasion."

"A true Sevalas." Harriet nodded, lifting her hand to signal a passing waiter. "And on that note, I think we all could use another drink."

And for once in my life, my grandmother and I were in total agreement.

Chapter 20

In Manhattan you can tell how long a person has lived in the city based solely on the name he uses to refer to certain places. Request the Pan Am Building and you'll find MetLife. Avenue of the Americas? You'll get an eye roll and wind up on Sixth Avenue.

Ask someone where the GE Building is and they'll most likely direct you to Rockefeller Center. But ask an old-timer and they'll send you to Lexington and one of my favorite art deco buildings in the city. And just to keep you on your toes—both new and old GE buildings were originally owned by RCA Victor. Go Nipper.

And go Philip DuBois. If one's success is mirrored by one's surroundings, DuBois had scored the equivalent of a coveted Michelin three-star rating in securing an office in the General Electric Building. I was supposed to be meeting him there at eleven o'clock. But unfortunately I was running late.

As I leapt from the taxi, straightening my pencil skirt and hiking my newly acquired handbag onto my shoulder, I prayed I looked as good as Bethany had assured me I would. Coco Chanel once said that it was best to be as pretty as possible for destiny. And I happened to subscribe to her way of thinking. What better way to prepare for battle than to dress to the nines?

So Bethany and I had done some serious shopping after my lunch at d&d. And now, thanks to Donna Karan and Christian Louboutin, hopefully I looked the perfect vision of Manhattan business chic. Black on black with my red Lambertson Truex handbag for accent. God bless Saks Fifth Avenue.

I ran across the sidewalk and pushed through the revolving door into the magnificent lobby of the General Electric Building, slowing as I reached the other side to try and catch my breath.

"You're late," Cassie said, rising from a small chair near the front desk. "I was beginning to worry that something was wrong."

"Everything's fine," I said, straightening my shoulders and pasting on what I hoped was a cool, collected smile.

"Where's Ethan?" she asked as we walked through the lobby toward the elevator bank.

"Already here, I presume. We decided that, under the circumstances, it would be better if we didn't arrive together."

Actually, at first it hadn't been a mutual decision. I'd wanted Ethan to come with me. I figured I could use the moral support and that it wouldn't hurt for DuBois to see which side of the fence Ethan was playing on. But Ethan had disagreed, arguing that it would be more professional if we kept our private affairs just that. We'd argued back and forth for most of the night, but finally, with the morning sunlight (and a lovely reminder of just how private said affair really was) I'd come around to his way of thinking.

"Probably a good idea," she said as we stepped into the wood-paneled elevator. "Best not to make DuBois feel as if we've ganged up on him."

"I don't see how he can feel that way. I mean, after all, he's got the upper hand. And Monica is going to be there, right?"

"Yes. I talked to her again last night. And she thinks he's interested, but wary."

"I can't say that I blame him," I said as the elevator lurched to a stop. "After all the confusion over Mathias Industries and where they stand with regard to our interview, I'd be ready to dump the whole thing myself."

"For God's sake, don't share that with DuBois," Cassie said. "In fact, you really need to be careful what you say in there. Sometimes you can get a little carried away."

"You think?" I asked, laughing. It really was a good idea to try and curb my tongue, but the truth of the matter was that it was almost impossible for me to actually do so.

"Yes," Cassie said, her mouth quirking upward into a smile, the gesture serving to remove the sting from her pronouncement. "I do."

"All right then," I sighed, following her down the hallway and into DuBois' offices. "I'll give it my best."

Five minutes, a receptionist, and two assistants later, we were ushered into an austerely appointed conference room. The man of the hour was seated at the head of the table, with Ethan sitting to his left and Monica on his right. Talk about a power play.

Everyone rose, and we moved forward as I swallowed and strove for a calm I was most certainly not feeling.

"I'm sorry we kept you waiting," Cassie said.

"Not a problem," Monica said. "You're here now." She took her seat again. And Ethan followed suit, the corner of his mouth tilting slightly as his gaze met mine.

"You must be Ms. Sevalas," DuBois said, coming around the table to offer his hand. In person he seemed even more vibrant than I remembered. Polished and smooth. Very French.

He had the steely-eyed gaze of a business tycoon and the sensitive hands of an artist, a contradiction in tone underscored by the severe cut of his gray suit and the soft lavender of his tie. Actually, on thinking about it I supposed the contradiction fit. The man was first and foremost a chef. But he'd also built a restaurant empire that spanned the globe.

"Yes." I nodded, taking his hand in mine, noting the strength in his grasp. I really hate men who think that they have to offer a woman a limp noodle instead of a real handshake. Fortunately, DuBois wasn't that kind of man. "It's a pleasure to meet you."

"And I you," he said, eyes narrowed as he studied my face. Then, without any warning whatsoever, he reached out to tip my chin upward, face to the light, making me feel a lot like an insect pinned to a corkboard. He shifted his head, then mine, and finally, with a small sigh, he stepped back. "You look just like her. It's as if I've stepped back in time. But then, that is impossible, no?"

I nodded, shooting a sideways glance at Ethan, who just shrugged and smiled. Maybe we'd just discovered the reason DuBois didn't do public appearances. The man was certifiable.

"Excuse me for being so forward." DuBois waved his hand, dismissing the words as he motioned for me and Cassie to sit down. "I'm afraid you caught me by surprise. Anyway, I believe you have a business proposition, no?"

"Yes," Cassie said, taking the chair next to Monica, "and we really appreciate your taking the time to talk to us."

I sat down next to Ethan, still trying to make sense of DuBois' curious behavior.

"Monsieur McCay was most insistent that I hear what you

have to say. And because I have great respect for his grandfather, I agreed. As I understand it, you're requesting an interview."

"Not in the formal sense," Cassie assured. "It's more of an appearance, really."

"You realize that I don't usually agree to that kind of thing. I have an aversion, as it were, to making a spectacle of myself."

"Monica made that more than clear. But we have absolutely no desire to make anyone a spectacle. And in all honesty, your absence from the public eye is what makes you so valuable as a guest." Cassie had clearly moved beyond any awkwardness, slipping effortlessly into business mode.

"In the beginning," DuBois shrugged, "I was not a commodity. Chefs were not considered celebrities. There was no Emeril Lagasse or Wolfgang Puck. Just superb food served in equally splendid restaurants."

"Most of them yours," Cassie said with a nod.

"Ah, now you flatter me." There was just the barest hint of a smile, the gesture softening his expression, and I found myself relaxing. "But it has never been about the cooking alone. In truth, I am no better or worse than any marketable chef. I am just smarter than most."

"And that's exactly why we'd like to feature you on *What's Cooking in the City*."

"But Monica said that the show is a combination of cooking and gossip." He looked to her for confirmation, and she nodded. "And as I just said, I am not interested in discussing my life with anyone, particularly on television."

"We just want to feature your cooking," I said, finally finding my voice again.

"But you do wish to talk about the business as well?"

"Yes, but not in any way that would be invasive to your personal life," Cassie said. "We're envisioning something more along the lines of discussing the clientele who patronize your many restaurants, the plans for Chère and your return to the city, and, of course, any anecdotes you'd like to share. But nothing that would make you feel uncomfortable."

"I've admired your work for years, and it would be a great honor to have you on the show," I gushed. "I've always been fascinated with food, particularly restaurant dishes and the people who create them."

"So you are also a chef?" he asked, his interest purely professional this time.

"No. Not even close."

"She's really quite good," Ethan said, just the sound of his voice buoying my courage.

"I don't know about that," I said with a grateful smile, "but I really do love to cook. Especially trying to re-create a fabulous dish I've tasted somewhere. It's sort of like a game, I guess. Trying to figure out what it is that makes a particular recipe so special."

"Then I think you are halfway there already," DuBois said. "It's almost like chemistry, is it not? The search for the perfect mix of ingredients?"

"Exactly." I nodded. This was common ground. "And sometimes the last bit—the most important—is what eludes you. I can't tell you how much of a thrill it is to finally pin it down. To know that you've re-created something using nothing but your wits and sense of taste."

"I can see that you are passionate about cooking."

"I guess I am. Although I never really thought about it like that before."

"Then perhaps you have missed your calling?"

"No." I shook my head. "I don't think I have the acumen to take on what is admittedly one of the most competitive industries around, especially today. I'm afraid that in making it business, I'd lose the fun of it, you know?"

Cassie frowned, and I realized I was talking too much. As usual.

But DuBois smiled. "I think you have hit the proverbial nail on its head. Business is not fun. And I have learned over the course of these many years that the challenge of finding the joy in my cooking becomes more difficult with every restaurant I open."

"So maybe cooking with me is a chance to find the joy again. Cooking for cooking's sake."

"Were we discussing a class or perhaps a personal lesson I would tend to agree with you. But a television show is very public, and as I've already made clear, I despise the public light."

"But why? You're such a success and there's so much you have to share with regard to the profession."

"I just choose to keep my life private."

"Because you have something to hide?"

Cassie was glowering now, and if my purse hadn't cost an arm and a leg I'd have stuffed the damn thing into my mouth to stop the verbal onslaught.

Again, however, DuBois surprised me. This time with laughter. "You are quite the pistol, Ms. Sevalas. Very blunt. But then I suppose I shouldn't be surprised."

"I'm sorry." Clearly I'd been considering stuffing the wrong accessory in my mouth as I'd apparently already stuck my Louboutin-clad foot in it. "I probably shouldn't have said that."

"Under the circumstances, it's a fair question." He shrugged. "But sometimes the past is best left in the past."

"You enjoy being an enigma, don't you?" I said, intrigued by the thought.

"I think that in most cases the mystery is more enticing than reality."

"But if we play it right," Cassie said, trying to gain control of the careening conversation, "coming on our show could be used to heighten the mystique. And promote the new restaurant, which has got to be a good thing."

"If I were interested in promotion, mademoiselle, I'd have said yes to Barbara Walters or Charles Gibson."

"I realize we don't have as large an audience," Cassie started.

"But it's a targeted one," I interrupted. "People who love good food. And that's something straight news shows simply can't give you."

"I think she makes a good point, Philip," Monica said. "You'd be opening yourself to an audience of people who already love you."

"Or at least my food." He shrugged. "But I'll admit that is part of the appeal of appearing on your show rather than someone else's."

"I'm sensing a *but . . .* ," Cassie said, shooting an appeal in Monica's direction.

DuBois shrugged. "As I've said, publicity of any kind is not something I invite."

"But Monica and Cassie are right," Ethan said, speaking for the first time. "You could use a push with the New York market. And this would be an ideal way to reach the right audience."

DuBois shrugged.

"Wait." I held up my hand, cutting him off before he could speak. "Before you say no. You need to understand the whole story. I don't know how much Monica told you. But the honest truth is that the network offered me a shot at prime time. Which is pretty much the crème de la crème in my business. But in order to secure that slot, I had to come up with an amazing idea for a show. And since you're pretty much the king of the culinary world, and the chef I've always admired most, I suggested cooking with you. And not surprisingly, the network brass jumped at the idea. So much so that now they'll only give me the slot if I can, in fact, produce you. Which means that you'd be doing me an enormous favor by appearing." Cassie was trying, not so subtly now, to get me to shush, but I waved her silent. In for a penny and all that.

"I know that you hate public appearances," I continued, "and there's nothing I can do to change the fact that coming on *What's Cooking in the City* is exactly that. But we've already established that this isn't meant to be an interview. I'm not out to get the skinny on your life. I just want you on the show. To enjoy some time together cooking. Maybe I'll even learn a thing or two."

I sucked in breath, feeling as if I were drowning, but I couldn't stop now. "I realize you don't know me. But you know Ethan. And you said you respect him. And *he* knows me, which has to count for something. So just promise you'll at least think about it. Please?"

"Does she always say just what she thinks?" DuBois asked.

"With alarming regularity," Ethan said, but he was smiling.

"I'm sorry." I sighed. "I just want this so badly."

"And when you want something you should go for it with everything you've got." DuBois nodded in agreement.

"Maybe not quite so vocally," I admitted.

"Because of our connection," he said, standing to signal the end of our meeting, "I'll consider your request."

I had no idea what he meant by "connection." Cooking, I supposed. Not that it really mattered. As long as he did the show he could be mad as the proverbial hatter.

"It was a pleasure to meet you," I said as he came around the table to offer his hand.

"The pleasure was all mine," he said, his dark eyes reflecting something I couldn't quite put a name to.

I nodded, grateful to be finally—blessedly—out of words.

Minutes later Cassie and I, along with Ethan, found ourselves in the same paneled elevator heading down.

"I'm sorry. I did exactly what I wasn't supposed to do. I ran off at the mouth. But I was nervous. He's sort of overwhelming in person."

"Actually, I thought he was a little odd," Cassie said, sounding as bemused as I felt. "But you did all right."

"She did more than all right," Ethan said, his fingers closing warmly around mine. "You were amazing."

"I think that might be overstating it. But it does actually seem possible that he might say yes."

"Don't get me wrong," Cassie laughed, "I thought you were at your motormouth worst, but you're right, DuBois seemed to like it."

"But he was still hesitating. I could feel it."

"Maybe there really is some dark awful secret in his past," Cassie said as the elevator doors slid open and we stepped back into the opulent lobby.

"If there is, we'll never know what it is." I shook my head. "The man's definitely not a 'spill your guts' kind of person."

"As opposed to you?" Cassie quipped.

"She speaks with her heart," Ethan said, still holding my hand. "I think that's a good thing."

"I do, too, actually." Cassie smiled. "And she always seems to manage to talk her way through whatever."

"So what do you really think?" I asked them both. "Will DuBois say yes?"

"I honestly don't know," Cassie said. "I'd have laid odds he was going to say no when you interrupted with your heartfelt plea."

"But now," Ethan finished for her, "thanks in no small part to your unbridled enthusiasm, I think there's a very good chance the man will agree to be on the show."

So let it be a lesson to all you naysayers out there: Motormouths occasionally do win the day. Or at least manage to drive it into submission.

PLEASE JOIN US TO CELEBRATE
THE ENGAGEMENT OF

Vanessa Eloise Carlson

AND

Mark Rutherford Grayson

6:00 P.M.

HOSTED BY STEPHEN AND CYBIL HOBBS   COCKTAILS AND HORS D'OEUVRES
THE PIERRE HOTEL   REGRETS ONLY

Chapter 21

I have a thing about elegant hotels. I think it started on my first trip to Europe. The one with Harriet. When we were in Vienna we stayed at the Hotel Sacher. It was amazing. Particularly the Blaue Bar (and yes, I was allowed a taste of champagne, which was probably responsible for the reprehensible life I live today). Anyway, with blue damask covering walls decorated with portraits of people in velvets and pearls, the bar—and the hotel—captivated me.

What can I say? I'm a five-star kind of girl.

And in my book, The Pierre, across from Central Park, definitely ranks right up there with the Sacher. It's the perfect place for an engagement party.

Vanessa and Mark's, to be exact.

Ethan and I were arriving fashionably late, which meant that the party was already in full swing. Unfortunately, the press hadn't gotten the message and were still loitering in full force.

The engagement was big news for any number of reasons, not the least of which involved my aunt and a certain bet.

"Ms. Sevalas," a reporter bellowed, shoving a microphone in my face, flashbulbs momentarily blinding me. "Can you tell us if it's true that Althea orchestrated the proposal?"

I shook my head and pushed forward, grateful for Ethan's protective arm.

"What about the wedding?" another reporter asked. "Will Althea be giving away the bride?" There was a swell of laughter as I gritted my teeth.

"Ms. Sevalas has no comment," Ethan said, ushering me up the steps and through the doorway.

"I'm very sorry, Mr. McCay," an unctuous hotel staffer offered, appearing at our elbow. "We've cleared the entrance twice, but they just keep coming back."

"No worries." Ethan shrugged, his manner cordial. "It comes with the territory. Besides, we made it in one piece."

"Thanks to you," I said as we walked through the lobby toward the stairs. "I just hope Althea managed to avoid the worst of it."

"I think that's the first time I've ever heard you defending your aunt," he said as we paused on the threshold of the Wedgwood Room.

"Just don't tell anyone," I said with a wry grin.

Ethan laughed and I felt my heart lighten. At least for the moment, life was good. I'd successfully dodged the paparazzi, Philip DuBois had all but agreed to be on my show, and I was attending the party of the year with one of Manhattan's most eligible bachelors.

Not that I was trying to tempt fate or anything.

We made our way through the assembled company to the bar, and as Ethan ordered a couple of drinks I allowed myself the luxury of perusing the crowd. The attendees read like *Who's*

Who of New York Society. The up-and-coming huddled in adoration around the already arrived, separated discretely from little clusters of born-with-it-alls. Society in miniature, a microcosm perfectly preserved within walls of delicate Wedgwood blue.

Which is, of course, where the room gets its name. Pale blue walls with white accents and strategically placed mirrors give the space the air of days gone by. While not as ornate as the Grand Ballroom, there's a seductive warmth that makes it perfect for a more intimate party. It's almost as if you stepped into one of Josiah Wedgwood's Jasperware creations.

Something like two hundred of Vanessa's and Mark's friends and family were in attendance. Although in all honesty, at least part of the crowd was here to see and be seen. In Manhattan society, even an engagement party is a spectator sport. Especially when one considered the circumstances surrounding said engagement.

Tables laden with all kinds of epicurean delicacies were strategically placed in the center of the room, with bars in the corners, and a champagne fountain taking center stage against the far wall. Catty-corner across the way, a carved mahogany table under one of the mirrors housed a small arsenal of wrapped gifts, many of them signature Tiffany blue. (Presumably, including mine—a ridiculously expensive and absolutely adorable martini pitcher. I'd known it was perfect for Vanessa and Mark the minute I'd spotted it.)

"I see my grandfather over there," Ethan said, interrupting my thoughts as he handed me a drink. "Come on, I'll introduce you."

I was secretly delighted that he wanted to introduce me, but it didn't pay to be too openly enthusiastic about that sort of thing. So instead I nodded, linking my arm through his as we made our way through the crowd, and in short order we were standing in front of Walter Mathias, the reigning patriarch of Ethan's family.

Although Walter had long left the springtime of his life, he was still a formidable man, standing well over six feet with a swath of white hair and a surprising twinkle in his faded blue eyes.

"Andi, this is my grandfather."

"Delighted to meet you," Walter said, enveloping my hand in both of his. "I hear you've been keeping my grandson on his toes. The office is still buzzing with talk of your dressing him down."

"It seems I jumped the gun—at least a little bit," I said, wrinkling my nose in embarrassment. "I sort of have a habit of doing that."

"Well, from the way I heard it, you had justifiable cause to be angry."

"Yes, but not at your grandson. Thankfully, he's forgiven me for that."

"All's well that ends well, I always say. But I am sorry about my granddaughter," Walter said. "She's got a mind of her own, that one. And I can assure you that she's been appropriately reprimanded."

"It's over now." I shrugged. "And thanks to Ethan everything is back on track."

Walter smiled fondly at his grandson and then turned his attention back to me. "You look a lot like your grandmother," he said, studying my face.

"She mentioned that the two of you were friends."

"I've known Harriet for practically ever."

"Since you were in short pants, to hear her tell it."

"Our families summered together in Newport. But our friendship continued beyond that. I was fond of Niko as well. Always thought he did Harriet a favor taking her away from her father. Old man was dogmatic as hell. She had a far better life with your grandfather. He had a way of making anything seem fun. I miss him."

"Me, too," I said, feeling the familiar tug of longing.

"So how is Harriet these days?" Walter asked.

"Traveling, mainly. She likes to say she's seeing the world one port at a time. She still misses Grandfather, but I think for the most part she's happy."

"Good for her," Walter said. "It's hard being on your own."

"Harriet's not exactly on her own, Grandfather," Diana said, appearing at Walter's elbow, Dillon hovering just behind. "She's got Andi, and Althea. And Melina. Although I don't know that she really counts, considering she so rarely puts in an appearance. Must be hard, Andi, not knowing where your mother is." She smirked at me, her expression goading.

Ethan's hand tightened on my arm, and I swallowed a retort. "My mother isn't any of your business."

"Diana," Walter said, his blue eyes suddenly icy, "be a dear, won't you, and go and get me another drink?" He handed her his empty glass, and I swear to God, if I could have taken a photograph of her reaction I would have. It was not a pretty picture, anger turning her face a nasty shade of red.

Without another word, she turned, glass in hand, and, with Dillon in tow, headed for the bar. I wanted to clap. Or cheer. Or maybe hit Instant Replay. It was that good. But, having been raised with better manners, I withheld the urge.

"I'm sorry, Andi," Ethan began, but his grandfather cut him off.

"What Diana said was utterly inexcusable. There is really no excuse. And unfortunately, no controlling her mouth."

"But," I began, for some reason feeling compelled to confess that Diana's antagonism toward me was at least partly my fault.

"Doesn't matter," Walter said, his wizened gaze hardening. "She shouldn't have attacked your mother that way. Or you, for that matter. All I can ask is that you don't hold her rudeness against the rest of the family. Particularly my grandson. He's a good man. But," he said, his eyes back to twinkling, "if I were you, I'd scoot before she comes back. Oh, and Andi," he called as we walked away, "do tell Harriet I asked about her."

"Your grandfather is lovely."

"And my cousin is a bitch."

"Well, there's clearly no love lost between the two of us," I said, pleased to hear him support me over Diana. "I'm just sorry you and your grandfather got caught in the cross fire."

"Seemed pretty one-sided to me. Your grandmother would have been proud of you."

"If she'd stuck around long enough to hear about it."

"She's gone already?"

"Not yet. But she's leaving soon. She's very like my mother in that way."

"I don't know your mother. But I've seen how much Harriet loves you."

"And I love her," I said with a sigh. "I suppose every family has its eccentricities. Mine just has a little more than most."

"We've got Diana," Ethan reminded me with a grin. "Which gives us quite a leg up on the competition. Anyway, if it's any consolation, Dillon seemed incredibly uncomfortable."

"He knows how I feel about my mother's leaving. And even though we're not together anymore, I can't believe he'd support Diana's dissing my mother."

"Of course not. And Grandfather was right. Diana speaks without thinking."

"We have that much in common," I said. "But this is a party and I'm not going to let Diana ruin it for me."

"A thought I completely concur with." Ethan nodded as Vanessa emerged from the crowd.

"Andi, thank goodness I found you," Vanessa said, looking

both relieved and resplendent in a gold-embroidered sheath that glittered as she moved. "I wanted to warn you. Diana Merreck is here—with Dillon."

"Too late," Ethan acknowledged. "We've just run into her."

"Oh, God. That's just what I was afraid of. Can you forgive me?"

"What's to forgive?" I shrugged with a wave of my hand. "Sometimes life is just messy."

"Well, if it gives you any comfort at all," Vanessa laughed, "I did get the best of her once. At Camp Adirondack. We were in sixth grade. She was going on and on about her lineage. And how her blood was bluer than any of ours. So Cybil and I stole her panties, and ran them up the camp flagpole. You should have heard her shrieking—underwear flapping in the breeze. And trust me, they weren't Pérèle."

"There's something absurdly comforting in that story." I smiled. "Although I'm not sure what that says about me."

"That you're normal," Ethan assured me. "And knowing Diana, she deserved the humiliation."

"Well, I don't know about that," Vanessa said. "But I have to admit it gave everyone else a good laugh. Anyway, Diana never should have been invited tonight. Not under the circumstances. But you know how adamant my mother is about following social decorum. She's all about propriety and she insisted it wouldn't be right to omit Diana when we were inviting the rest of the family. And I never dreamed she'd actually come."

"Well, in this case," I said, "I think your mother's right. But you're sweet to have worried about me."

"I just hate to think that I caused you any more pain."

"But you didn't," I said, shaking my head. "I'm fine. Honestly."

"So score one for the good guys," Vanessa said. "I know she's your cousin, Ethan, but I've never really liked her."

"She seems to have that effect on people," he observed dryly.

"So where's the man of the hour?" I asked, changing the subject. Not that I was against a little Diana bashing, but she was Ethan's cousin and I hated the idea of us continuing to run down a member of his family—even if it was Diana.

"He's over there with my father and his cronies." She nodded toward one of the bars and a crowd of older men, Mark at the center, holding court. "Considering the age difference, it's remarkable how well he fits in." Not to mention the fact that Mark made his fortune strictly on his own without the benefit of an East Coast pedigree.

"Actually, Mark can run circles around most of them," Ethan said. "I suspect they're salivating just to have the chance to pick his brain."

"He is pretty amazing, isn't he?" Vanessa asked, smiling as she watched her husband-to-be. "But they do seem to be hovering and, other attributes aside, Mark isn't the most patient of men. What do you say we go and rescue him?"

"Good idea," Ethan said. "Andi?"

"I'll be there in a minute. I want to try and find Bethany. She's here somewhere."

"All right," he nodded, dropping a kiss on the top of my head, "but don't be too long."

I nodded as they moved off to rescue Mark. I'd lied, actually. I wasn't looking for Bethany. I just wanted a moment alone. The run-in with Diana had affected me more than I really wanted to admit.

Sucking in a deep breath, I headed toward a quiet corner and a potted palm. Very cliché, but exactly what I needed—a place to gather my scattered thoughts. Once there, I closed my eyes, waiting for calm to descend. Nothing happened. But then what had I expected? Advice from on high? *Hate Diana. Love Ethan. Forget about Dillon?*

"Andi?"

Speak of the devil. With a sigh I opened my eyes and turned slowly toward the sound of Dillon's voice, bracing myself for the worst. So much for finding refuge.

He stood in front of me, rocking on the soles of his feet, his discomfort obvious. "You, ah, look really beautiful tonight."

I searched his face, looking for some sign that he was leading me on, but I saw only sincerity. "Thanks. I'm happy."

"Are you? Really happy, I mean?"

"Yeah. I think so."

"With Ethan."

The name hung between us for a moment, and then I nodded, realizing that it was the truth. Ethan did make me happy.

"I see," he said, staring down at his immaculately polished wingtips.

"So where's Diana?" I asked, purposely keeping my tone light as I tried to ignore the tension stretching between us.

"I'm not sure," he said. "Mingling somewhere. I sort of ditched her. I wanted to find you and apologize for what she said earlier."

"It's a nice thought. But I hardly think Diana's on board with that idea. And she's really the only one who can apologize."

"Well, that's not going to happen. She's really got a thing when it comes to you," he said, looking even more uncomfortable. "I've no idea why. Something about your success, I think."

"My success?" There was a novel thought. Diana Merreck being jealous of me. I dismissed the notion as the overworking of Dillon's very masculine mind. "I don't think so."

"I'm serious," he said. "But it doesn't matter. I didn't come over here to talk about Diana."

"You can't have Bentley, if that's what you're getting at."

"I don't want the dog, Andi."

"Well, I certainly wouldn't have guessed that from your phone calls. Honest to God, I was afraid you were going to swoop in and kidnap him or something."

"I'm sorry I made you worry," he said, his discomfort still apparent. "I should have let you have him from the very beginning. He's always been more your dog than mine. But it was a connection and I guess I'd hoped . . . Look, the real reason I came over here was to talk about us."

"There isn't an us, Dillon."

"Maybe not like that. But we do still share a history. And surely that's not completely wiped out?"

"If you're asking if we can still be friends, the answer is no. At least not now. You really hurt me."

"I know. And believe me, if I could take it back, I would."

I wasn't sure what he was saying and I wasn't sure I really wanted to know. My life was confusing enough as it was.

"Look, Dillon, I appreciate your wanting to apologize for Diana. It means a lot. And I'm relieved to know that we're not going to have custody issues when it comes to Bentley. But I don't really think there's anything else for us to talk about."

"Are you sure?" he asked, tucking his hands into his pockets. It was a gesture I'd always thought charming, but surprisingly, in the moment, I felt nothing.

"Actually," I said, "I am." And with a half smile, I turned and walked away.

The fact was that at that moment there was only one man I wanted to talk to. And it most definitely wasn't Dillon.

Chapter 22

As I searched the crowd for Ethan, I marveled at how nothing really had changed. People were still laughing. Champagne was still flowing. And yet despite all the sameness, everything was different, in that indefinable way life has of shifting sometimes without any warning at all.

One minute you see the world as completely blue and the next minute it's all greens and purples. Okay, maybe that's not the best analogy. But you get the idea. I'd been worrying so much about losing Dillon that I'd completely missed the fact that I'd *found* Ethan.

And, at least temporarily, lost him again. Although it was impossible to see anything much in this crush.

"Hey, you," Clinton said, appearing at my elbow, carrying two vodka tonics. "I saw you talking to Dillon and figured you might could use this."

"Just what the doctor ordered," I sighed, accepting the drink gratefully.

"Are you all right?" Clinton asked, his brow furrowed with concern.

"I'm fine." I smiled up at him. "Better than fine, actually."

"You sure?" He frowned, clearly not certain what to make of my newfound euphoria. "I debated about interrupting you but figured under the circumstances you were probably better off on your own. So I toddled off to get your drink and then hightailed it back in case you needed me to pick up the pieces."

"Nothing to pick up," I assured him. "Dillon just wanted to apologize for Diana's behavior."

"I'm not sure that an apology would cover it. Even if it came from Diana herself."

"That's pretty much what I said. But even so, you have to admit it was a nice gesture."

"I suppose." He shrugged, his loyalty touching. "So is that all he wanted?"

"He gave me full custody of Bentley," I said, attempting to duck the question.

"Andi—," Clinton prompted, not about to let me get away with dodging.

"Fine," I said, with just a hint of exasperation. "He said he was feeling badly about how things went down between us."

"Badly as in 'I want you back'?" Clinton frowned, putting voice to my earlier suspicions.

"I don't know. I shut him down. Told him that I'm happy with my life the way it is now, and that there really wasn't anything for us to discuss. And then I came to look for Ethan." I took a sip of my vodka and tonic, the bittersweet concoction suiting my mood perfectly.

"Last I saw he was talking to Mark." Clinton waved a hand in the direction of the champagne fountain. "They were looking really intense and bandying words like 'leveraged' and 'synergy.'"

"Sounds less than fascinating."

"Exactly," Clinton said, his expression smug. "Anyway, there was an older man there as well. Distinguished looking."

"Gray suit. White hair. Impressive eyebrows?"

"And a conspicuously understated necktie." Clinton nodded. "Sounds like you know who he is."

"Walter Mathias. Ethan's grandfather. Ethan introduced me earlier."

"I should have recognized him. His picture is certainly in the papers often enough."

"At least he only graces the financial pages. Unlike Althea, who seems to have taken up permanent residence on Page Six. Did you have to run the gauntlet outside?"

"Kind of hard to avoid it. Fortunately, the paparazzi aren't all that interested in the opinions of an old restaurateur."

"I think you're underrepresenting yourself."

"Well, someone did ask me what Althea was wearing to the wedding."

"And I'm sure you had an educated guess."

"Dior," he sighed. "But it's not like it was a trick question. Anyone who's anyone knows she always favors Dior."

"Actually, I hadn't a clue. And she's my aunt. I'm telling you, it's a gift."

"I hardly think your not knowing something about Althea makes me a prodigy. I'm just more observant. And clearly you're not all that interested in anything having to do with Althea."

"Probably true," I admitted. "But this is a party and I'm not here to talk about my aunt. Or my feelings about her. So where's Bethany? I haven't seen her yet."

"She's here," he said. "Arrived the same time as I did. We started out together, but I lost her somewhere after her third cosmo."

"Nothing like a couple of cocktails to dull one's pain."

"You said it, not me. To be honest, I'm not sure she had any business coming tonight."

"Sometimes it helps to just try and forget. Put the bad stuff behind you."

"As long as you don't make a fool of yourself in the process."

"I take it there's something more than the cosmos?"

"Alexander Kerensky. She's been in the corner with him for the past half hour."

"But he's—"

"Lower than slime?" Clinton finished for me. "Exactly my thoughts."

Alexander Kerensky was a notorious playboy. Of questionable breeding, he was known for bedding and abandoning women of a certain age, all of them with money. Bethany wasn't his type, but that didn't mean he wasn't above plying his charms.

"Is Michael here?"

"I've no idea. But I'm hoping not. If there's any chance at the two of them working things out, it isn't going to survive Michael seeing Bethany play kissy face with Alexander."

"I still can't understand why Michael was so quick to end things. It wasn't as if she wanted to break up."

"I guess in his mind, not wanting to move in was the same thing."

"Well, making out with Alexander Kerensky isn't going to solve anything. Maybe I should talk to her?"

"I think talking might actually just make things worse. Why don't you just let me keep an eye on her? I promise I'll keep her from doing anything she'll regret."

"Okay, but I'm here if you need me."

"You just enjoy the evening," he said with a suggestive arch of his eyebrows.

"Ethan, you mean."

"Well, if the shoe fits . . ."

"You're incorrigible," I said, slapping him playfully on the shoulder.

"And proud of the fact. But as much as I'd like to stay and trade insults with you, I think our Bethany needs me." He tipped his head toward the corner, where she was only halfheartedly fending off Alexander's carefully honed moves. "Clinton to the rescue." He laughed, then made a beeline for Bethany.

I watched for a moment as he effortlessly separated Bethany from Alexander's embrace and, gesturing wildly, began some story or another as he pulled her away, leaving Alexander fuming in the corner.

I smothered a laugh, and turned back toward the fountain. Ethan was visible now, still deep in conversation. Only the group was larger now. Mark, Walter, Vanessa's father, and a couple of other men I didn't recognize.

Ethan, as if sensing my attention, looked up and smiled. My heart rate immediately ratcheted upward. The man was giving me palpitations and he was standing halfway across a very crowded ballroom. Clearly, I had it bad. With a half wave, I tilted my head toward Vanessa and Cybil chatting by the bar. He followed my gaze, nodded, and then, with another quick smile, returned to his conversation.

I took two steps toward Vanessa and company and then did an about-face. I'd had enough small talk for the evening. In all honesty, I'd had enough talk, period. The best thing to do was head for the ladies' room and a quick freshen up, then hopefully Ethan would be ready to call it a night. At least as far as the party was concerned.

Smiling, I made my way out of the ballroom.

The hallway outside was quiet and I stopped for a moment to catch a breath. The Pierre has always reminded me of a French palace, elegance and refinement surrounding one with a feeling of luxury and good taste. The perfect place for a tryst or an illicit affair. Except that the hotel sits on one of Manhattan's busiest corners. Shaking my head at my flight into romantic nonsense, I started to turn the corner into the main hallway, but stopped at the sound of voices.

Diana and her friend Kitty Wheeler.

Just what I needed—the devil and her cohort in crime. I wasn't about to turn tail and run (although I'll admit the idea had its merits), but taking Diana on wasn't the best of ideas, either. This was a public hotel and there were at least three dozen reporters camped outside. Better to just hold my head high and hopefully sail right past them without engaging.

On the other hand, maybe Bethany needed me.

I started to turn around, but something in the sound of their voices made me stop. Careful not to make any noise, I leaned forward, listening.

"Oh my God," Diana said. "You're never going to believe what I just found out. You know how weirded out I've been about my cousin seeing Andi Sevalas?"

Okay, this was the stuff of nightmares. They were actually talking about me. I pressed closer to the wall, knowing I would probably regret eavesdropping, but totally incapable of stopping myself.

"Of course," Kitty said. "If it hadn't been for him being involved with her, your plan to ruin her television show would have worked like a charm."

"And my grandfather would have seen just how brilliant my business acumen really is. I still can't believe he took Ethan's side over mine. It's not like I did anything illegal. I just suggested that DuBois might be happier if he worked with Mathias instead of doing a spot on that insipid little show."

"Well, at least you have Dillon."

"Big consolation. I mean, he's great in bed and everything, but he's hardly the kind of man I'm going to spend the rest of my life with. Half the fun was taking him away from Andi."

"I still think it's pretty wild that Andi wound up dating your cousin. I mean, that's a pretty small world even for Manhattan."

A woman in a black Prada suit walked out of the dining room and I bent to fiddle with my shoe, avoiding any chance of eye contact. My head was pounding, and I knew I should go. But it was like being caught in headlights: You want to run, but you've somehow become glued to the spot.

Prada lady turned the corner away from Kitty and Diana, and once she was out of sight I straightened, fighting to control my rioting emotions as I strained to hear the rest of the conversation.

"Actually, turns out it's not wild at all," Diana was saying. "That's what I'm trying to tell you. It was all planned. A setup. Althea asked Ethan to go out with Andi. She was trying to keep her niece from looking pathetic. As if that were possible. Anyway, after my cousin rescued Andi from the garbage dump, Althea figured why not make the most of the moment. Boost Andi's ego by making her believe Ethan was interested in her. Isn't that priceless?"

"So the whole thing was fabricated? And Andi has no idea?"

"None at all."

"Who told you all this?"

My stomach was churning, the resulting bile rising in my throat, while some disembodied part of my brain warned that it wasn't the done thing to throw up in the hallway of The Pierre.

"That's the best part. I got it straight from the horse's mouth. Althea was discussing it with one of her cronies, and I just happened to overhear. She was crowing about how brilliant she was and how well it was working."

"Maybe not," Kitty said. "I saw Andi talking to Dillon earlier. And they looked pretty intense."

"Oh, please, Dillon isn't interested in her. Probably still just trying to wheedle his way into getting that stupid dog back. I'm far more interested in my cousin's antics."

"So you think Ethan's just pretending to like her?"

"On some level he probably believes that he cares about her. He's always picking up strays. But basically, yes. This is just a game. And when Ethan's tired of it, he'll toss her aside. He's done it before. Playing Prince Charming has its limitations. Besides, I'm certain Althea's promised Ethan something in return for plying his favors, as it were. I'm betting it's something for Mathias Industries. Althea has a lot of contacts and I suspect she's privy to a lot of very interesting information. And Ethan will do anything to curry his way into Grandfather's favor."

"So are you going to tell Andi?"

"I don't know. Eventually. But for the moment I'm quite enjoying watching her make a fool of herself."

There were tears dripping down my nose, and I angrily wiped them away with my hand. I couldn't believe what I was hearing. The idea that Althea had asked someone to pretend to like me so I wouldn't feel as devastated by Dillon's betrayal—well, there just weren't words.

It was the ultimate humiliation.

I couldn't decide who I was angrier with—Althea for setting me up, or Ethan for agreeing to the charade. Just at the moment I hated them both.

Although not as much as I despised Diana Merreck.

"Damn it all to hell," I whispered, still swiping at tears, praying that The Pierre's floor would magically open up and swallow me. But of course nothing happened, except Diana and Kitty started walking in my direction.

"Honest to God," Diana was saying. "I can't believe she was stupid enough to fall for any of it. She can't even see when she's being set up."

They both laughed and some basic instinct for preservation made me whip around the corner, but not before Diana saw me, her smile laced with malice.

Thinking only of escape, I headed for the staircase leading to the ground floor and the beckoning freedom of Fifth Avenue. My mind was whirling, emotions crescendoing, anger and shame blending together. Diana was right; I'd allowed myself to be duped into believing my meeting Ethan was fated. That we were supposed to be together. And to make matters worse, I'd actually begun to think I might be falling for the man.

Pushing past a tuxedo-clad partygoer, I tried to order my tumbling thoughts. How could Ethan and Althea have done this to me? And how had I not seen it for what it really was?

Althea had known I was going to the park. In fact, I'd specifically mentioned Conservatory Water. Which meant that Ethan had known where to find me. And Althea had probably told him just what to say. She knew how I felt about Dillon's betrayal. And how much I'd welcomed Ethan's rescue. God, I'd played right into her hands. It had all been a setup. Nothing but lies and manipulation.

I was halfway down the stairs when I remembered the horde of reporters waiting outside the front door. The last thing I needed was to deal with paparazzi. I stood on the first-floor landing, indecision holding me captive. There was probably a back way out but I didn't frequent the hotel enough to know where it was. And I wasn't about to ask; talking to anyone would most likely push me right over the edge.

"Andi?"

I was beginning to hate the sound of my name. I spun

around, fighting for composure. "Dillon. What are you doing here?"

"Looking for you. Diana told me that you overheard her talking about Althea setting you up."

"So what, you've come to rub salt in the wound?" I hadn't meant to sound so harsh, but Dillon wasn't exactly my idea of a knight-errant.

"No. Of course not. I know how much you hate being manipulated. Especially when it comes to your aunt."

"Oh, God, Dillon, they've made a fool out of me," I said, still fighting tears. "And now, thanks to Diana, everyone is going to know about it."

"It isn't that bad," he said, his expression contradicting the words.

"It's horrible and you know it."

"Well, it's not good. But it's also not your fault. And people will see that. Hell, if anything they'll blame me." He stared down at his hands, then lifted his gaze to meet mine. "Look, Andi, I know how badly I hurt you, and that you probably don't think you can trust me. But if it helps at all, I was a complete and total ass. And for what it's worth, I told Diana to go to hell."

I gave him a watery smile, feeling like I'd come full circle somehow.

"Come on," he said, slipping an arm around me, "let's get you out of here. I know the back way."

Chapter 23

I woke the next morning to the sound of the downstairs buzzer and the sight of my bra and a man's tie looped together over the lamp shade. Never a good sign. Especially when the exact details surrounding their removal were a bit hazy.

It had been a late night. A lot of talking and copious amounts of alcohol. I distinctly remember making a third pitcher of vodka tonics and then abandoning the mixers altogether. Dillon and I had talked about us. About life. About Ethan and about Althea.

I'd dodged phone calls from both of them and fielded worried questions from Clinton and Vanessa. Neither of whom had approved of Dillon's conciliatory visit. But I hadn't particularly cared. I'd needed comfort and he was offering it.

And apparently, judging from the articles of clothing strewn everywhere, all that comforting had led to a *When Harry Met Sally* moment. In all honesty, when you're hurting sometimes any old port will do.

Unfortunately, my memory wasn't cooperating.

Which isn't meant to be a diss against Dillon. More an advisory against drinking too much vodka.

Anyway, there you had it.

Not exactly the best ending to what already had been a horrible night.

The buzzer sounded again, and I rolled over to wake Dillon, only to find that he wasn't there. Which only served to remind me of another morning, another man, and a completely different kind of night.

Damn it all to hell.

I stumbled out of bed, pulled a sheet around me, and screamed "I'm coming" to no one in particular. Bentley poked his head in the bedroom doorway, bright eyes inquisitive. I suspected he'd gotten more than an eyeful last night, but then it wouldn't have been the first time. And at least I hadn't dragged home a complete stranger.

I walked into the living room just as Dillon, wearing only his pants, was pulling open the door.

Ethan stood on the other side, his eyebrows registering his surprise with almost comic timing.

Oh, God. I'd walked into the middle of a Noël Coward play.

Only this one wasn't going to have a happy ending.

"I just came by to see if you were all right," Ethan said, his icy gaze assessing the situation. "But clearly, you're fine."

"Of course she's not fine," Dillon said, his voice tight with anger. "Thanks to you, she's been made a laughingstock. Thank God I found her before the press did."

"What the hell are you talking about?" Ethan said, his brows drawing together in confusion.

"You and Althea," I said. "You set me up. Or are you going to deny it?" I waited, a part of me praying that he'd tell me Diana was a liar.

"How did you find out?"

I felt as if someone had punched me. As if all the air inside me had been sucked out in an instant. And I realized that until just this moment some part of me had actually believed that it wasn't true.

"Diana," I whispered, words nearly impossible.

"Goddamn her," Ethan bellowed, his fists clenching in anger.

"I don't think you can lay this one at her feet," I said, my whole body shaking with reaction. "This one is all on you. And Althea. You promised me there were no more secrets. But you lied."

"Andi, I . . ."

"I don't want to hear it," I said, raising a hand. "Believe me, your cousin has done enough talking for both of you. You deserve each other. And to think that I was actually. . . . So, what did Althea say to convince you to sign on? That poor little Andi was devastated over losing her boyfriend? That you were just the ticket for making her feel all better? Rescue the poor pathetic loser. That must have played to your nobility. Or was Diana right and Althea promised you something in return?"

"Apparently, you've got it all figured out," he said, his eyes cutting from my sheet to Dillon's bare chest. "I'm sorry to have intruded on your morning."

He made a little half bow, which only reinforced my feeling that I'd been dropped into the middle of an English farce, and without another word spun on his heels and was gone. I tightened my grip on my sheet and fought the urge to throw up.

"Good riddance," Dillon said, slamming the door.

"How the hell did he get up here anyway?" I asked, still staring at the door. "Did you buzz him in?"

"Of course not." He shook his head, heading over to pour himself a cup of coffee. "When I saw it was him, I didn't answer. He must have followed someone in."

I nodded, finding speech too difficult. Besides, there wasn't anything to say, really.

It was over.

Had been last night.

Anything I'd done was only icing on an already top-heavy cake.

But just at the moment, the thought wasn't comforting.

"You've got to go," I whispered, not certain where the thought had come from, but absolutely sure it was the right one.

"What do you mean?" Dillon frowned, looking—quite fairly—surprised. "Aren't we going to spend the day together? I thought after last night . . ."

"No," I said, shaking my head. "There is no 'after.' I will always be grateful to you for what you did last night. Rescuing me from what was an indescribably awful situation. But nothing's changed between us. We're not a couple, Dillon."

"But we talked it all through."

"Maybe we did. To be honest, I don't remember a lot of it. But standing here—right now—I know that it's never going to work between us. We just want different things."

"You want Ethan," he said, his jaw tightening as he said the name.

"Trust me, that ship has sailed," I said, meaning every word. It was breaking my heart, but it was the cold hard truth. "This isn't about Ethan. It's about you and me. It just isn't going to work. And you know I'm right."

"Maybe I do," he agreed. Almost too easily. "But I do love you. And you should know that—"

"No more words," I said, hiking up my sheet. "Just go. Please."

"Right." He nodded, grabbing his shirt from a chair and heading for the bedroom.

I stood in the same spot, apparently incapable of moving, my mind yelling that I was making a terrible mistake. That Dillon and I had been through too much to simply throw it all away. But the truth was that it'd been thrown away a long time ago. Before Diana. Before Ethan. We'd simply been too stubborn to face the truth.

It was a surprisingly adult moment.

I don't have them all that often.

And quite honestly, it wasn't at all enlightening. Just really depressing.

"So," Dillon said, coming back into the living room, "this is it?"

I nodded, and leaned over to kiss his cheek. "Thanks again for last night." I wasn't completely sure that I meant it. At least the biblical part. But he had come to my rescue when I'd really needed it. And that had to count for something.

"Be happy," he said.

I didn't have an answer to that. But then maybe under the circumstances that was for the best. Dillon walked down the hall, looking back once, and then, with a sigh, I closed the door.

Still wrapped in my sheet, I leaned back against the cold metal door, sliding down until I was sitting on the floor, fighting the waves of emotion racking through me. Bentley, sensing my distress, moved into my lap, his head resting on my knee. I let my fingers tangle in the silky softness of his snowy fur.

"So," I whispered, the tears finally beginning to flow, "it's just you and me now."

Self-pity has its limitations, however, and after an hour or so of wallowing, I realized I'd had enough of my own company. And so, after a much-needed shower, I pulled myself together and headed over to Bethany's. Misery loves company. And her night hadn't been much better than mine. Although at least she'd managed to avoid going to bed with the wrong man.

Me, apparently, not so much so.

Bethany lived in a fabulous co-op on the Upper West Side. Just a block from Riverside Park in the Seventies. It was an old building with a part-time doorman, an ancient elevator, and subway-tiled foyers. Each apartment had twelve-foot ceilings and separate service entrances. One of the perks of being in real estate was that you got first shot at some of the best properties in Manhattan. And Bethany had definitely capitalized on the fact.

"Hey," she said, opening the door. "You look worse than I feel."

"And I feel worse than I look," I laughed, "but I brought something to ease the pain. Cookies." I offered the package I'd picked up at Dean & DeLuca on my way over.

"Eleni's. My favorite."

Eleni's cookies are simply the most wonderful cookies in Manhattan. I love them. Sugar cookies with enough icing to cause permanent sugar shock. They don't call the frosting "white death" for nothing. Perfect for whatever ails you.

And to make them even more special, the cookies come in all kinds of fantastical shapes. Baby carriages, designer dresses, Kate Spade purses, even breast-cancer-awareness ribbons. Today the cookies were shaped like little pink hearts, and believe me, there was going to be something quite cathartic in breaking them into bite-size pieces.

"I figured we could use the sugar rush." I settled on the sofa, opening the box while Bethany headed into the kitchen, returning with two tall glasses of milk.

"Next to Ben and Jerry's, of course," I said, dunking the cookie in my glass, "this has got to be the best 'feeling sorry for ourselves' food on the planet."

"We seem to be making a habit of pity parties of late," she said, dropping cross-legged onto the floor. "I woke up this morning wishing I was dead."

"At least you woke up alone."

"Thank God for Clinton," she said with a delicate shudder. "Can you imagine waking up to Alexander Kerensky?"

"Believe me, it's only slightly more revolting than realizing you broke up with your current boyfriend only to wind up in bed with your ex. Not exactly my finest moment."

"At least Dillon isn't a letch. And Ethan gave you plenty of reason to move on."

"I know, but I still feel guilty somehow. You should have seen his face when he saw the two of us standing there half naked. It was almost too cliché to be true." I reached for another cookie.

"So maybe you should talk to him. Maybe there's still some hope for the two of you."

"Not a chance." I shook my head. "Even if I could get over the whole setup thing, there's still the fact that he lied about it. I gave him the opportunity to come clean when he admitted being related to Diana. And he didn't. In fact, he promised me that there weren't any more secrets."

"At the risk of making you throw things," Bethany said, snapping a frosted heart in two, "you made your feelings about setups pretty damn clear. I can't imagine anyone would have found it particularly easy to come clean in light of that."

"I'll admit there's some truth in what you're saying." I shrugged.

"But it doesn't matter. My forgiving Ethan isn't going to make it all better. There's still the little matter of my sleeping with Dillon. Which means that even if I could convince myself to forgive Ethan, he's never going to forgive me."

"But there were mitigating factors."

"Doesn't matter." I shook my head. "You didn't see his face. It's definitely over. But I still think there's hope for you and Michael."

"I don't know how you can say that. He broke up with me. Remember?" She popped a bite in her mouth, closing her eyes in pure ecstasy. "These are so good."

"I know," I said, reaching for another. "But we were talking about Michael."

"Past tense."

"Maybe not. You didn't sleep with anyone else. And as far as I know, he wasn't at the party and so didn't get to see you swapping spit with Kerensky."

"God, when you put it like that," she said, making a hideous face, "it sounds so nasty."

"Well, as public displays of affection go, it wasn't your finest hour. Not that I'm in any position to pass judgment."

"No," she said. "You're absolutely right. It was a stupid thing to do. I'd had too much to drink."

"Join the party. I don't even remember sleeping with Dillon. Fortunately, I've been down that road before so it's easy enough to fill in the blanks. But still—"

"Face it, we're both sluts." We laughed and simultaneously reached for more cookies, which made us laugh even harder. There was something to be said for girlfriends. Especially the kind you could share your worst moments with.

"I still think there's some hope with Michael," I said. "I mean, sure he was angry when you turned him down. But maybe there's a reason he overreacted. Maybe it's not even something to do with you. You said he was really shy. And I know that Althea said something about him not being overly confident with women. Maybe your rejection was just more than he could handle."

"But I wasn't rejecting him."

"Maybe *he* doesn't know that. I know sometimes when I'm hurt I strike first, without thinking, in an effort to protect myself against something that hasn't actually happened yet. And more often than not, I regret it. Because I never really know for sure how things would have turned out. I'm too busy making sure I don't get hurt. And if that's what Michael's doing, then he could be at home right now, regretting the whole thing."

"You really think that's possible?" Bethany leaned forward, an uneaten cookie in her hand. And the flicker of hope in her eyes killed any desire I had for a friend to share my misery. Better one with a happy ending.

"I do," I insisted, "I really do. I think you just need to go and talk to him. Tell him that you're scared, but that you don't want to lose him. And for God's sake, Bethany, if it's a deal breaker and you really care about the man, move in with him. I mean, why the hell not? We don't get that many chances at happiness. You know?"

"You're right. It's just so scary to put myself out there like that."

"It beats the heck out of sitting here with me, eating yourself into a sugar coma."

"Well, I don't know that I'd go that far." She reached over and squeezed my hand. "But I'm going to do it. I'm going to go over there, and tell him that he's got to give me another chance."

"Here's to success," I said, lifting my milk. "Now go and get dressed. I'll wait and walk out with you."

She smiled, looking giddy but determined, and I smiled back. At least one of us had a shot at being happy.

I leaned back against the sofa, and was reaching for another cookie—hey, I was still working on that pity party—when the jarring tinny sound of "Macarena" filled the room. Great, someone calling. Probably the press. Althea's latest antics had made all the columns, which included speculation as to Ethan's real motivation. It made for gripping reading.

If you weren't the one living *la vida loca.*

I produced the offending phone and flipped it open, noting Metro Media's number. Not exactly a call I was expecting. Still, at least it wasn't *Page Six.*

"Hello?"

"Andi, Monica Sinclair here. I'm sorry to bother you on a weekend."

"Not a problem," I said, "but shouldn't you be calling Cassie?"

"I thought maybe that under the circumstances, it would be better if I called you."

My heart stuttered to a stop. "That doesn't sound good."

"It's not. I'm sorry, Andi, but Philip isn't going to do the interview."

"I see." I hadn't thought I could feel any worse than I already did. I was wrong.

"Look, I probably shouldn't tell you this, but maybe it'll help you understand Philip's position. The reason he turned you down is because of your aunt."

"Excuse me?"

"I know it doesn't really make any sense. He didn't go into any further detail. Just said it had to do with Althea. You know how he is about keeping his image private. And I'm thinking he's worried about his name being linked with yours. And by association your aunt's. Considering today's columns I'm sure you can understand why."

And I could. That was the really sucky part.

My aunt and her notoriety had killed my television show. Or

if not that then at least perpetually trapped it in the obscurity of daytime cable television.

In short, she'd ruined my life—again.

And, believe me, there weren't enough cookies in the world to make that pain go away.

Chapter 24

After bolstering Bethany and sending her off to conquer Michael, I marshaled my anger and called Althea. I don't know what exactly I thought I was going to say. But in the end it didn't matter because no one answered. And under the circumstances, although tempting, leaving a message was out of the question. So I disconnected and hailed a cab to my grandmother's.

I wasn't sure if she was still there, but I really needed someone to talk to. And she knew Althea better than anyone.

The taxi let me out on the corner of East Eighty-fifth and East End and I walked along the park side of the street, letting the familiar sights and sounds surround me.

Manhattan sometimes feels like it's all about what's coming next—the newest, the best, the brightest—but in my opinion, some of the most wonderful things come in rather dated packages. Like my grandmother's building. It's just got that old Manhattan feel. When I was little there was even an elevator operator. Frederick. I loved him. He'd let me run the controls. It was great fun.

Of course, even then he was an anachronism. But it was a lovely reflection of what must have been a very elegant time.

I've seen pictures. My grandfather and grandmother dressed to the nines. Harriet in furs. My grandfather in a white dinner coat with a carnation in the lapel. They were off to the theater or to a dinner club or maybe uptown for a bit of jazz.

Wonderful memories, with Harriet's classic six all that remains to remind her of the life she and Niko once led. Six perfect rooms in a fading building with a spectacular park view.

Like all of Manhattan, the neighborhood is being revitalized, and sooner or later all traces of my grandmother's world will no doubt disappear. But for now, I can still imagine the building and its occupants in all their former glory.

I crossed the street and waved at Diego, my grandmother's doorman, thankful that some things at least never seem to change. He'd been on the door as long as I could remember, to the point where you actually felt compelled to open your own door in case the exertion proved too much for him. Diego lifted his cap as I walked into the building and headed up to my grandmother's apartment.

"Harriet?" I called as I let myself in, my heels clicking on the herringbone floor. "It's Andi." The apartment always smells like Murphy Oil Soap and Fleur de Rocaille, my grandmother's favorite perfume. It probably sounds like an incongruous pair, but to me, at least, it smells like home.

"She's not here," Bernie said, appearing in the doorway to the dining room. "She left for Paris this morning."

"Just like that," I sighed. Even though she'd told me she was going, I'd somehow hoped that maybe this time, under the circumstances, she'd have stayed.

"It wasn't a spur-of-the-moment trip, Andi. People were expecting her."

"Yeah, well, maybe I needed her, too." There was nothing to be gained in taking my disappointment out on Bernie, though. "So, what are you doing here?"

"Closing things down. Harriet always leaves everything a mess. So I figured I'd tidy up a bit and make sure everything's in good shape for her return. Why don't you come into the kitchen and let me fix you something to eat. Some food will do you good."

"I actually had a bunch of cookies at Bethany's. So I'm not all that hungry."

"Cookies aren't food," Bernie sniffed. "Especially those sugar bombs you buy at Dean and DeLuca. Let me make you some eggs. And I think there are still some muffins."

It was the closest I was going to get to mothering, so I accepted, following her through the dining room and into the kitchen.

My grandmother's kitchen was probably my favorite part of the apartment. Windowed, with enough room for a butcher-block island, it had been privy to the recounting of many childhood and adolescent tragedies. Skinned knees to broken hearts, the kitchen had witnessed them all.

I made myself a cup of tea and perched on the ancient yellow step stool that sat in the corner while Bernie gathered ingredients to make an omelet.

"So I gather it wasn't a very good night," she said, whisking eggs, salt, and pepper.

"Not my best, no," I said as an ugly thought occurred to me. "You didn't know, did you? About Althea's arrangement with Ethan, I mean."

"Hadn't a clue." Bernie shook her head. "You know Althea doesn't talk business with me."

"Business," I snorted. "That's a laugh. I'm her niece, not her client, for God's sake."

"It was a setup, Andi. That's what Althea does."

"Yes. But usually both parties are in on the fact. And I most certainly didn't agree to anything. Althea knows how I feel about her meddling in my life. I can't believe she'd do this to me."

"She did what she thought was best." The eggs sizzled as Bernie dropped them into the pan.

"Well, then she's seriously delusional. And thanks to her meddling, she's ruined my life."

"Surely that's overstating things a bit."

"Maybe," I shrugged, "but she's managed to make me a laughingstock. Did you see the papers?"

"I saw the *Post*," she said, adding some Gruyère and green onion to the omelet.

"Well, the *Daily News* was just as bad."

"So that's what's got you upset," she asked. "The paparazzi?"

"Well, it's not as if I enjoy public humiliation. But no, of course that's not the main reason I'm upset. I'm devastated that everything about my relationship with Ethan was a lie."

"Surely the fact that it was a setup doesn't make the whole thing a lie."

"But it does. Especially if Diana was right about Althea offering him something in return for his *services*, so to speak."

"Do you know for certain that Diana's telling the truth?"

"No. But I don't see any reason why she'd lie."

"We're talking about Diana Merreck."

"Yes, but she didn't know I was listening," I said, my heart feeling like it had been run through a shredder. "Anyway, even if he only agreed to do it out of pity, it still makes the whole thing feel like a sick joke."

"I can understand your feeling that way. But you're not being fair to Althea," she chided, as she slid the omelet onto a plate and set it in front of me on the butcher block. "Althea had good intentions. You know she did."

"Yeah, well, it didn't quite work out that way."

"So have you talked to her?" Bernie asked.

"No," I said. "I tried to call, but she wasn't there. Which was just as well since I'd have only said things I'd probably regret. Better to wait until I have time to process what's happened." I took a forkful of omelet, the cheese and onion mixing with the egg to form a perfect creamy bite.

"I'm not sure she'll give you that kind of time," Bernie said, handing me a plate of muffins. "Look, I understand that you're angry. But you can't avoid her forever. She's family and she raised you."

"Well, she's not my mother if that's what you're getting at." The words were bitter, but I was beyond sugarcoating. "Melina is my mother. And if Althea hadn't run her off, *she* would have raised me."

"You have no idea what you're talking about," Bernie said, with a hint of rebuke.

"I was there. I heard them arguing."

"You were just a little girl. And believe me, whatever you think you heard, it was just the tip of a very large iceberg."

"What are you talking about?"

"The truth. I've kept quiet all this time because it wasn't my place to tell you, and because Althea wanted to protect your memories of your mother. But I think it's time. The lies have gone on long enough."

"I don't know what you're getting at," I said over a bite of muffin. "But nothing you can tell me will change the way I feel about my mother." I sounded defensive, but I'd been facing more than my fair share of realities of late, and I wasn't sure I was

ready for another revelation. Being angry at Althea was all that
was holding me together at the moment. That and Bernie's
cooking.

"Maybe not. But you still need to hear the truth." She sat down
across from me, her eyes kind. "Your grandfather used to say that
your mother was like a butterfly, flitting from flower to flower,
never staying long enough to leave an impression. She was beautiful. Like you, Andi. And even I have to admit, it was pure pleasure
just to watch her."

"I remember thinking that she had a smile like sunshine," I
said, the image floating through my mind.

"She was fearless," Bernie continued. "And it scared your
grandparents. But Althea always seemed to be there to watch over
her sister. So gradually, without realizing what they were doing,
they made Althea responsible for Melina."

"But Mother was older than Althea," I said, still thinking of
my mom.

"Yes. Which makes it all the more unusual, I suppose. But
Althea was always a nurturer. I think that's why she's so good at
matchmaking. For all her spouting about 'like attracting like,' I
think deep down she really believed in the power of love."

"I'm sure you'll understand if I choose to disagree with that,"
I said.

"Things aren't always what they seem, Andi."

"All right. Fine. We'll stipulate that at some point Althea
believed in love. But you used past tense, so I'm assuming you're
saying she doesn't believe in it anymore?"

"Just hang on. I'm getting there," Bernie said, taking a sip of
coffee. "So, where was I?"

"Mother as a butterfly," I prompted.

"Right." She nodded. "Anyway, the older Melina got, the more
distracted she became. Although I'm not entirely sure that's the

right word for it. I guess in a lot of ways Melina was like Harriet. They both choose to see the world through rose-colored glasses, and while that makes life a lot of fun, oftentimes it can hurt the people around them."

"Like Harriet not being here now." I hated the thought but I couldn't avoid it. My grandmother loved me. I knew that. But she wasn't ever really there for me. Not in the way I needed. And as much as it hurt to admit it, the same was true of my mother. Only more so.

"Exactly," Bernie agreed. "But we're talking about your mother. You have to understand that Melina was given free rein. She did pretty much exactly what she wanted. Which led to some rather indiscreet moments."

"Me, you mean," I said, taking another bite of muffin.

"Well, certainly the events leading up to you being born. But there was quite a bit more. As I said, Melina wasn't afraid of anything. Including experimentation of all kinds. For the most part she managed to walk the line, but there were definitely moments when she pushed things a bit too far."

"So you're saying Mother did drugs?" I asked. "Who hasn't?"

"Me, for one." Bernie smiled. "Anyway, there were other things. But none of them are really important except that they can help you understand how close Melina danced to the fire."

"I know Mother was wild, but what does that have to do with Althea sending her away?"

"What makes you think Althea sent her away?"

"I told you, I heard her. They were yelling. Althea told Mother she wasn't fit to be a parent. And the next morning Mother was gone. What else could I have thought?"

"That there was more to the story."

"How in the world was I supposed to have thought that? I was eight."

"Well, you're not eight anymore." Bernie's tone was gentle, but I felt the rebuke nevertheless.

"Fine, then," I said, crossing my arms over my chest mutinously. "Tell me what really happened."

"You have to understand that Althea didn't have much of a life in those days," Bernie said. "Keeping up with Melina was a full-time job. And then when your grandfather died, she had to take care of Harriet as well. Not to mention you."

"So now you're casting Althea as Cinderella?"

"No. I'm telling you that she didn't have much of a life outside of this family, until she fell in love."

"Althea?" The idea seemed almost ludicrous. She was so into everyone else's love lives that it had never occurred to me that she could have had one of her own.

"Yes. And for a little while at least, she was really happy."

"Who was he?" I asked, surprised to find that I had trouble picturing Althea young and in love.

"Philip DuBois."

Everything went silent as I tried to digest the idea.

"Althea had a relationship with Philip DuBois," I finally squeaked, surprised that I'd managed any sound at all. "My Philip DuBois."

"Yes." Bernie nodded.

"So that's why he refused to do the interview," I said, more to myself than to Bernie. "He told Monica it had something to do with Althea. I just assumed it was all the bad press."

"I'm not privy to the workings of Philip DuBois' mind, but if he made the connection between the two of you, it certainly makes sense, under the circumstances, that he'd not want to further the relationship."

"You make it sound so dire. And I still don't see what any of this has to do with the argument I overheard the night Mother left."

"It has everything to do with it." Bernie paused, her expression grim. "Melina ran away with Philip."

"Oh my God." My heart lurched and tears filled my eyes. No matter how angry I was at Althea, she didn't deserve that kind of betrayal.

"Philip was young. And very French. He'd asked Althea to go away with him. To Paris. Despite his success in New York, he missed his home. And so he asked Althea to come with him. And she wanted to go. I know she did, because I heard her crying about it, but when I tried to comfort her, to get her to talk about it, she just said that things would be fine."

"But she didn't go," I said, pushing away my plate, my omelet forgotten.

"No. In the end she chose to stay with you. As I said, Harriet was never really much on mothering. And Melina even less so. Althea knew you needed her. So she begged Philip to stay. To make their life in New York. He refused. And so Althea turned him down."

"Because of me?" I said, feeling oddly guilty for something that had happened when I was only a little girl.

"Yes. Philip was adamant and so was Althea. It was a complete impasse. But then Melina came to Althea with a solution. She offered to let Althea take you with her to Paris."

"I don't believe you," I said, my voice shaking.

"It's ugly, but it's the truth, and Althea has paid for Melina's carelessness for far too long. Melina's offer came with a price. She'd managed to run up a rather large debt. As you know, Niko left most of his money to Harriet. But there were trusts for both of his girls, as well as one for you."

"I used part of it to buy my apartment."

"Yes, well, your mother blew through hers in a matter of months and she wanted Althea to cover her debts."

"And so Althea demanded me in return for the money," I said, still valiantly trying to defend my mother. The one who apparently never really existed at all.

"No, Andi." Bernie shook her head, her eyes filled with compassion. "Althea refused altogether at first. But Melina could be quite convincing when she put her mind to it. And so finally Althea agreed to discuss the idea with Philip."

"But he said no, didn't he?" I asked, suddenly afraid that I knew how the story ended.

"Yes, he did. And so Althea refused to give Melina the money."

"And that's what they were fighting about the night I heard them."

Bernie nodded, her wrinkled hand closing around mine. "The next morning we woke to a note telling us your mother had run off with Philip. To Paris."

"Oh, God, Althea must have been crushed," I said, my stomach knotting at the thought of her pain.

"That's the funny part of it," Bernie said. "I know that she must have been devastated. But instead of moping about or trying to do something to stop them, she just threw herself into raising you. Genetically, Melina may be your mother, Andi, but in every other way, the ones that really count, it's Althea who's always put you first. Althea who's always been there for you. Even when she goes about it all the wrong way."

"And she didn't want me to know any of this?"

"No. She wanted to protect your feelings for your mother."

"And the cards Mother sent?" I asked, a nasty realization forming in my head. "The gifts?"

"They were all from Althea."

"I suppose I should have known. Everything was always so perfect. The little French doll. The African rug in its perfect shades of green. The painted platter from Bellagio. All things I loved. Things only someone who really knew me could possibly have chosen." I blew out a long breath, trying desperately to reorder a world gone suddenly topsy-turvy. "What about DuBois? Did he stay with my mother?"

"No." Bernie shook her head. "They went their separate ways after only a few months. And I've always felt that he must have regretted the choice he made. But maybe that's just wishful thinking."

I reached for another muffin, taking a bite as I tried to make sense of everything Bernie had just told me. Althea had chosen me over the man she loved. And my mother had chosen Philip over me. Hell, she'd chosen everything over me. And I'd gone right on believing Althea was the enemy.

Althea, who'd always been there. Through all my ups and downs. Maddeningly pushy, overbearing as all get out, but *always* there.

I swallowed the last bit of muffin, everything finally coming into focus. And it hit me. As clear as if it had been highlighted in neon. "It's lime zest," I said, amazed that it could really be so simple. "The missing ingredient is lime zest."

"And?" Bernie prompted.

"And—you're right. Althea is my mother. In every way that counts. I've just been too stubborn to see the truth. But what do I do now?" I asked, finding myself on uncharted ground.

"You go and talk to her. And you try to understand that whatever she does, right or wrong, it's because she loves you."

Chapter 25

On a good day the walk from Harriet's apartment on East End to Althea's on Fifth is about twenty-five minutes. It took me two hours. Partly because I was trying to digest everything Bernie had told me. And partly because I kept getting distracted by favorite epicurean haunts.

The Upper East Side, for all its haughty attitudes, is home to some of the best markets in the city. There's Agata and Valentina, Eli's, Citarella, and Grace's, just to name a few. And I visited several. Strolling up and down aisles of produce and freshly baked breads is soothing to me in the way being surrounded by racks of couture or tables full of Manolos, Maddens, and Jimmy Choos is soothing for other women.

The fact that I hadn't arrived on Althea's doorstep with arms full of plastic and Styrofoam is testament to the fact that I was completely and totally distracted by my confusion.

On the one hand, I was still really angry at what she and Ethan had pulled. But on the other, I was shaken to the core with what Bernie had divulged. I'd never really stopped to see things from Althea's perspective, my perceptions colored by the argument I'd overheard that night long ago. Maybe it was a stupid mistake, or maybe I had just wanted to believe in my mother. But either way I'd managed to keep Althea at arm's length despite the fact that she'd chosen me over happiness with someone else.

And then there was the fact that that "someone else" happened to be Philip DuBois. The man who held my career in the palm of his hand. Okay, maybe not so much my career. But at least my chance at prime time.

No wonder he'd thought I looked like someone he'd once known. Even though people said I looked like my mother, the truth was that I was a ringer for Althea when she was younger. I must have been a real blast from the past. And not a particularly good one.

When he'd blamed Althea for his saying no to my request, he hadn't been thinking about the paparazzi. He'd been thinking about the woman he'd dumped. For her sister.

Talk about tangled webs.

I walked into the lobby of Althea's building and took the elevator to the twenty-eighth floor. But I still couldn't bring myself to knock. Instead I just stared at the door. So much so that Mildred DiGrassi, my aunt's eighty-five-year-old neighbor, had poked her head out in suspicion. Although I assured her I had absolutely no interest in making off with her Hummel collection, I could still hear her, just on the other side of her door, eye glued to the peephole.

Of course, Althea had to know I was out there, too. The building was the kind that double- and triple-checks security— even though I'd been coming in and out since Althea had first moved in. I guessed she was just giving me time to compose myself. And I should have felt grateful, but all I really felt was lost.

I'd spent the past couple of hours trying to make sense of all of it, and hadn't come up with a thing. So here I stood in the hallway, annoying Mildred DiGrassi, without a clue as to what it was I really wanted to say.

But in the end, it didn't matter.

Althea opened the door and simply held her arms out and I was there in three seconds flat.

There's something so comforting about a maternal hug, no matter how mad you are at the woman giving it to you. A thousand memories rushed through me. Althea braiding my hair. Althea taking me to fit my first bra. Althea beaming at my first, and only, dance recital. They'd given parts out according to talent. I was a gate. Which basically consisted of my standing in second position, and swinging a hula hoop in and out. Needless to say I was not the star of the show, but Althea had clapped as if I were a prima ballerina on opening night.

There were lots of memories there. I'd just never recognized them for what they were.

"I'm still really angry at you," I said, pulling back.

"I know. And you have every right to be. I should have handled it better. But I was only trying to help."

And there you had it. The purest of all motives. Even in the face of the disaster that was my life, I couldn't help but respond to the honesty in her voice. She did love me. That much I was suddenly very certain of.

"So what have you brought me?" she asked, purposely lightening the moment.

"Bernie's muffins," I said, holding out the foil-covered plate. "The missing ingredient was lime zest."

"She finally told you?"

"No." I shook my head. "I figured it out myself. Along with a few other things."

"I knew you'd get it eventually." Althea smiled, her words holding a multitude of meanings. "You always do."

"Yes," I agreed. "But I can be a little slow."

"Sometimes it takes a crisis for us to be able to see what's been right in front of our faces all the time."

"I do seem to have been enduring more than my share of late," I said, sitting down on the sofa. The room was decorated with a light hand. Everything in shades of cream, teal, and rose. It just felt like Althea. "Although, quite frankly, some of them have been my own fault."

"Well, at least you can admit it. Not many people can," she said, setting the plate of muffins on the table. "And for what it's worth, I'm really sorry for my part in all of it. I honestly didn't set out to hurt you."

"I know." I nodded. "I'm not saying it helps. But I do know."

We sat for a minute in silence and then, with a sigh, I jumped right into the hard part. "Bernie told me about what happened. With Philip DuBois and my mother."

"I know. She called to tell me."

"To warn you, you mean," I said, offering a weak smile. "I was pretty upset."

"And I don't blame you. I probably should have told you the truth a long time ago. I just wasn't sure there was really a need. And I hated the idea of ruining your perception of your mother."

"No. It was important for me to understand what really happened. Seems I've been carrying around a lot of misperceptions. In fact, I think it might be my specialty."

"You just want to see the best in everyone. There's nothing wrong with that."

"Well, I didn't see the best in you. I blamed you for what happened with my mother. I thought you drove her away."

Althea laughed. "As if I could have. Melina has never done anything she didn't want to do."

"Including abandoning me." I hated the bitterness in my voice, but I couldn't help it. Reality bites. "All this time I believed in a person who doesn't exist."

"She does exist, Andrea. On some level. Your mother lives in the moment. And when you have the chance to share that moment with her, it can be magical."

"Do you really believe that?"

"Yes," she said. "I do. People are what they are. And we have to accept them for that. Otherwise, we're doomed to be disappointed. But there's no doubt in my mind that Melina loves you. She just doesn't know how to be a mother."

"You weren't afraid to step up to the plate. And I wasn't even your child."

"You were always my child, Andrea." She smiled, reaching over to squeeze my hands. "From the first time I saw your tiny little face. There was never a contest in my mind. It wasn't a sacrifice."

"But you loved Philip."

"And he ran away with my sister. But the past is just that— the past."

"So, do you ever talk to her? Melina, I mean?" I hadn't consciously chosen to use her given name. It had just slipped out. But with the pronouncement, something inside me shifted. I let some of the pain go, the relief actually palpable. Like the moment after you jump off the high dive when your fear morphs into elation. I knew it probably wouldn't last. That there were still emotions I had to deal with. But for the moment, at least, the sensation was freeing.

"Not often." Althea shrugged. "We don't really have all that much to say. Mother keeps me up-to-date, and that's enough."

"You must hate her."

"It's not that simple. She's my sister. And I accepted her for who she is a long time ago."

"And Philip? Have you talked to him?"

"Since he's been back in New York? No. Although I probably should have. It might have made things easier for you. But you like to do things on your own, and you seemed to have things under control."

"Now there's a misperception." I laughed, marveling at how comfortable I felt sharing with Althea. For a moment I considered that maybe this wasn't my aunt. Maybe this new, softer woman was a pod person or a clone or something equally nefarious. Or maybe, for the first time, I was just seeing things for what they really were.

"Everything seemed to be progressing well the last time we talked," Althea was saying. "Has something happened?"

"He turned me down. His publicist said it was because of you. I thought she meant all the brouhaha surrounding the bet and Vanessa and Mark's engagement. But of course she was talking about you and Melina."

"Well, that just isn't going to do," Althea said, her expression hardening. "I simply won't let something that happened a lifetime ago impact you in a negative way."

"I'm not sure there's anything you can do about it. And even if you could, I'm not sure that I'd want you to. I mean, the man is slime. After what he did to you, I have no interest whatsoever in working with him."

"What happened to me happened a long time ago," she said, her voice soft. "It was humiliating, and painful, and something I'd have just as soon had been left buried. But the real truth of it is that Philip DuBois was the loser. Not me. I got you. He got Melina."

It was perhaps the nicest thing anyone had ever said to me. "I appreciate the sentiment. But no matter who got the better deal, I am still not comfortable working with the man."

"What about prime time?" she asked, cutting right to the heart of the matter.

"I'll just have to get there some other way. If not now, then later. We've got a good show. And we don't need Philip DuBois to prove it. The powers that be will just have to get a grip."

"I love you for saying that," Althea said, "but there's no point in cutting off your nose for the sake of my face. Or something like that."

"It's a mixed-up metaphor but I get the point." I was kind of liking this "Althea and Andi against the world" thing.

"So you'll let me talk to him?"

"I don't know."

"I can get him to change his mind," she said. "I mean, worst case, I can just threaten to air his dirty laundry."

"You don't mean that."

"Well, only as a last resort. This isn't a vendetta. But I won't allow what happened between Philip, Melina, and me to negatively impact you any more than it already has. I want your show to succeed. And if cooking with Philip DuBois is part of the package, then I'll do whatever is necessary to make sure it happens." Now here was the Althea I knew and loved. The queen of manipulation. Only this time she was on my side—or maybe she'd always been on my side and I'd just been too blind to see it.

Anyway, there was really no arguing with Althea once her mind was made up. "All right, then. Talk to Philip. Do your worst."

"Or best." She smiled. "It all depends on how you look at it."

And that was, of course, exactly the point. It was all about point of view. And mine had been seriously askew. My mother might look at the world through rose-colored glasses, but I'd been wearing blinders. And it was past time to get rid of them. To accept my life for what it really was. I wasn't my mother. And I wasn't Althea. I was hopefully the best of them both. And more important, I was me. Andi. And that had to count for something.

"So," Althea said, pulling me back to the conversation at hand. "It's settled. I'll call Philip. But before I do that, we still have one more thing we need to talk about."

My newfound maturity headed south. The last thing I wanted to discuss was Ethan. Better to just close the door and move on. "Honestly, Althea, I don't think there's anything left to say."

"There's a lot to be said, Andi." I don't think Althea had ever actually called me Andi before. I know it's not that big a deal, but it felt good. Right, actually. "And up until now the only person talking has been Diana Merreck."

"Believe me, she said enough for everyone."

"But she didn't tell you the whole truth. And if I've learned anything today, it's that it's important to be completely honest. So I'll admit that I helped to set you up with Ethan. But I didn't approach him. He came to me."

"What do you mean?" I asked, my stomach going creepy crawly on me.

"He came to me that night in the hospital. He was intrigued. But he knew you were in a bad place. What with Dillon and the breakup and everything. So he asked me for advice. And initially I agreed that it probably wasn't the optimal time for a new man in your life. But he was quite insistent. And so I came up with the idea of arranging for him to seemingly accidentally run into you."

"At the park. I can't believe I didn't see it for what it was."

"A man so interested in a woman he's willing to ask her family for help?"

"You make it sound so normal."

"Well, if you put aside my profession, it is normal. And because I liked him and I love you, I agreed."

"To set me up."

"To facilitate the two of you coming together."

"But Diana said—"

"Diana doesn't know squat. There were no ulterior motives. Except maybe the fact that I wanted to make things better for you. How could I not? Dillon hurt you badly, and you have to know by now that I'd have done anything to make that better. Including shooting the boy if I thought that would have helped."

"You never liked Dillon."

"It doesn't matter what I thought. *You* loved him. And I know what it feels like to have someone you love hurt you."

"So you were just trying to help ease the pain?"

"Yes." She nodded. "And I thought—still think, actually—that Ethan could make that happen."

"And Ethan, he really just wanted to go out with me?"

"That's pretty much it. You fell into the cellar and he fell for you."

"So you're saying that everything that happened, everything I said, I got it all wrong—again? I blew my chance at happiness because I believed what Diana said?"

"It doesn't have to be over," Althea said. "There might need to be a little groveling on your part. But he was in the wrong, too. He did lie to you."

"Because I was so obsessed with the idea of you meddling in my life that I drove him to it."

"It wasn't your fault. I do meddle. It's part of who I am. I can't help myself. That's why I'm a good matchmaker. And maybe not such a good aunt?"

"You're better than good. I just wasn't seeing things in the right light."

"Anyway," she said, "the point is that there's hope for the two of you."

"No, actually, there isn't," I said, staring down at my hands. "You see, Dillon helped me get out of The Pierre last night. And then he sort of stayed over."

"I take it he didn't sleep on the sofa."

I shook my head. "He was really wonderful. He told Diana off, snuck me out the back way, and then apologized for everything that had happened. We talked and drank—a lot. And one thing led to another . . . Anyway, Ethan arrived to find Dillon without a shirt and me wearing a bedsheet. It wasn't pretty."

"Did you and Ethan talk at all?"

"Yeah. Sort of. I let him have it. And he . . . well, he didn't have much to say. Which I guess, considering the circumstances, was understandable. Anyway, you can see now that our getting back together is out of the question. I pretty much sealed the deal, so to speak, when I slept with my ex."

"And what about Dillon?"

"I'm not sure what you mean?"

"Are the two of you getting back together?" she asked, brows drawn together in concern.

"No. I don't know why I ever thought we had a chance. You were right. We have nothing in common."

"You loved each other."

"But that's not enough, is it? There has to be something more. Something to build on. And with Dillon, there just isn't anything there."

"But you still slept with him."

"I was devastated and drunk," I said, being completely honest with her.

"Not a good combination," she acknowledged.

I shook my head. "I don't really remember all that much. But I guess I just needed to know that someone cared. Anyway, I knew the moment I saw the two of them standing there this morning that what I had with Dillon was over. And as soon as Ethan left, I told him as much."

"Sounds to me like you've got your head on straight. I'm just sorry it had to play out the way it did. And I honestly regret setting the whole thing in motion by not telling you about Ethan's interest in the first place."

"You had good reasons to handle things the way you did. It's no one's fault. It just is what it is. And it's time for me to move on. It's like you said, sometimes it's better not to dwell on the past."

"I was talking about something that happened twenty years ago. You and Ethan . . ."

"Althea . . ." I crossed my arms, glaring at her.

"But I was only—"

"Trying to help?" We both broke into laughter, and suddenly the whole world seemed brighter. Out of all the bad something intrinsically good had arisen. I'd found my mother. My real mother. And the funny thing was, she'd been right here under my nose the whole time. Sometimes one really can't see the trees for the forest. Or however that goes.

"All right," my mother said, still smiling. "I promise. No more meddling."

It was a brave statement. And I think in her own way she probably meant it. At least in that moment.

But I knew better.

Some things just aren't that easy to change.

Chapter 26

New York in the springtime is like a beautiful reawakening. Especially after a rain. Blustery winds and gray clouds give way to budding branches and bright blue sky, everything smelling fresh and sweet.

And there's no prettier place, in my opinion, than the Ramble in Central Park. The long winding paths are the perfect place for thinking. And, eventually, when you spill out onto the far side of the boat pond, it's almost like walking into a postcard. Rowboats idyllically bob in the pond as pedestrians amble along rain-washed pathways, the soft hollow wail of a saxophone carried on the breeze.

Althea had worked her magic. It had taken a bit of persuasion, but Philip DuBois had agreed to do the show. I still wasn't sure that we wouldn't have been better off just forgetting the whole thing, but in some weird kind of way I think talking to him had given her closure. And Cassie and Clinton were over the moon.

Cassie had taken the news to the big guns and word was that we had the inside track on the prime time special.

Don't get me wrong—I was really happy about the show—but funnily, it didn't seem to matter as much as it had a month ago. Shifting priorities, I suppose. Anyway, we were all celebrating tonight. Althea's treat. Craft. Which, as I've already noted, has the most amazing food. But before facing my friends, I'd wanted a little time on my own. And so I'd left Althea's and headed for the park.

So much had changed. Not the least of which was me. I had been so certain that I knew what I wanted in life. That I had a handle on where I was going and where I'd been. Turns out I didn't have a clue. Everything had been based on a version of my life that didn't actually exist.

I'd spent years rejecting everything Althea stood for. And now, it turned out, she was my true north. I'd spent my whole life chasing after an image of my mother. An ideal I'd created of a free spirit. And yet, in the end, it turned out that she'd simply been running away. Hiding from reality. Pretending that mistakes she'd made didn't exist.

Mistakes like me.

But Althea had stepped in. She'd loved and protected me. And driven me insane. Pretty much the definition of a mother. Right?

Only I'd refused to see it, clinging instead to a fairy-tale person who didn't exist. Trying to emulate her. When in reality I wasn't anything like her at all. Real or imagined.

I'd chosen Dillon because he seemed to embody the ideal I sought. But I'd lied to myself. Pretended I wanted the same things he did. When in truth, I yearned for stability. For a family. For a place where I truly belonged.

Then Ethan had come along and, despite all my misguided notions, he'd showed me what life could be like when someone really cared. Only I'd thrown it all away with my preconceived judgments and overreactions. Not to mention the horizontal pity party with my ex.

I'd been afraid. Pure and simple.

And so I'd blown my chance at happiness by refusing to see it for what it really was.

I sighed and settled down on a bench by the edge of the water, just as my cell rang. I pulled out the phone, my heart quickening. Maybe . . .

It was Bethany.

"Hey there," I said, swallowing my disappointment. "I was wondering when I'd hear from you. I've been leaving messages."

"I'm sorry," she said. "I've had my phone turned off. I've been with Michael."

"So tell me?" I asked, holding my breath, praying for a positive answer.

"Everything is great. I finally convinced him that I didn't want to break up. That I was just scared about moving in. Anyway, he's willing to give it another try. So I guess that means we're officially back together again."

"That's wonderful," I said. "Honestly, Bethany, I'm so happy for you."

"Thank you. I can't quite believe it myself. But I never would have gone to talk to him if it hadn't been for you. If I didn't know better, I'd say you were turning into Althea."

Twenty-four hours ago, that comment would have pissed me off. But now—well, amazingly, it felt like a compliment. Not that I was going into the family business, mind you. "I'm just glad it worked out. You and Michael belong together."

"I wasn't sure I should tell you. I mean, I wanted you to know, but under the circumstances I thought . . ." She paused, her voice hesitant.

"That I couldn't deal," I finished for her. "I can see why you'd think that. But you're wrong. I couldn't stand not knowing how things turned out. That's one of the reasons I've been leaving messages every five minutes."

"Well, it's all wonderful," she gushed. "In fact, we're even re-visiting the idea of moving in together."

"That's huge."

"I know. But I'm working off what you said. That we have to grab on to chance when it comes by. Anyway, enough about me. What about you? Last time we talked you were off to wring Althea's neck."

"Fortunately for me, she didn't answer her cell," I said, laughing at the thought. "I'm sure I would have just said something I regretted. Anyway, since she wasn't around, I decided to try Harriet's and wound up talking to Bernie instead."

"Always the voice of reason."

"More than you'll ever know. She gave me a lot to think about, and, as a result, I wound up having a long talk with Althea."

"For the good, I hope."

"I think so. But it's too long a story to tell you over the phone. I'll save it for when we're together. Which brings me to the other reason I called. I actually have some good news. Philip DuBois agreed to do the show."

"You're kidding? That's great."

"I know. And even more amazing, it's all Althea's doing. Anyway, she's taking Clinton, Cassie, and me out to celebrate. And I wanted you to come, too."

"If it were any other night, I'd be there in a second, but—"

"You have plans with Michael."

"Yeah," she said. "We just need a little time for ourselves. Is that okay?"

"Of course. I totally understand."

"And you're certain you're all right?" she asked, her tone worried. "I can change my plans."

"You're sweet to offer. But it's not necessary. If I sound a little off it's only because I'm still dealing with the fallout from everything that's happened. But I promise, I'm going to be okay."

And for the first time since falling down the rabbit hole, I actually believed it was true. I might not have gotten a perfect ending. But it was definitely a new beginning. And that had to count for something.

"You're sure?" Bethany asked, still sounding unconvinced.

"Yes. I am," I assured her. "Now go. Be with Michael. We'll talk later."

I disconnected and then slid my phone back in my pocket with a sigh. Althea had been right again. Bethany and Michael belonged together. They completed each other in a way that I couldn't possibly have seen—until now.

I closed my eyes, content in the moment. The soft breeze caressed my skin as the sun beat warm upon my face. Sometimes joy was found in the smallest of pleasures.

"Is this seat taken?"

Like the voice of someone we love.

"No, I . . . no," I said, our gazes colliding as I opened my eyes.

Ethan was here. Right here.

Standing beside me.

In the flesh. As if I'd just conjured him up from my imagination.

"Please," I stuttered, struggling for words, "sit down."

He sat next to me on the bench as I tried to sort through my agitated thoughts. "How did you know I was here?" I asked, as if I didn't already know the answer.

"Althea," he said.

I nodded. "She has a way of sticking her nose in."

"Hopefully where it's wanted?" Ethan sounded so tentative, my heart actually skipped a beat.

"Definitely." I nodded, certain that we weren't talking about Althea anymore. "I . . . Oh, God, Ethan, I'm so sorry. I never should have . . . the things I said . . . I . . ."

"You had good reason," he said, a muscle in his jaw working overtime. "None of this would have happened if I had just told the truth. I never should have let you believe that our meeting in the park was an accident. I should have come clean about Althea's involvement from the very beginning."

"She said it was your idea. Our getting together, I mean."

"It was. In fact, as I recall, I was quite insistent about it."

"That's pretty much what she told me."

"Well, it's the truth. I just wanted to be careful about how I handled things. My timing wasn't the best. What with everything that had happened. I didn't want you to think I was taking advantage."

"Actually," I said, "I was just thinking that sometimes we have to grab on to opportunity when it presents itself. No matter the circumstances. Anyway, I certainly didn't make things easy. I second-guessed our relationship every step of the way. And when I found out about the setup, I immediately jumped to all the wrong conclusions. I should have known that Diana wasn't telling the whole truth."

"We've both made mistakes."

"Some more unforgivable than others," I said, watching the rowboats glide by. "I didn't mean to . . . at least I don't remember . . . I shouldn't have slept with Dillon. It was stupid. And I'm so sorry."

"Andi," Ethan said, reaching over to cover my hand, "it's okay—"

"No, it's not. It's horrible. But it didn't mean anything. I don't want Dillon. I want you." The words came out of their own accord and I stopped, horrified at what I'd just admitted.

"Sweetheart," Ethan said, his hand covering mine, the endearment making my heart flutter so rapidly I thought it might actually take flight, "you didn't sleep with Dillon."

"I didn't?" Hope like some stupid neon light blinked in syncopated rhythm with my heart.

"No. You didn't."

"But how, I mean . . . you can't possibly . . ." I trailed off, apparently totally incapable of coherent thought.

"Dillon told me."

"You spoke with him?" Talk about a crazy shift in the cosmic existence.

"He was worried about you. And about what I'd think. So he called to tell me that nothing happened. He apparently tried to tell you, but you were too busy throwing him out to listen."

"That seems to be my modus operandi of late."

"It's one of the things I find most charming about you."

"Really?" I said, chewing on the side of my lip. "I thought it was my worst fault."

"Well, sometimes it's a bit of both." He shrugged with a crooked smile. "So, tell me, did you really mean it? The part about wanting me?"

"I did." I was back to nodding. The man was going to think I was a bobble head.

"Well, then," he said, lacing his fingers with mine, "what do you say we give it another try?"

"Yes," I said, certain that in this moment anything was possible. "Definitely yes."

He leaned forward, I closed my eyes, and—well, that's really none of your business, is it? Let's just say it was absolutely perfect, and that when I opened my eyes, Ethan was smiling, the sun was shining, and somewhere out there Althea was probably doing handstands.

"You know, of course," he said as I snuggled into his arms, "now that we're giving it a go, Althea will probably expect me to pay for the match."

"No worries," I said, smiling up at him. "I'll be more than happy to write that check."

"Great and decadent fun!"

—Julia London, *USA Today*
bestselling author of *Wedding Survivor*

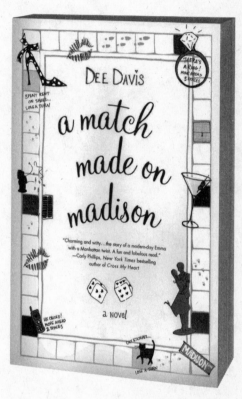

Vanessa Carlson's matchmaker business is giving her biggest rival (and best friend) a run for her money. So, to prove once and for all who's the best matchmaker in town, they enter a competition to see who can send playboy Mark Grayson walking down the aisle. Seems simple enough, but emotions often have a will of their own, and Vanessa learns that her rules don't always apply.

"A thoroughly modern homage to Emma populated with wonderful characters and overflowing with wit, charm, and heart. This one is most definitely a keeper!"

—Julie Kenner, *USA Today* bestselling author of *Carpe Demon* and *The Givenchy Code*

 ST. MARTIN'S GRIFFIN

Now available